Crushing on Love

THE BRADENS AT PEACEFUL HARBOR

LOVE IN BLOOM SERIES

Melissa Foster

ISBN-10: 194148042X
ISBN-13: 9781941480427

Cover Design: Natasha Brown and Elizabeth Mackey

WORLD LITERARY PRESS
PRINTED IN THE UNITED STATES OF AMERICA

A Note to Readers

Steve and Shannon are wickedly naughty in a primal, playful, oh-so-delicious way. They definitely controlled the ink on these pages, and I was merely along for the sexy ride. I hope you love them as much as I do! ~ Melissa

Sign up for my newsletter to keep up to date with new releases and to receive an exclusive short story.
www.melissafoster.com/News

The Bradens are just one of the series in the Love in Bloom big-family romance collection. Characters from each series make appearances in future books so you never miss an engagement, wedding, or birth. A complete list of all series titles is included at the end of this book.

Love in Bloom Subseries Order
Snow Sisters
The Bradens
The Remingtons
Seaside Summers
The Ryders
Billionaires After Dark (Wild Boys, Bad Boys)
Harborside Nights

Visit Melissa's Reader Goodies page…
www.melissafoster.com/reader-goodies
—Download **FREE**: Love in Bloom series order and checklist
—Get **FREE first in series** Love in Bloom ebooks
—Keep track of your favorite characters with the essential Love in Bloom Series Guide

For my fab Fan Club member Alexis Bruce
Because shirtless, sweaty, ax-wielding men
spark too many hot conversations
to go unnoticed

Chapter One

STEVE JOHNSON TOOK off his sweaty shirt and guzzled a bottle of water. Nothing beat a predawn run, especially after a shitty night's sleep. He set the empty bottle and shirt on the steps leading to his rustic log cabin and crossed the yard to the chopping post, determined to work the remaining tension from his body. A six-mile run on the rough terrain of the Colorado mountains should have worked out all his piss and vinegar, but not this morning.

Sun beat down on his shoulders as he centered a slab of wood on the tree stump that served as his chopping post, trying to ignore the reason he'd been unable to sleep last night. He filled his lungs with the scents of nature and tranquility. He knew every sound and smell of the area, could differentiate every species of animal and plant in the forest, and anticipated inclement weather well before it hit. His body was attuned to the mountains as if he were a part of them.

He hoisted the ax over his shoulder, thoughts he was trying to ignore pushing back in like adamant thieves. He swung the ax. A loud *crack* echoed in the forest—and in his head—rattling the truth of his angst free. Shannon Braden was back—and she'd come home last night wrapped around Cal Hayden on the back of his horse.

He ground his teeth against that reality and set another log in place.

Smart, sexy-as-sin, talks-a-mile-a-minute Shannon. He'd known her for years. His sister, Jade, was married to her second cousin, Rex. Shannon had spent weeks doing research on red foxes in the mountains. She'd been staying at her uncle's ranch in Weston, but he knew the company she was working with had made arrangements for her to stay at the vacant cabin just around the bend for the remainder of the project. He swung the ax, thinking of the weeks she'd spent flitting in and out of his peaceful life, full of energy and never-ending conversations— mostly one-sided, which she didn't seem to mind. Truth be known, neither did he. Listening to Shannon rattle on about *anything* was hot. She tangled up his thoughts in ways no other woman ever had, which was just his luck. Steve wasn't into meaningless hookups, and Shannon's life was in Maryland, while his was there on the mountain, which rooted Shannon Braden firmly in his off-limits zone.

The past couple of weeks had been quiet while she'd re-turned home to Maryland to attend her brother's wedding, and the fact that Steve had noticed, and disliked it being quiet, had thrown him for a loop.

His mind reeled back to last night again. He'd heard Cal riding back down the mountain about two hours after he'd arrived. As he swung the ax, he wondered if Shannon had done some hands-on research with Cowboy Cal last night.

He set another log in place, telling himself it was none of his damn business if she had, and split the log so hard the two halves flew ten feet from the stump. Another log, another split. And so became his stress-relieving pattern as the sun sailed higher, taking the bite off the chilly spring morning.

A mass of birds took off from the treetops. Steve paused midswing, a smile tugging at his lips. *Shannon.* He split another log, trying to ignore his accelerating pulse at the thought of her flitting back into his life.

The sweet sounds of her humming floated into his ears, and he tried harder to deny the thrum of heat racing down his spine. He heard the crunching of leaves and his smile widened further. Damn, he needed to get a grip.

"Hey there, mountain man."

He forced the foolhardy smile from his lips, replacing it with what he hoped was a less lustful one, and turned to find the all-too-chipper and insanely hot brunette. Her hair was piled on her head in a messy bun, a few dark tendrils curling past her shoulders. She held a mug in each hand. Curls of steam rose into the air. Her pink shirt hitched on her breasts, and he chalked that up to the list of things he was futilely trying not to react to. But his body wasn't on board with the off-limits plan, and it brimmed with heat. It had been a hell of a lot easier to be around her when she was staying at her uncle's house in town. At least then by the time he saw her she had a freaking bra on.

He dropped his eyes to avoid staring, but her flannel pajama pants hung low on her hips, revealing a sliver of taut skin just below her belly button. Christ, she was gorgeous. Striving for a safe view, he looked at her leather boots. Boots were safe. There was nothing sexy about boots. Bright pink laces hung loose over the dark leather, her pajama pants bunched around the tops, showing another flash of skin. He pictured her shoving her bare feet into them before jaunting out the door with her mind-blowing smile in place. There must be something wrong with him, because he found that sexy, too.

"You should lace those up." He ran a hand through his hair, grinding his teeth against the way his entire body was buzzing like a live wire.

"Well, *Mr. Safety*. I missed you, too." She thrust a mug toward him with a coy smile. "Just the way you like it. Bitter as weeds."

She was too damn cute, too damn social, and too damn temporary for the likes of him.

He reached for the mug. "Thanks, Butterfly." The nickname flew off his tongue without thought, just as it had the first time she'd flitted into his yard, turned his insides to fire, and flitted back out. He was surprised to realize he'd missed saying it while she was gone.

"No prob, Grizz."

Grizz. Hell if he hadn't missed that, too. Her eyes dropped to his bare chest, lingering long enough for him to feel it lower. *Much lower.* Her cheeks flushed, and she slid those gorgeous hazel eyes to his ax—the one in his hand, not the one in his pants.

"Preparing for a cold night, or thinking about becoming a serial killer?"

I wouldn't have cold nights if you were in my bed. As if on cue, his body stirred again, reminding him it'd been far too long since he'd been with a woman.

"As *interesting* as becoming a serial killer sounds, I don't think I'm cut out for it."

"Right. It would require human contact."

"I missed that smart mouth of yours," he said sarcastically. He'd been fantasizing about her full lips and sassy mouth ever since they'd reconnected at Rex and Jade's wedding several months ago. But she was only there until her project ended, so sarcasm it was.

"Heard you ride in with Cal last night. How long are you here for?" He hadn't just heard her arrive. He'd gone out to see who was riding up the mountain and had seen her arms wrapped around Cal from behind as they rode past the overlook. In the moonlight they'd looked like a frigging Hallmark card.

"A few weeks. Four and a half, I think. Something like that." She stretched one arm, flashing even more of her midriff.

Torture. Pure, exquisite torture.

"You could have called me to bring you up the mountain." He shifted his eyes away, trying to figure out who had taken possession of his mouth. *Called me?* He had nothing against Cal. He was a nice guy and was one of the most respected horse trainers around. And he shouldn't give a shit who Shannon was with. Sure, she was hot, smart, and he liked her ballsy attitude, but he liked his life just the way it was. The last thing he needed was a social butterfly like her bringing noise and chaos into his life, telling him what to do or how to live.

"I know." She kicked at the dirt, her eyes downcast. "Treat and Max stopped by in the afternoon and I went into town with them to visit my uncle Hal and my cousins. Cal was there and he offered to drive me back, since he lives in Preston. It was only once we got back to his place that he suggested we ride up on horseback. Besides, you don't exactly love going into town."

Great, now he was stuck envisioning her at Cal's sprawling horse ranch.

He finished his coffee and handed her the mug. "Thanks. It was perfect." He turned to set another log on the stump. "You ought to be careful bringing guys up to your cabin," he said with his back to her.

"I thought I left my overprotective big brothers at home." She sighed. "I hardly think Cal is a threat. He's known Rex forever."

Steve rested the ax over his shoulder, weighing his response. The last thing he wanted to be was her big brother, and he'd known Cal forever, too. Cal wasn't the kind of guy to take advantage of a woman, but that didn't stop Steve's gut from churning at the thought of them cozied up together.

"He's a *friend*, Steve." She narrowed her eyes as he drew the ax back. "Don't even try to pretend you don't bring women up to your cabin."

He arched a brow. That would be a big *no fucking way*. He liked his privacy.

Her jaw gaped. "What? Don't you ever get bored? Lonely?"

"Not really," he said as he swung the ax. It was a damned lie, at least since Shannon had flitted into his life, making him feel things he'd once been adept at ignoring.

"Why not? That's not normal." She finished her coffee and set the mugs on the ground as he split the log and set another one on the stump. "What do you do for sex?"

He laughed under his breath. "Seriously, city girl?"

"I'd hardly call Peaceful Harbor a city. It's a beach town, and you're avoiding the question."

"Maybe because you're asking questions you shouldn't be asking." He swung the ax and split another log.

She smirked. "Look at you, all big and brawny and afraid to talk about sex."

"What's gotten into you?" He set the ax-head on the ground and leaned on the handle. Before she'd gone home, he'd gotten away with a strategically placed *Uh-huh*. "I'm pretty sure you weren't this curious about my sexual habits the last time you were on the mountain."

Her eyes rolled over him, and he couldn't tell if she was assessing or enjoying the view.

"I don't know," she said with a mischievous grin. "You're standing there like a lumberjack. Six...what?"

"Three," he said with a sigh.

"Right. Six three of shirtless, sweaty muscle, with your hair all tousled." She moved her hands around her head, causing her shirt to lift up again. "You haven't shaved in who knows how long, and you look like the guys on 'Seriously Sexy Hot Guys' Pinterest boards. A guy who looks like you *can't* be going without." She shrugged and her cheeks pinked up. "It made me wonder..."

"How about you wonder a little less?" *Because hearing you talk about my sex life makes me want you in it. Front and center.* "Pinterest? What the heck is Pinterest?"

Her eyes widened with disbelief. "I forgot you know nothing about the *real* world. Pinterest is this awesome social media site—"

"Never mind. That's so far from the real world it shouldn't exist. People nowadays are content to sit inside and stare at screens, talking with people they don't know instead of living their lives. Bodies are meant to *move*, Butterfly. Weather is meant to be *experienced*. If people were more like animals, the world would be a better place."

He saw a hint of hurt in her eyes and felt bad. Sometimes he forgot that he wasn't the only one protective of their lifestyle. He tried to change the subject to a lighter one.

"What are you doing out here so early anyway?" he asked.

"The company offered me a new project, and my boss at my real job gave me a leave of absence to do it. I thought that was pretty cool of him. I'm going to be comparing the habits of gray and red foxes, and I'm here to scout the grays. You know how red foxes prefer edge habitats and grays prefer mountainous forestland?" Edge habitats were the boundary of two habitats, like field and forest. She didn't wait for him to respond before continuing with her explanation. "They're similar in life and history in almost every way, except for grays being shier and slightly smaller and where they make their dens. I'm going to study them to see if their behavioral patterns reveal reasons for the difference in habitat preference. I was hoping you'd have time to show me where I can find them."

The request took him by surprise. She'd spent weeks researching red foxes and hadn't once asked him to help her.

"No can do today, Butterfly." He had a busy day planned. He'd caught a group of twentysomethings partying by one of the rock ledges last week and he'd spotted a few of them again yesterday. He needed to make the rounds to ensure they weren't back and getting into trouble, and he had to head down the mountain to meet with his old buddies Mack and Will Cumberland. Yesterday he'd learned the Cumberland ranch was going up for sale: two hundred acres in Weston, adjacent to the national park where Steve had worked as a ranger and wildlife consultant for a decade. Steve had grown up in Weston, and though he lived two towns away now, his small-town roots ran deep. He wanted to try to convince his buddies to put the land into conservation instead of selling.

"Bummer. I was looking forward to catching up on all the crazy shenanigans you were up to while I was gone." She waggled her brows with the tease.

He smiled and shook his head. "Be careful out there. I caught some kids partying recently. They're probably harmless, but guys and alcohol…Just be careful. You got that Mace I left in your cabin?"

"That was you?" She narrowed her eyes and said, "You do realize I'm a grown woman, right?"

Christ, had he ever.

SHANNON WATCHED STEVE swing his ax. He was built like the very mountains he loved: strong and stable, with layers of hard-earned muscles born from honest, hard work. *Pure perfection*. And that hair? *Lord*. What would it be like to fist her hands in his hair and kiss him? To touch all those hard planes of muscle? To discover the man behind the walls? She told herself those were *wants* not *needs*, no matter how much they felt like it. *The kind of unrelenting wants that bring a girl to reach beneath the sheets and satisfy her fantasies.*

Down, girl.

Shannon had been surprised by how much she'd missed Steve when she'd gone home for her eldest brother Cole's wedding. She and Steve hadn't spent more than a few stolen moments together during the weeks she was here for her first assignment. Usually she'd catch him working on equipment, or in his yard, before she returned to her uncle's ranch in the evenings. He'd captivated her with his passion for, and endless knowledge about, all things wilderness related. And he was different from most of the guys she knew. He wasn't hung up on his looks or material things. He was *real*, with a strong set of values and priorities. Somehow, between their almost daily conversations and weeks of hoping she'd see him, she'd become completely and utterly taken with him.

When she'd been offered the assignment *and* the cabin, she'd accepted without hesitation. She'd missed Steve too much to deny the attraction, and she wanted to see if something might come of it.

Now that she was here, her body was thrumming at the mere sight of him. Given that she'd actually asked him about his sex life—and nearly died on the spot when the question slipped out—she desperately needed to rein herself in.

He wiped sweat from his brow, his tanned skin glistening in the morning sun. "Need anything from town?" he asked, setting another log on the stump.

She couldn't pry her eyes from his rippling abs and his bulbous biceps flexing with every move. "Town?"

He cocked a smile and hoisted the ax again. "Town. You know, the place where people who like *Pinterest* live?"

She forced her eyes away, glancing at the trees swaying in the breeze, the rocks at her feet, anywhere but at him.

"I know what town is. I'm just surprised you're going there." Everyone knew Steve hated to leave his precious mountain.

"Gotta take care of some business."

Going into town was a big deal. Unlike a quick trip to the store from her apartment in Peaceful Harbor, the drive into town took at least thirty to forty-five minutes, depending on which town he was going to. She'd realized last night she'd forgotten two very important supplies. Pop-Tarts and toilet paper. She could probably live with the single roll of toilet paper she had in the cabin for another few days if she needed to, but Pop-Tarts were pretty much a necessity. Besides, maybe she could convince Steve to help her scout gray-fox habitats at dusk. *Perfect!*

"Can I come with you?" she asked hopefully. "I need to pick up a few things."

"I'll get them for you. What do you need?"

She bit her lower lip, willing herself not to fib. But if she asked him to pick up what she really needed, he'd leave and she'd have to go searching for habitats by herself. Now that she'd thought about going later with her yummy mountain man, she'd already settled on it in her mind.

"It's girl stuff. You won't want to get it." So much for not fibbing. "Can I please go with you?" She gave him her best pleading look. "I promise not to talk your ear off." *Fib, fib, fib!* She had no control over what came out of her mouth, especially around him.

He muttered under his breath and set the ax against the stump. "I'm not making a hundred stops."

She leapt with delight and ran over to hug him. Her heel slipped out of her boot and she stumbled into him in a half hug, half full-body-draped-over-Steve embrace. His skin was hot, his body was hard, *and getting harder by the second.* He smelled like man and musk, and…she was still plastered against him.

She cleared her throat and managed, "Thank you." Using his chest for leverage—*yum, yum*—she found her footing and pressed her heel back into her boot. "One stop. That's it. Promise."

"You're excited to get those supplies." He picked up the logs he'd chopped and piled them on his forearm like they were toothpicks.

"I'm just excited to be back. Maybe at dusk you can help me map out the habitats? It'll be fun to scope them out together."

He gave her a curious look. "Haven't heard anyone describe hanging out with me as fun in a long time."

"Then you're hanging out with losers, and I'm taking that as a yes." She grabbed the coffee mugs, unable to stop smiling.

"I'm leaving in twenty minutes."

"I'll be back lickety-split." With a bounce in her step, she headed toward her cabin and heard him mutter, "Lickety-split," followed by a chuckle.

Chapter Two

BEFORE THEY GOT in the truck, *dangerous* wasn't a word Steve would have used to describe sweet and effervescent Shannon, but as they drove down the mountain, the scent of her perfume filled the cab. It was simple, understated, and feminine, contradicting the complicated woman who hadn't stopped talking since they left. As constant as her chatter was, something about the excitement in her voice, combined with her tantalizing scent, made him want to shut her up with a kiss. *Dangerous* quickly became synonymous with *Shannon*.

"You should have seen Cole and Leesa walk down the aisle. They were be-au-ti-ful!" She sighed as if she were caught up in a fantasy. "Oh, and did I tell you Sam and Faith got engaged? I can hardly believe it. I got to watch him propose over Skype while I was at my uncle's. It was so romantic, and Faith cried, which made us all cry. Nate and Jewel are getting married in September. It's so hard to believe I'll have two married brothers and one who is engaged. It's like cupid got arrow happy."

Steve knew her close-knit family, and he liked hearing about them, despite the fact that they were a constant reminder that her life in Colorado was only temporary. If she'd moved there, wild horses couldn't keep him away, but he was too drawn to her to open a door he might not be able to close.

"Hello?" Shannon touched his arm. "You were totally spacing out. Thinking about how many trees you had to hug or something?"

"Something like that." He returned her smile, stealing a quick glance before pulling on to the main road. She'd changed her clothes, and looked hotter than the summer sun in her skinny jeans and a cranberry-red sweater. She wasn't like other girls, who matched their shoes to every outfit and wore so much makeup it looked painted on. Shannon wore the leather hiking boots she'd had on earlier, with the pink laces tied this time, and just enough makeup to set off her hazel eyes and high cheekbones.

When did I start noticing women's clothes and makeup?

"You're a bit of a tree hugger yourself," he said to distract himself from his thoughts.

"I know, but I'm kind of rethinking my career at the moment."

"I thought you liked what you were doing. And you're back again, so you must like something about it."

She nibbled on her lower lip. "I love the work, but I'm not like you." She looked at him with a thoughtful gaze. "I need people."

"Most people do," he admitted. Their differences were yet another reason he had to keep his lips to himself. Their families were too close for him to mess around with Shannon when it couldn't lead anywhere.

"I still don't get how you *don't* need people," she said. "It's not natural to want to be alone all the time."

He didn't have to look to feel the heat of her gaze. He didn't have an answer, at least not one he felt like talking about right now, so he focused on driving. Main Street in Weston was built to resemble the Wild West, complete with hitching posts in front of stores and old-fashioned, hand-carved wooden signs. To an outsider, life in Weston looked simple, quiet, easygoing, but that's not how Steve saw it. There had never been anything simple about growing up in a town where everyone knew everyone else's business and his father's bad decisions clouded people's judgment. At least that's how he had always felt.

"I'm not alone all the time, and I happen to like my life the way it is," he told her, just as he had a hundred times before. Wanting to change the subject, he asked, "Where are we headed? Grocery store or the corner market?"

"Oh! I just realized we're close to the bakery. Can we *please*, please stop there? I know I said just one stop, but it's only two, and I'm starved. Do you mind?" She turned hopeful eyes toward him, and he felt a pull in the pit of his stomach. "Please? Saralou makes those yummy chocolate- and fruit-filled croissants. Come on. We'll get your favorite. What is your favorite anyway?"

Laughing at her never-ending sentences, he shook his head and pulled down the next street, heading for the bakery. "Is there anything you don't get excited about?"

"I don't know. Should there be?" She tilted her head and smiled. "I take life as it comes, and usually it's pretty fun. I know people who are Negative Nellies, and they're such bores. I hope I never become like them. I can't imagine being negative all the time."

He parked in front of the bakery and relaxed back into his seat.

"You're not coming in?"

The disappointment in her voice was palpable, but he needed a moment to pull his head together. He thought he'd had his attraction to her under control, but he wasn't even close. She was still right there under his skin. Every moment they were together was like a tug-of-war between wanting to get closer and needing to keep his distance.

"It's your thing," he said. "Go ahead."

"But I don't know your favorite flavor." Her full lips curved down into a perfectly orchestrated pout that tugged at his heartstrings—reiterating his need for distance.

"It's okay. Grab whatever you like." He reached for his wallet. "Need some money?"

"No, I don't need your money," she huffed as she climbed out of the truck, and he closed his eyes.

He startled when his door was yanked open. "What the—"

Shannon grabbed his hand and pulled—hard.

"You're already in town," she said with a look of fierce determination. "Get your butt out of the truck and pretend to be sociable. If I needed a chauffeur, I would have called one. I think you've lost some of your marbles up on that mountain. I wanted your company, dumbass."

"Dumbass?" he muttered, stepping from the truck. "You're not quite as sweet as I thought you were."

"Get over it." She flashed a haughty smile and dragged him toward the bakery.

"What happened to you in Maryland? Did someone shoot you up with pushiness?" He held the door open and followed her in. The sweet aroma of sugary goodness filled his senses.

"Heaven have mercy. Look who the cat dragged in." Saralou Carmell, the owner of Sweet Sensations Bakery, came around the counter and hugged Steve. He had gone to high school with her daughter, Krista. She drew back with a warm smile that reached her blue eyes, which were currently scanning his face. "Sweetheart, you need a trim, but you are just as handsome as ever."

"Thanks, Saralou," he said pleasantly. "I haven't had time to get it cut. How's Krista?"

"Just dandy. Her little boy is cute as a button. Did you hear about the Cumberlands' ranch? I hear there's a development company sniffing around. As if those Cumberland boys don't have enough on their plates these days."

Steve gritted his teeth. He'd thought he'd have time before the vultures swooped in, but who was he kidding? Probably half the town already knew about this. He should come into town more often, just to stay in the loop. Not surprising, that town gossip was one of the reasons he didn't like hanging around. That and the fact that it took forever to get in and out of anyplace he went. Everyone wanted to chat.

Before he could answer, Saralou said, "Jade was in the other morning with baby Hal. Goodness gracious, your nephew is the spitting image of his daddy, isn't he?"

"That he is," he said with a smile, thinking of baby Hal's sweet face.

Saralou winked at Shannon. "And you, Ms. Braden. I have no idea how you got him off that mountain, but you did a good thing, honey. What can I get y'all?"

"Let's see..." Shannon leaned over the pastry display and began humming. She twisted a lock of hair around her finger as she looked over the cupcakes, croissants, pies, and cakes. She crouched to see the cookies on the lower shelves, and her tongue moved back and forth over her lower lip. Her eyes narrowed in concentration.

Christ. The hair? The tongue? The happy little humming?

He seriously needed to walk straight out that door and keep going until he was too far away to even *think* about her. Since that wasn't an option, he hoped to at least hurry her up and lessen the lip licking, hair twirling, sexy-sweet torture she was doling out.

He crouched beside her. "Big decision?"

"Mm-hm."

"You said you wanted croissants," he reminded her.

"I know." She began humming again.

He pointed to the croissants. "Right there."

She gave him a deadpan look. "Can you really look at all this deliciousness and make a decision that fast? I mean, *look* at those cookies. And that pink frosting on those cupcakes? Don't you just want to dip your finger in it and suck it off?"

Holy. Hell. Like *that* image wouldn't run rampant in his mind all day.

"And look at the pies," she said a little breathlessly. "And the muffins…"

Nope. No pies or muffins or acts of God would erase the image of Shannon sucking frosting off of her finger.

"It's a wonder you don't weigh three hundred pounds." He wasn't into string-skinny girls, and Shannon had curves in all the right places. Another thing he was trying not to think about. But the truth was, even if she'd weighed three hundred pounds she'd still be irresistible. It was her essence, her vivacious personality, and that sassy, brazen wit that called him on his shit that he was drawn to.

He took her hand and rose to his feet, bringing her up beside him.

"Saralou, we'll take a chocolate croissant, a cherry croissant, a blueberry muffin, a cranberry muffin, one of each type of cookie, and"—he would surely be struck by lightning for this one—"one of those cupcakes with pink frosting, please."

Shannon squealed and hugged him again. "Thank you. I knew you would want something."

You have no idea how much something *I want.* He couldn't look at her mouth without picturing her sucking…*Christ.* What was it about her that had him thinking about sex every time she was near? He was usually so good at keeping those thoughts locked away. She grinned up at him as if she were innocent of the mental lock picking she was doing.

"Those aren't for me," he finally said, and paid for the pastries, trying to ignore the way Saralou was eyeing the two of them approvingly. *There's nothing to approve of here. Carry on.*

"I can't eat all that," Shannon insisted as they left the bakery. "I didn't invite you in so you could pay for everything either. I'll pay you back."

"You didn't invite me in. You dragged me." He opened the passenger door, and once she was settled in, he climbed into the driver's side and opened the bakery box. "If it were left up to you, we'd have stood there all day debating pastries. Now you have choices."

"But you don't even know if I like all of these."

Was there any point she wouldn't argue? With the meeting with the Cumberlands looming, and the freaking inferno she stoked in him, he was a hot mess. *Here comes lightning strike number two.* "No, but I knew you wanted to taste the pink frosting."

"SERIOUSLY? YOU BOUGHT that cupcake just so I could

taste the icing? You have just risen to favorite mountain man status. That was really sweet of you." She dipped her finger into the thick, creamy pink frosting.

"Not really," he mumbled as he started the truck.

She put her finger in her mouth and closed her eyes, savoring the sweetness as it melted on her tongue. "Mm."

When she opened her eyes, his heated gaze was locked on her mouth—with her finger still in it. A wolfish grin lifted his lips, and she nearly burst into flames.

"You just paid me back," he said in a low voice that ignited even more heat.

Her finger dropped from her lips with a *pop*. "You..." *Holy hotness*. She had no idea how to react to *that* look. "I can't believe you did that."

He laughed as he drove away from the curb. "Hey, you're the one who planted the idea in my head."

"Planted the idea? You're a pig!" She scooped up another fingerful of frosting and turned away. "To think I was going to offer you a taste. *Tsk*."

He grabbed her hand, both of them laughing as she struggled to pull it away. He kept one hand on the steering wheel while pulling her finger toward his mouth.

"Don't you dare—"

He captured her finger in his mouth and swirled his tongue over it, sucking ever so gently and sending rivers of heat slithering through her, silencing her laughter along with every other thought in her head. He stopped at a traffic light, holding her gaze as he withdrew her finger from his mouth and licked his lips. It was all she could do to remember to breathe.

"You're right," he said seductively. "That was mind-blowingly good."

The light changed, and he shifted his eyes to the road, chuckling. "So, where to?" he asked casually. "Did you really need to get anything at the store, or did you just want to pick up your requisite sugar fix?"

She closed her gaping mouth, still hung up on how strong and soft his tongue had felt as it slid over her finger, like it was made for giving pleasure—*to my finger? Oh my God. I'm losing it.*

She forced herself to square her shoulders and lift her chin, regaining a modicum of control. "You have no idea where my finger's been."

"Sure I do." He slid his slate-blue eyes her way, and another wave of heat consumed her. "I watched it go in that smart mouth of yours just before it went in mine."

Holy cow, you are so hot.

"Don't get all weird on me. I was just messing with you." He slowed at the corner of Main and South and asked, "Which way? Grocery store or corner market?"

Messing with me? Heck yeah, you were messing with me. You made my whole body hot. Another second and I would have had to change my underwear.

"Corner market." She glared at him, but he didn't seem to notice, which also annoyed her. What kind of game was he playing?

He parked at the market and got out of the truck.

"You're coming in?" she asked.

"I'm suddenly feeling hot. I thought I'd get a nice cold drink." He put a hand on her lower back and nudged her through the door. "Don't worry. I won't watch you buy your lady things."

Oh shit. She'd forgotten about that ruse. It didn't matter

now. She wasn't about to buy *lady things* in front of him. Especially after what he'd done. There was no way she wanted him thinking she was on her period. No way. She wanted him to have sexy thoughts about her.

She snagged the Pop-Tarts and toilet paper, thinking twice about the toilet paper. That wasn't exactly sexy, but it was necessary. Maybe he'd think that was what she'd been referring to. She walked through the aisles trying to think of something sexy to buy. They didn't even have lip gloss. ChapStick would definitely not do the trick. Too bad they didn't sell sexy lingerie.

After ten minutes of searching for something sexy, she gave up and carried her purchases to the cashier. She spotted Steve outside talking with Rachel Gray, a local hairdresser. Rachel had worked wonders for Callie, her cousin Wes's wife, on their wedding day a few months ago. Rachel was a pixie of a girl at barely five feet tall, with gorgeous green eyes and silky blond hair. Shannon had met her at the wedding. She was sweet *and* smart, a total package. It was no wonder guys waited weeks just to sit in her chair.

And she's smiling flirtatiously at Grizz.

Jealousy she had no right feeling prickled her skin. She paid for her purchases and headed out to the truck.

"Shannon? Oh my gosh!" Rachel touched Steve's forearm, said something Shannon couldn't hear, then hurried over and hugged her. "I had no idea you were back in town."

"I'm staying up on the mountain for a while, doing another research project."

Steve glanced at her on his way back to the truck, and her blood ran hot.

"Lucky you," Rachel said. "It's beautiful up there. Maybe we can get the girls together while you're here. Have you seen

Callie's baby bump? She's just started showing, and I swear she's the cutest pregnant gal around!"

"I saw her at my uncle's barbecue last night. She looks amazing, and Wes is over the moon." Steve started the truck, and Shannon took the hint. "I'd better go. He's my ride home."

"Oh," Rachel said with an inquisitive light in her eyes. "You're even luckier than I thought." She leaned closer and lowered her voice. "He wasn't always quite so reclusive. Maybe you can bring him out of his shell again."

Don't I wish. She had the urge to ask if he was always hot and cold, or if that was new, too. But she bit her tongue, knowing the small town's rumor mill plucked gossip from the air like flies to fly strips.

"I can try," she said, and headed for the truck. She set the bag on the bench seat and climbed in, wondering what had made Steve turn to the wilderness instead of people. She'd assumed he'd always liked his solitude.

He peeked into her bag and pulled out the Pop-Tarts. "Seriously? I bought you a box of homemade goodies and you buy this garbage?"

She snagged them from his hands and put them back in the bag. "They're power food. And they're shmores, which are fitting since I'm staying in a cabin."

"Power food." He smiled and shook his head. Pulling out of the parking lot, he said, "S'mores, without the 'h.'"

"That's what I said. Shmores."

"S'mores," he repeated, emphasizing the 'm.'

"Whatever. I've never had them, anyway."

He looked over with a furrowed brow. "You've never had s'mores? I thought you lived in a beach town."

"I do. We have bonfires, and we roast marshmallows, but

I've never done the whole shmore thing. You'll probably make fun of me for this, too. I've never had a Happy Pack."

He laughed again. "A whatty what? That sounds dirty. Maybe I can help you out with whatever *that* is."

Her heart spun with the offer, but she knew he was probably messing around again, so she forced herself not to dwell on how incredible it would feel to do dirty things with her muscle-bound grizzly man.

"A Happy Pack. You know, at McDonald's."

That earned her another deep, sexy laugh. "You mean a Happy Meal? A *kid's* Happy Meal?"

"Yeah, a Happy Pack. With those cute toys, you know."

He shook his head, laughing under his breath. "We'll have to change that. Everyone should experience s'mores. It's like a rite of passage. And you're not missing much with McDonald's, but you should experience a Happy Meal, too."

She tried not to hold on to the *we* part of what he'd said, but inside she was doing a happy dance at the prospect of spending more time with him. She was dying to ask him about what Rachel had said. Did he really prefer a more solitary lifestyle, or was there more to it? But despite his flirty comments and sucking her finger—*God, sucking my finger!*—his private life was none of her business.

"I'll put shmores and a Happy Pack on my bucket list." She opened the bakery box and tilted it in his direction. "Do you want one of these?"

In the space of a breath, his eyes flashed with heat. "No, thanks. They couldn't possibly be as sweet as my last taste was."

He ran hot and cold like a faucet, and she was in the mood for a steamy bath. She eyed the chocolate croissant, wondering if she should switch to the pink-frosted cupcake. *I was just messing with you.*

Ugh! She refocused on pulling her mind out of the gutter.

"So…" she said. "Where are we heading now?"

His expression turned serious, and Shannon wondered if the coy look had actually been there, or if it had simply been her wishful thinking.

"To meet with the Cumberlands."

"Who are they?"

"They own two hundred acres of land adjacent to the park near my parents' place. They're putting it on the market, and I want to try to convince them to put it into conservation land instead of selling." The muscle in his jaw jumped. "It might be a while, and I'm not sure how they'll react. Do you want me to drop you at Hal's, or somewhere else?"

No, she didn't want to go to Hal's. She wanted to learn more about him, to see what was stoking his fire. Aggression was rolling off of him like the wind, and it had come on so fast, she *had* to see him in action when he handled it.

"I don't mind going, unless you'd prefer I didn't." She took a bite of a chocolate croissant and he arched a brow. She looked down at the croissant. "I'm powering up to have your back."

"I'm sure I'll regret this later," he said with a hint of a smile, "but I don't mind you coming along. Just let me do the talking."

"No problem. You'll do all the talking. I'll stand by nodding supportively and I won't say a word. Not one single sentence. Can I give them the stink eye or—"

He shot her a narrow-eyed look.

She shoved the croissant in her mouth and pretended to zip her lips closed and lock them. He turned his hand palm up and motioned with his fingers. She feigned setting the key in his palm.

He curled his fingers over hers and said, "Thanks, Butter-fly."

He tucked the invisible key in his shirt pocket while she tried to remember how to chew.

Chapter Three

THE CUMBERLAND RANCH was nestled at the base of the mountains. Rolling pastures gave way to pockets of forest. It was one of the prettiest properties around. Not that there was an ugly acre in all of Colorado as far as Steve was concerned, but this was definitely right up there as one of his favorite spots. When he was younger, he and the two oldest Cumberland brothers, Mack and Will, had run wild, exploring every inch of the property.

"Is this the plan?" Shannon asked. "Stare out at the land and hope the owners change their mind via brain waves?"

He pulled the keys from the ignition and breathed deeply, readying for a conversation he wasn't looking forward to having with his two old friends. Mack and Will had lost their mother two years ago, and their father had passed away last winter. Their parents had been good to Steve, treating him like one of their own, and he missed them. He was sure his friends were still grieving, and he imagined handling their parents' estate was making things even more difficult. He didn't want to add stress to their difficult time, but there would always be reasons not to take a stand. If he waited for a good time to present itself, it might be too late.

"That's what's wrong with you city dwellers. You're always in a hurry to get to the next thing, when the most compelling things are right in front of you." He shoved the keys in his pocket and tried to shake his uneasy feeling about the impending conversation with his friends. He'd also flirted more than he would have liked with Shannon, and he knew he was sending her mixed messages. But he had too much on his mind to think clearly.

He motioned toward the gorgeous property. Every few years another parcel in Weston was sold, another farm was subdivided. It pained him to see the sprawling landscape chopped up into communities and meted out as if land were expendable. He'd been fighting the good fight for long enough to know one person *could* make a difference. But with a property of this size and an asking price of nearly 2.4 million dollars, he knew it would take a lot more than good intentions and a little rallying to keep it out of the hands of developers, unless his friends agreed with his idea.

"I'm not a city dweller. I'm a beach dweller." She glanced at him, then out the front window. "Are we getting out of the truck?"

"In a sec, Butterfly. I'm just taking it all in. I played frontier with Mack and Will Cumberland in those fields. Sneaking out at night, spending hours climbing trees, finding snakes and frogs and scaring my sister with them." He laughed with the memory. "We used to hide in the hayloft in that barn down there. I remember the sound of their father sliding the heavy wooden doors open and the feel of my pulse racing, the pungent smell of hay as we buried ourselves in it. The way the smell invaded my lungs and tickled my throat and I had to choke back coughs." He rubbed his forearm. "I can still feel the scratches it left on my arms and legs."

He opened the truck door and met her intense gaze. "Can you get that on your Pinterest boards?" He walked around the truck and opened her door, offering her a hand to step down.

"Pinterest has pictures of everything."

She took his hand as she stepped from the truck, and he led her to the fence surrounding the pastures, nodding in the direction of the woods in the distance toward their left. "At night we used to meet in those woods with our flashlights. I love this land, and I really don't want to see it fall into the wrong hands." Even back then he'd wanted to live in the mountains, and he wondered whether Shannon saw the beauty he saw, or like so many others who didn't grow up there, if she saw land ripe for development. "What do you see when you look out there?"

She was quiet for a moment. "I see majestic mountains, pastures, trees." She smiled and her gaze dropped to their joined hands.

He hadn't realized he was still holding her hand, and released it.

She lifted her eyes to his and said, "And I see a guy who gets lost in those things."

The way she was looking at him made his thoughts stumble. "And that's a bad thing?"

"No. It's a *curious* thing. Do you ever wonder if you're missing out on things? Technological advances? Things like that?"

He shrugged. "I read the news. It's not like I don't have the Internet. But I don't live *for* the news, or for what anyone else is doing. I think you and I live in different worlds, Butterfly."

She stepped closer, bringing with her that scintillating scent he already knew by heart. "Do we? Or do we look at the same world differently?" Before he could come up with an answer, she asked, "Why do you call me 'Butterfly'?"

"Isn't it obvious?" He held her gaze, taking pleasure in the way her cheeks pinked up.

"Not to me," she said sweetly.

She went from mouthy to sweet, and that sweetness got to him every damn time. "Why do you call me Grizz?"

She laughed and brushed her fingers through the ends of his hair. Her hand slid to his cheek, grazing his whiskers. "Isn't it obvious?"

Her hand was warm and soft against his cheek. Despite how nice it felt, despite his mounting desire to gather her in his arms and finally take his first taste of the woman who was slowly driving him out of his mind, he knew he had to find that elusive space he desperately needed. He placed his hand over hers, enjoying the smooth, delicate feel of it before reluctantly drawing it away.

"We should go get this over with." He nodded toward the house.

"Right." She blinked several times, as if he'd confused her as badly as his actions confused him.

He forced himself to break the spell and headed for the cedar-sided home where he'd spent many nights of his youth.

Mack came around the side of the house and waved them over. "Hey, buddy! Come on back."

Steve tried not to dissect the fact that his hand immediately took up residence on Shannon's lower back as they approached his friend.

Mack pulled him into a manly embrace. "I missed you, man." At six two, Mack stood nearly eye to eye with Steve.

"Me too, bro," Steve said. "How are you guys? How's Casey?" Casey was Mack and Will's younger brother. A late-in-life baby for their parents, at twenty-two Casey was thirteen years younger than Mack. He'd been just a boy when Mack and Steve had gone off to college.

"Casey's good. He's living with me, finding his way. You know. We're all back to the bump and grind of the business world. Trying to wrap up Dad's estate." Mack had moved away from Weston after college to work for a computer software development company and had settled in Allure, a neighboring town. He glanced curiously at Shannon.

"This is Shannon Braden." Without any cognitive thought, Steve placed a possessive hand on her back again. "She's doing research up on the mountain."

"Related to Hal?" Mack asked, flashing the killer smile. He and Will were a year apart, and they looked like twins, with deep-set pale blue eyes, olive skin, and jet-black hair, all of which made them chick magnets. Their outgoing personalities helped with the ladies, too.

"He's my uncle," Shannon said, flashing her own pearly whites.

"He's a good man," Mack said, pulling his phone from his pocket. "Let me get Will up here. He's down at the barn." He thumbed a text and shoved the phone in his pocket, then winked at Steve and said, "He's probably up in that loft."

Steve laughed. "Good times, Mack. Good times."

"Come on. Let's sit down and talk. Can I get y'all a drink?" Mack led them to the slate patio. "Soda? Water? Beer?"

"Shannon?" Steve asked, pulling a chair out from beneath the glass table for her.

"I'm okay, thanks." She sat down, and he claimed the seat beside her.

"I'm cool, too. Thanks for making time for me today, Mack. I know you're busy."

"Man, you're like our brother." Mack took the seat opposite Steve. "You know we'll always make time for you."

"You can't imagine how much that means to me. You know I feel the same way." Steve rose to his feet as Will came up the hill. Will's eyes made a beeline for Shannon, who looked radiant with the sun beating down on her beautiful face. Steve set a hand on the back of her chair, hating himself a little for laying claim to a woman who wasn't his.

"Steve!" Will opened his arms and yanked him in tight. "Damn, I've missed you."

"Missed you, too, bud." He hadn't seen them since a few weeks after their father passed away.

"Who's this gorgeous creature?" Will bent down on one knee beside Shannon and kissed her hand.

"Get up, you fool," Mack said. "Can't you see she's spoken for?"

"No, I'm not," Shannon said, wrinkling her nose in confusion.

Steve tried to remember why he'd thought it was a good idea for her to come along when he knew damn well Will and Mack would be crazy not to try to pick her up.

"Will, Shannon Braden. Shannon, Will Cumberland." Steve grabbed Will by the arm and lifted him to his feet. "Braden. As in Rex will kick your ass halfway across the state if you mess with her."

Will laughed and sat across from Shannon. "As I remember it, he kicked your ass for saying you wouldn't mind getting a piece of his sister, Savannah."

"Yeah, let's not go there." Steve scrubbed a hand down his

face.

"Really?" Shannon's eyes lit up. "Oh my gosh, you have to tell me about that."

"No, I don't," Steve said, hoping to throw her off the scent of that particularly embarrassing story.

"Rex is *so* possessive," Shannon said. "You should see him with their new baby, Hal, named for Rex's father, of course. I swear that baby is attached to Rex every minute he's not running the ranch, and half the time when he is. He's so freaking adorable. Anyway, Rex is the same way with his nieces and nephews. He's always got kids clinging to him. No one messes with Rex Braden's family." She grabbed Steve's arm and leaned in so close her breath became his. "I want every last detail. Did you put up a good fight, at least?"

"Wow, you don't let up, do you?" Mack said with a grin. "She definitely has Braden blood."

"Thank you," Shannon said with a proud smile.

"She's tenacious," Steve agreed. "Since we're not here to talk about old times, how about I share that with you later?" *Like in a million years.*

"Oh, right." She pressed her lips together but failed in containing her contagious smile. She lowered her voice and whispered, "But if you don't tell me, I'll ask Rex."

Will and Mack burst into laughter.

"Damn, you are a wild one," Will said. "How'd you like to have a drink with me tonight?"

Mack's brows rose with amusement. Steve's slanted in anger.

WOW. STEVE KNEW how to pick his friends. Mack and Will were smokin' hot. They looked like a double shot of Henry Cavill, complete with matching dimples in their chins. But they had nothing on her grizzly man. She shifted her eyes to Steve, who had a death stare locked on Will. He quickly tried to mask the threatening look with splayed hands and a halfhearted smile.

With hope that he wasn't messing with her after all, she said, "Actually, I'm supposed to scout locations for my research with Steve tonight."

"That's okay," Steve said, shocking—*and upsetting*—her. "The mountain isn't going anywhere."

Her thoughts came to a sudden halt. He wanted her to go out with Will? Then what was that look? She didn't want to go out with Will. She wanted to go scouting with Steve.

"So, it's settled, then." Will pulled out his phone. "Put your number in there, sweetheart. I'll pick you up around seven?"

"Um…" She gave Steve what she hoped was a look that said, *You really want me to go with him?* and *Please say no.*

He shrugged.

What the hell did that mean? She picked up Will's phone and reluctantly put her number in his contact list. "Can we make it nine? I want to try to do some scouting first." *And figure out why Steve is playing with my head.*

"Anytime you want." Will grinned and slipped his phone into his pocket.

"I'll bring her down the mountain so you don't have to try to navigate up at night," Steve offered. "I'm coming back into town anyway."

"You are?" Shannon asked. Did he have a date? Her mind trailed back to the image of Steve and Rachel talking and the way Rachel had touched his arm. She wondered if he had a date with her. Wouldn't Rachel have said something if she were seeing Steve?

Steve nodded and turned back to his friends. "Anyway, the reason I wanted to talk with you guys was about the ranch."

Holy cow, she'd nearly forgotten this wasn't a social visit. He'd changed gears so quickly she wondered if he was upset with her for Will asking her out. His tight jaw and rigid back told her he was purposely trying not to look at her, and that stung.

"I was hoping you'd consider putting the land into a conservation trust," Steve said with a serious tone.

"We thought you might want to discuss that," Mack said. "Nothing personal, Steve, but we're done with the ranch, the land, the whole deal."

"Done with it?" Steve asked. "It's been in your family for generations."

"Buddy, so has your old man's property," Will said. "But I don't see you clamoring to get on board."

The pained expression that came over Steve's face made Shannon want to reach for his hand, softening the sting of his pushing her toward Will. His rigid exterior was obviously due to this conversation and not the fact that Will had asked her out.

"The truth is," Mack said, "we need the money from the sale of the ranch. We're keeping our mom's family's little house near town, trying to rent it out at the moment. But, Steve, while you're up on that mountain living off the land, the world is getting more expensive by the week. I want to settle down and have kids one day, work a regular job, and not sweat it out on the ranch from dawn until dark, worrying about animals and agricultural costs. And Casey wants to get his master's degree. We're just not married to the land the way Mom and Dad were."

"I forgot your parents also owned that little house near town. I'm glad you're keeping it," Steve said. "And I get it, about needing the money. I just thought it was worth a shot."

"We appreciate that," Mack said thoughtfully. "You should know that CRH Enterprises is nosing around."

Steve sank back in his seat, grinding his teeth together. "Please tell me you're not considering selling to them. They're a conglomerate of land-raping assholes. They'll strip the land and turn this place into a housing development quicker than you can cash their check."

"We're not doing anything yet," Mack assured him. "The property won't formally be on the market for another sixty days. Our agent just said they were sniffing around."

"Can you do me a favor and keep me in the loop?" Steve rose to his feet, tension billowing off of him.

Shannon pushed from her chair. She had so many questions, but she'd already opened her mouth once, and that had landed her a date with the wrong man.

"Of course," Mack said, rising to his feet. "We're not trying to screw Weston, Steve."

Steve nodded. "I know. You've got to do what you've got to do. Just give me those sixty days to see what I can come up with."

"No worries, buddy." Will put a hand on Steve's shoulder. "I don't know what you have in mind, but if you have a way to put the land into conservation and we can still get the equity out of it, you know we're behind you. And I'm sorry about the comment about your pop's ranch. I was just making a point."

"No worries," Steve assured him. "We'll see you around."

"Right. Tonight," Will reminded him. "You're bringing

Shannon down the mountain?"

Steve turned a possessive gaze to Shannon that nearly stopped her heart.

"Yeah," Steve said. "Right."

"Cool." Will smiled at Shannon. "See you tonight, sweetheart."

"Can you send me a text real quick?" Shannon asked Will. "That way I'll have your number in case I get hung up or something." She didn't want to make things any more uncomfortable by telling Will she didn't want to go out with him now, but she had every intention of canceling their date. She'd already spent two hours talking to Cal last night when she'd really wanted to connect with a certain other man. The man who was currently looking at her like he didn't know if he wanted to claim her or curse at her.

The ride back up the mountain was tense. Steve looked like he was chewing on nails. She knew he was upset over that company looking into purchasing the land, and tried to lighten the mood.

She opened the bakery box, scooped frosting on her finger, and held it out to him. "Can I entice you into a little sugary delight?"

He managed a smile, and his gorgeous, troubled eyes shifted to her, but his smile didn't alleviate the darkness she saw in them.

"Come on. Sugar fixes almost everything. Just try it." She pushed her finger in front of his mouth. "You know you want it."

"Shannon," he warned huskily.

She touched the frosting to his lips, earning a soft laugh. "Come on. Open up. Just don't do that sucking thing."

He held her hand and took her finger into his mouth, sucking harder than before and doing that swirly thing with his tongue that sent shivers straight to her core. She snapped her mouth shut to keep a sound of pleasure from escaping and cleared her throat to try to mask her emotions.

"Better?" Her voice cracked.

"Mildly," he said a little angrily.

"Want to talk about it?"

"The frosting? Yeah, I do," he said. "The pink-frosted cupcake stays at my cabin tonight. It's not going anywhere near Will's mouth."

"I meant the land!" She laughed, but her stomach was doing flips with the hint of jealousy he'd just revealed.

"Oh." He stared out at the road with a serious expression. "No."

"Why not? And why do you care if I go out with Will?"

His tense expression gave nothing away.

"Steve," she urged.

He stared straight ahead.

"God," she said, exasperated. "You're like a child."

"I assure you, I'm all man."

She rolled her eyes. "It's not like *you* want to go out with me, so why do you care?"

He gave her the deadpan look again.

"*Whatever.*" She wondered if he knew how crazy he was making her, or if he was too tied up in knots over the land to realize it. "Why won't you talk about the land? It's obviously bugging you."

"Because I don't have an answer."

"That's why we should talk," she said sharply. "That's what friends do, you know. They talk about things, figure things out."

They rode the rest of the way in tense silence. At his cabin, he helped her from the truck and she kept hold of his hand.

"Talk to me," she urged.

"I need to get out and do my rounds. Check on those partying kids." He freed his hand and reached into the truck for her grocery bag and the bakery box. "I'll carry these up for you."

"I can carry them."

He stalked off toward her cabin with the bags in hand, leaving her no choice but to fall into step beside him. The big, brooding pain in the butt. They followed the narrow path through the woods, weaving around rocks and trees. Her quaint log cabin and rented Jeep came into view. Her cabin was smaller than Steve's, with a front porch barely big enough for two people. She unlocked the door, acutely aware of his close proximity, and he followed her inside the cozy living room. A beige sofa sat against the far wall with an end table on one side, taking up most of the space. The tiny kitchen had a stove with a microwave above it, a sink, and enough counter space for a coffee machine and two plates, or a grocery bag and a bakery box. She hoped. Opposite the kitchen, the refrigerator was tucked into an alcove beside the bathroom, and on the other side of the bathroom, a narrow staircase led up to the bedroom loft above the kitchen. It was small to begin with, and with Steve's broad shoulders, it felt even tighter.

"You can set those on the counter," she said. "Care to tell me why I'm getting the silent treatment?"

"I'm sorry. I don't mean to be a prick." He looked around, and she wished she knew what he was thinking. He walked over to the end table and picked up the framed photograph of her family she had set there. A small smile settled on his lips.

"Do you miss them, being so far away?" he asked.

"Always. When I'm in my own apartment I miss them, and believe me, I know exactly how silly that sounds. But when you grow up in a big family, you're used to noise and people and talking about everything, because everyone always wants to help and be part of your decisions." She leaned against the counter, thinking about her family. Before coming to Colorado for the initial research project, Shannon had felt restless, oppressed by her close-knit hometown and living under the constant watch of her four older brothers. She'd had a hard time figuring out what she wanted out of life separate from what those who loved her wanted *for* her. At the suggestion of her older sister, Tempest, she'd taken the assignment and come to Colorado as an exercise in introspection. She'd thought she would love doing research, but all that time alone on the mountain had made her realize that loving the work wasn't enough. She didn't just enjoy being around people; she *needed* social interaction, and she wanted *more* from her work. She wanted to make a bigger difference. More *what*, she wasn't sure, but the solo research wasn't doing it for her.

He set the picture down, and his expression turned solemn. "And I've just made you lonelier by clamming up. I'm sorry. I was just thinking about the land."

He was so complex—hot, cold, stoic, sensitive. She found him even more intriguing because of it. Some people were open books, like her and her mother, while people like Steve needed to be finessed and pushed through every page, like her father and her brothers Sam and Nate. Tempest always said they were the most interesting people. *The ones that loved the hardest.*

"You know my cousin Treat is a real estate investor," she offered. "You could probably talk to him about it."

"The feud between my family and your uncle Hal's taught me not to do business with people you care about," he said casually.

"That's a pretty crappy rule." She knew his father and her uncle Hal had purchased land together and his father had somehow broken Hal's trust, which was the impetus for what had become a forty-year feud between the families. She didn't know all the details of their reconciliation, but she knew Rex and Jade's relationship had brought it all to a head. After they'd made amends, Rex and Jade had bought the property the two men had been feuding over and had built their home on it.

"It is, isn't it?" He shook his head. "Crappy but important."

"What are your alternatives?" She didn't know what Steve earned, but she didn't think it was enough to purchase the estate.

He shrugged. "I'll talk to a few connections, see if I can get them interested in purchasing the property and putting it into a conservation trust."

"Maybe I can come up with something."

He ran an assessing gaze over her.

"What?" She was good at coming up with solutions for other people's problems. It was her own she had trouble with.

"Nothing. You're just not like anyone I know." He reached into the box and grabbed the cupcake. "This is coming with me."

She followed him to the door. "You're seriously going to hold my cupcake hostage? For a man who says very little, that says a heck of a lot."

He stepped closer. So close his chest touched hers when he inhaled.

"What exactly does it say?" he challenged.

"That maybe you don't want me to go out with Will." She didn't recognize her breathy voice.

His eyes narrowed, and he lifted the cupcake with a devilish smile. "Or maybe it says I like pink frosting."

She wasn't going to let him off that easy. "I think it says you like me."

"Do you?" He dropped his eyes to the cupcake, then shifted them to her mouth, lingering there so long her lips tingled with anticipation.

Kiss me.

"Yes," she whispered.

He didn't move. Didn't blink. Didn't do a freaking thing, and her entire body ached for his touch. He raised a brow, silent as the day was long. Damn him. No man had ever had this effect on her. She had to break their connection before she took the kiss she so desperately wanted.

"Should I come by later?" she finally managed.

His eyes grew sinfully darker.

"To look for habitats." The words flew from her mouth and he smiled. *Ugh!* He was messing with her again!

"See you later, Butterfly."

She watched his perfect butt as he walked away. She needed to up her game if she was going to figure out how to beat him at it.

Chapter Four

AFTER TAKING CARE of his duties, Steve made a few calls to the contacts he thought might take an interest in the Cumberland property. He knew it was a long shot, but he wasn't going to give up before trying everything he could. When Shannon came over to ask him to go with her up the mountain, she was too sweet—*If you come with me, I'll go with you when you traipse all over the mountain tomorrow doing whatever it is a grizzly guy like you does*—and too insistent—*Grizz, you know you want to see those cute little foxes. You can't tell me you don't want to trek up the mountain one more time. You love doing that*—to deny.

They'd been scoping out fox habitats for the past two hours, and she'd been tossing out ideas to help him save the Cumberland property. She was as excited about the prospect as he was frustrated by it.

"There are tons of nonprofits that could probably help raise funds," she said, stepping around a big rock. "What about private investors? There are lots of philanthropists who are interested in land conservation. I bet we could find a list of them with a quick Google search."

She was an anomaly to him. Astute and animated. She'd pointed out animal prints, scat, and markings on trees without missing a beat in sharing her ideas for the land. The more time they spent together, the more difficult it became for him to keep a sense of distance between them.

"I've made some calls, put some feelers out." He looked up toward the darkening sky, and his gut fisted. "Shouldn't we head back so you can get ready for your date?"

"Not yet." She ducked beneath a branch. Her hair got tangled and she inhaled a sharp breath, bent over beneath the branch.

"I've got you." Steve began untangling her hair. The scent of lilacs rose from the silky strands. Without thinking, he said, "Your hair smells like spring."

"Uh-huh. Want a real turn-on, mountain man?" she said teasingly. "It's organic."

"You do realize I could give your hair a tug for that crack." He'd like to give it a tug, all right, when she was naked and on her knees. Or in his bed. Or right here against a tree...

"Careful, you never know what a girl likes."

Great. Now he was hard.

In an effort to distract himself, which wasn't easy with her bent at the waist in front of him, he said, "You should tie your hair back when you're out here working." *So my mind doesn't wander.*

She poked his stomach. "You could have mentioned that an hour ago."

"You were out here researching for weeks. How'd you get untangled then?" He unwound the last strand. "Okay, you're free."

"Thank you." She straightened her spine and ran her fingers through her hair. "I remembered to tie my hair back when I was working alone." Her eyes slid down his body. "You're a bit of a distraction."

He'd like to distract her, all right, but she had another man waiting for her tonight, and it was his own damn fault. He could have stopped it.

"Maybe you're just too excited about your date to concentrate." His gut twisted at the thought of Shannon going out with Will, but he couldn't afford to get any more tangled up in her than he already was.

"Hardly," she said, pulling him back to the moment. "Are you sure this is gray fox territory?" She walked around a group of pine trees.

He'd guided her to this area because he knew that just ahead, beyond a thicket of trees, there was a fox den, but he'd given her no forewarning, wanting to enjoy her reaction. When he'd been out looking for the partiers earlier, he'd checked on the dens, and was happy to see they were all in use again this year.

She rounded another group of trees and turned a wide smile to him, pointing to scat—fox poop—on the ground. The sun was just beginning to set, casting an orange glow behind her.

"This whole mountain is fox territory," he said. *And I'm looking at the foxiest thing around.*

She took a notebook from her backpack and began taking notes and sketching the area. Evening brought a different sort of peacefulness to the mountain, as diurnal creatures settled in safely for the evening, giving way to nocturnal wildlife. The air turned crisper, stealing the vanilla-butterscotch smell of ponderosa bark and bringing out sharper, earthier scents.

"Hey," she said. "You look like you've disappeared into some far-off land."

"Nope. Right here with you." He didn't understand how

anyone could stand in this forest and not lose himself in the beauty of it.

"What about crowdfunding?" She stepped over a large branch, and he grabbed her arm, steadying her.

"Crowd whatting?"

"Crowdfunding. Surely you've heard of it. It's when you list a project online and promote it to groups who you think will want to take part in the effort." She moved around the thicket, searching the ground. "Lots of little donations can equate to a massive amount of money. I read about a family who raised two hundred thousand dollars for their daughter's surgery. Crowdfunding is used for everything from buying a car and making a music video to buying property or taking care of bills after accidents or when someone falls on hard times."

"Online begging. No thank you."

She glared at him. "It's not like that. People don't see it that way. They want to help."

"I didn't take you for naive, city girl."

"If by naive you mean not thinking the worst about others, then I guess you *would* consider me naive. There are good people out there. Like the connections you already reached out to."

"Those are people I know and trust. They aren't strangers."

"So you only trust people you've met?" She took a step behind the thicket and stopped short. She held her finger over her lips and pointed to a kit—a baby fox—peeking its fuzzy little head out from the base of a hollow tree. Her shoulders rose, and she shivered with excitement. She had no idea what her gleeful reaction did to him. This was nature's foreplay at its best.

They watched the kit peek its head out, then disappear into

the dark den. A few seconds later two kits poked their heads out. Their fur had already begun turning russet behind their ears and on their legs. The rest was gray with patches of white around their beady dark eyes.

Shannon squeezed Steve's hand and mouthed, "Oh my God! So cute!"

They were cute little critters, all right, but not half as cute as she was, bouncing on her toes behind the thicket. They watched the kits poking their heads out, sniffing the air, then ducking back into the den. As darkness fell over them, they left as quietly as they could, though the foxes returned to the den the moment they moved.

Shannon clung to his arm as they made their way down the dark mountain.

"Did you see how cute they were? What do you think, eight or nine weeks old? I wonder how many kits there are. They start going out with the vixen—the mother—around five weeks for short forays. They're already eating solid foods. If we can find a few more sites, we can figure out the best places to watch them from."

She spoke so fast, he wondered if she realized she'd said *we*.

"Did you know the gray vixens have eight nipples and the red only have six? That's interesting to me. Isn't it to you?" She didn't pause for a response, and that was just fine with Steve. There was nothing she could tell him about the animals he didn't already know, but he enjoyed listening to her. "They're monogamous, too. For life. Did you know that? Of course you knew that. Did they use that same den last year? Do you know? Are we heading to another den now?"

She launched into another one-sided discussion about how humans could take a lesson in monogamy from foxes, and she didn't show any signs of slowing down. He knew he had to take her down the mountain for her date, but for a split second he debated not bringing it up and allowing her to get so lost in her excitement that time would slip by, her date forgotten. But Will was his friend, and it was a selfish thought. One that could lead only to hurting both Will and Shannon, which was why he stopped walking and gently touched her face to draw her attention.

Her sparkling eyes met his, the corners of her mouth curled up. "I'm sorry. I'm rambling."

She was so beautiful, with the moonlight at her back and that sweet, excited look in her eyes. How would he survive the night knowing she was in Will's arms?

"You're excited," he said, intensely aware of her hand on his forearm and how close they were standing. "There's a difference between being excited and rambling."

"You're just saying that to be nice." She lowered her gaze, and her hair fell forward, hiding her face.

He tucked a lock behind her ear so he could see her more clearly. When she lifted her eyes, gone was the excitement, replaced with a darker, more alluring look. Her fingers curled tighter around his arm. The urge to lean down and kiss her was so strong, his muscles burned against his restraint. He didn't do casual sex, and he knew there would be nothing *casual* about being buried deep inside Shannon. She stroked something dark and deep inside him. Something no one else ever had. Every minute with Shannon was a battle of self-control, and he was hanging on by a thread. If he kissed her, touched her, let himself do the things he wanted to with her, his feelings would only magnify. He knew, beyond a shadow of a doubt, there would be nothing left to hold on to. Nothing to keep his head on straight.

Nothing to protect his heart—or hers.

She licked her lips, chipping away at his resolve. He ground his teeth together, struggling to rein it back in.

"Shannon," he managed.

They both stepped closer, their thighs brushing. This was wrong. She had a date, and he'd agreed to bring her to his friend. But he could feel desire rolling off of her, and like a moth to a flame, he couldn't pull away. He didn't want to pull away. As he reached for her, her words came back to him. *I'm not like you. I need people.*

The thought sent the gears in his mind churning again, and he reluctantly stepped back. "It's getting dark."

She stepped forward. "Yes."

Her whisper sounded more like an invitation than an agreement about the sun's rapid departure, and hell if he didn't want to accept. But he'd never be the type of guy she needed. This couldn't go anywhere, and he was already teetering on a precarious edge. It took every ounce of his willpower to do the right thing.

"We should head back. You have a date." He took another step away, and she grabbed his arm, keeping him in place.

She looked at him through long, thick lashes and said, "I canceled it."

STEVE'S FOREHEAD WRINKLED in confusion, and the conflicted look in his eyes made Shannon's pulse race even more than their close proximity was causing.

"Why would you do that?"

Definitely not the response she'd hoped for.

"Because I didn't want to go out with him. I never even agreed to it. He assumed I wanted to go, and you just sat there like you didn't give a darn one way or another."

He wrenched his arm free. "I wish you hadn't done that. Will's a nice guy. He would have treated you well and you would have had a good time."

"You didn't hear what I said. I didn't *want* to go."

He looked at her with the pained expression she'd seen earlier when Will had made the comment about Steve not working with his father. He ran a hand through his hair and turned away. Had she totally misread him? Had he honestly been messing with her all day?

"We should get going," he said gruffly.

"Wait." Needing answers, she reached for his hand, and he stilled. "Did you really want me to go out with him?"

He didn't steal his hand away, but his serious expression sent a chill down her back.

"What I want doesn't matter."

Doesn't matter? "I don't understand. You've been hot and cold all day. One minute you're sucking my finger, the next you're telling me to go out with your friend. I have no idea where you stand."

"Where I stand?" He stepped closer. "Where I stand is right here on this mountain. Where I'll always stand."

She crossed her arms against the sting of rejection. "Come on, Steve. We've been playing this game since Rex and Jade's wedding, which was months ago."

"I don't play games," he said sharply.

She lifted her chin, meeting his gaze. "Then what do you call it? You *took* my cupcake, for God's sake, and whether you want to admit it or not, you definitely have been flirting with me."

"Why does it have to be called anything?" He turned away and ran his hand through his hair again. She realized it was a nervous habit. If he was nervous, that had to mean something.

"It doesn't, but…"

He turned toward her again. "But?"

"But…I don't know. Now I feel foolish for bringing it up."

His gaze softened and he grumbled a curse. "Well, don't feel foolish, for Christ's sake. I do like you." He reached for her hand and tugged her closer. "But I also respect you."

"But…?"

"We're saying that word a lot, aren't we?" His lips curved up in a smile. "But you're a social butterfly, and I like my solitary life. It doesn't matter if I like you, or if I find you insanely sexy. Nothing can come of it, so it's better if we don't torture ourselves with it."

She stepped closer and slipped her finger into the waistband of his pants. "You find me insanely sexy?"

"Shannon," he warned, and put his hand on hers to move it from his waist, but she curled her finger tighter.

"That's why you wanted me to go out with Will, isn't it? So I wouldn't want to go out with you? Or so I would be off-limits?"

He didn't respond, but his hand tightened around hers.

"So you wouldn't want me?" She closed the sliver of space between them. "Because you'd never hit on your friend's girlfriend. That's not who Steve Johnson is."

"For the record, your being with Will wouldn't stop me from *wanting* you. It would piss me off, but at least I'd know I didn't hold you back."

"From?"

"From the life you want. The life you deserve." His face went hard, tense. "Stop this, Shannon. This can't happen."

"Why?"

"Because it can't go anywhere."

She heard the words. She even processed them, and she didn't do flings, but her heart was so full of Steve, not one ounce of her wanted to give up the chance to get closer to him.

"Do all relationships have to go somewhere?" It was a stupid question, because she knew everyone wasn't looking for a lifelong commitment, but she didn't care about everyone. She cared about him.

He closed his eyes for a second, and when he opened them, she saw a renewed struggle.

"You're asking the wrong guy." He dropped his gaze from her eyes to her mouth, and his entire body seemed to rise and expand. He grimaced, and just when she was sure he was going to turn away, his arm circled her waist and he tugged her against him.

Heat surged through her with his conflicting messages. He was looking at her like he wanted to devour her, but he gritted his teeth like she was the enemy. Breathing hard, her nerves tingling like pinpricks, she forced through her fear of being turned away and tried one last time to entice him over to the dark side.

"So," she said shakily. "Let me get this straight. You're attracted to me, but since we like different things, we can't"—she licked her lips, feeling his body flex against her—"kiss?"

His lips parted and his eyes narrowed.

"We can't"—she pressed her hand to his chest—"touch?"

"Shannon," he said gruffly. "I'm trying to do the right thing."

How come every guy she wanted to do the right thing inevitably did the wrong thing—like he was doing now?

"You think you're trying to do the right thing, but your definitions are mixed up, Grizz. The way you're holding me? That *is* the right thing." She held his gaze, their bodies instinctively moving closer. His long fingers splayed across her back, searing heat through her shirt.

"Damn it, Shannon. Don't you get it?" He pressed his cheek to hers, his whiskers scratching her skin as his hot breath rolled over her ear. "It's not wrong. Not by any stretch of the imagination."

He touched his lips to her cheek, and she closed her eyes. His lips brushed along her jaw, over her lips. His hips pressed forward, every hard inch of him sinking into her.

"Feel what you do to me with nothing more than your voice, a single touch, your sexy-as-hell eyes."

She couldn't respond, could barely think past the feel of his hands on her body, the power and frustration in his voice. Lord help her, because she wanted to feel that power wrapped around her.

"You *know* I want to lay you down right here and memorize every sweet curve of your body. I want to taste your pleasures, waylay your fears, discover your vulnerabilities, your secret pleasure points." His lips brushed over hers again, along her cheek, to her other ear. "Even when we're not together, all I can think about is what it would be like to be inside you."

Yes, yes, yes. Oh Lord, yes.

He drew back, and she opened her eyes. Her knees weakened at the desire welling in his eyes. Then his hands left her body, and she heard herself whimper. He placed his hands on her cheeks, angling her head up so she had no choice but to give him her full attention. And boy, did he have it. Every inch of her body was waiting for his kiss.

"You have no idea how much I want you. *I* had no idea how much I've wanted you. I've been trying to deny it, but I've wanted you since Jade's wedding."

Hope soared within her.

He brushed his thumb over her lips. "God, I love that sassy mouth of yours. But in a few weeks you'll go back to your real life, and I'll still be right here on this mountain." He paused, and his words settled in like lead. "Sorry, Butterfly, but I'm not that selfish."

He laced his fingers with hers and led her away from the spot where she'd been sure they were going to share their first kiss. The spot where she'd left her legs, her hope, and a piece of her heart.

Neither one spoke for a long time. When her brain began to function, anger replaced disbelief. She couldn't take the silence anymore and said, "That's it?"

"Pretty much." He lifted their joined hands as she stepped over a rock.

"Don't take this the wrong way, but you're kind of a jerk."

He laughed. "I've been called much worse."

"Seriously, most guys would have been all over me up there."

He slowed, clenched his jaw, then continued walking.

Ugh! "Most guys would see it as a blessing that I'm not going to be a noose around their neck forever."

"It should've tipped you off that I'm not like most guys when you saw where I live. Besides, if you're the type of girl who wants to be fucked by a guy who won't give a shit about you the next morning, then I made the right decision."

"What? I'm not…That's not what I meant." She shoved a branch out of her way and stomped over a pile of twigs.

"Maybe you should choose your words more carefully." He guided her through a nest of cottonwood trees, and she knew they were nearing her cabin. She didn't want the night to end like this. This was worse than before he'd said anything. At least then she'd still wondered whether he liked her, but now she knew he did—and he was *choosing* not to act on it.

"All I meant was, most guys would have at least kissed me."

He mumbled something, then said, "You should have gone out with Will and gotten your kisses."

"I don't *want* to kiss Will. I want to kiss you, dumbass."

He stopped short and tugged her against him so hard she smacked into his chest. "You know, it's amazing you get any guys with all the compliments you dole out."

"Doesn't *anything* ruffle your feathers?"

"Yes. A certain mouthy brunette ruffles a hell of a lot more than my feathers."

She pressed her lips together and drew upon every ounce of courage she could muster. "Then why won't you kiss me?"

He brushed the back of his fingers down her cheek, fluid and gentle, but the look in his eyes was rough and possessive. The man was a walking contradiction.

"Shannon, you are a gorgeous woman," he said softly. "You're smart, seductive, and playful in a way that I'm not at all used to and find so freaking hot, you drive me out of my mind."

Hope slipped in again, and she dared to hang on to it.

"But for a girl who thinks she's got *most guys* figured out, you haven't got a clue about *this* guy."

Chapter Five

IT WAS HELL not popping over to see Steve in the morning, but Shannon needed to get her head on straight about what was, or wasn't, going on between them. She spent the entire day vacillating between being embarrassed by being blown off and turned on by all the sexy things he'd said. She tried to focus on her research, but her mind kept circling back to being in his arms and the hungry look in his eyes as he'd said those seductive things to her. Hours later, after she'd traipsed over half the mountain collecting data, she still couldn't make sense of it. But she was a researcher. And damn it, she'd figure him out one way or another.

By the time she'd finished for the day, she was fit to be tied. There was only one way to make sense of a man she wanted this badly, and that was to let her girlfriends do it for her. Two phone calls and half an hour later she was dressed in her cutest outfit and out the door, heading for Buckley's, a local bar.

She hummed as she drove down the narrow mountain road. *Do not even glance at his cabin. No looking. Just drive right past.*

Steve's truck was parked at the end of his driveway with the hood up, and he was bent over, peering into it. Denim stretched across his perfect ass. He rose to his full height as her Jeep neared, and she lost her breath. Why, oh why, did he have to be shirtless? Couldn't he wear a ski parka? Or even better, full-body armor?

He sauntered toward the road, and she had no choice but to stop or look like a bitch. He peered into her open window, his eyes drifting to her miniskirt. "Hey there, Butterfly. Where're you off to looking so pretty?"

She felt herself swooning. *No swooning!*

She wasn't going to get swept up in him any more than she already was.

"Meeting friends at Buckley's."

His eyes narrowed. "Buckley's? That's where Cal hangs out, isn't it?"

"I don't know," she said flippantly, although now that he'd said it, she remembered it was true. Good, let him get jealous. Served him right.

"Jade's coming, and she promised to tell me *all* your dirty little secrets." She was only teasing. Jade would never offer up anyone's dirty secrets.

The muscles in his neck corded tight. His eyes drifted down her legs, stirring all the heat she'd spent the day trying to pretend didn't exist. She didn't have a chance of not swooning over him when all it took was one look to make her go crazy.

"Good luck with that," he said with a smirk, moving away from the window and straightening up, giving her a mouthwatering view of his bare chest.

She tried to look away, but her eyes were glued to him. After last night, she wondered if he had any dirty secrets at all— or so many she'd be better off *not* knowing.

"Have a good time, Butterfly, and be careful on these roads. Turn on your headlights, and if you have any trouble, you know how to reach me."

She wondered what would happen if she called him from her bedroom. *Hey, Grizz, I need some wood...* Would he blow her off or turn her on?

"Thanks, Grizz." How did he go from raging inferno last night to casual neighbor today? She couldn't even stay irritated with him long enough to spin wheels and drive away. God, this crush was turning her into a wimp. "Everything okay with your truck? Need a ride somewhere?"

He wiped his hands on a rag she hadn't noticed. "I'm good."

"You know, you should get out and have some fun sometimes. It's good for you." She realized he'd said he had to go into town last night, and he'd never gone. She wondered if he'd made that up just so Will wouldn't end up in her cabin. That thought brought rise to the emotion she was starting not to trust—*hope*.

He raised his arms out to his sides. "Look around you. This *is* my fun."

She sighed. "Are you at least going to the barn dance the night before I leave?"

"Sorry, but these legs don't dance."

She rolled her eyes. "You could if you tried."

"Not my thing, Butterfly."

"Too bad. I'm going, and I *love* to dance."

"Have fun with that." He turned and walked away.

She stewed all the way to Buckley's. *The only one I need rescuing from is you.*

She'd put herself out there last night and he'd turned her away. She should have spent the day returning Cal's and Will's calls, not stewing over a man who said he's *not selfish enough* to get involved with her. But every time she'd picked up her phone to return one of their calls, she'd lost service. A sign from the universe? She was a scientifically minded woman and wasn't supposed to believe in things like cosmic signs. But her girly heart apparently didn't care about her advanced degree. It had clung to the silly universe idea and refused to let go.

Tempest would be so proud.

She smiled at the thought of her older sister, who loved all things cosmic and spiritual. She'd probably write a song about it. As a music therapist, Tempest wrote songs about everything. Shannon often found herself thinking, *WWTD?* But her What-Would-Tempest-Do frame of mind often led her to do the opposite, since they were so different. Tempest was reserved and practical. She held her tongue more often than not and *always* thought things through before speaking. Even though they were different in many ways, Shannon still found her mind going back to her sister time and time again. Tempest was her measuring post of how far she could stray, and even though she was pissed off at the moment, she was glad she'd taken her sister's advice about coming to Colorado. Of course, Tempest would give her a hard time for throwing herself at Steve, as would her four older brothers. Sam would have her wear a chastity belt if it were up to him. He had always been the most protective of her brothers, which was precisely why she hadn't called Tempest today to talk over the issue with Steve. She didn't need Sam catching wind of whatever *wasn't* going on. She had enough to deal with trying to weed through the hot-and-heavy confusion of the Steve-Shannon puzzle without her brother butting in.

At Buckley's she took several deep breaths before heading inside. She'd come to Colorado to figure out who she was *apart* from her family. She needed to stop worrying about them, or Steve, and focus on having fun tonight.

She walked inside and realized she'd called the emergency girls' night because of Steve. Forgetting about him was obviously *off* the table.

The dimly lit bar was loud, crowded, and smelled like too much perfume and testosterone, contrasting sharply with the pine-scented mountain air she'd already gotten accustomed to.

She spotted Jade and Max on the dance floor. Jade's long black hair hung nearly to her waist. Dancing to the fast-paced country song in her skinny jeans and cowgirl boots, she looked like she'd never had a baby. Max leaned forward, her brown hair sweeping over her shoulders, and said something. Jade's smile widened. They looked carefree. Why wouldn't they? They were happily married with adorable children, wonderful husbands, and careers they loved, while Shannon's career had turned out to be too solitary and not as fulfilling as she'd hoped—and to top it all off, the only man she wanted was harder to pin down than the foxes she was researching.

The girls waved and hurried off the dance floor.

"The cavalry is here!" Jade announced as they both hugged her.

"And we're all ears," Max said. "We'll figure out whatever's got your panties in a bunch."

Good luck with that. They led Shannon to their table, where Rachel and Savannah were waiting with eager smiles and alcohol. *The perfect combination.* This was just what she needed. The tightness in her chest eased.

"Hey, Rach. Savannah, what are you doing here?" Savannah lived in New York with her husband, Jack, and their new baby, Adam. Shannon hadn't seen her in weeks.

"Jack had a flight, so I tagged along." Jack was ex-Special Forces and now worked teaching survival courses and as a bush pilot. "We got in this morning. My dad was missing his grandson and was thrilled to watch Adam tonight." Savannah rose to greet her and pushed her auburn hair over one shoulder before hugging Shannon. "Nothing could've kept me from seeing you tonight."

"I'm so glad you're here." Shannon slid into the booth beside Rachel and hugged her. "Thanks for coming, Rach."

"Are you kidding? I've been dying to know what is going on up on that mountain ever since we ran into each other." Rachel slid her drink to Shannon. "Drink up, because we want details."

"Thank you." Shannon took a long pull of Rachel's drink. It was sweet and burned all the way down. *Perfect. Even the drink is a contradiction.* Could she make it through one minute without thinking about Steve?

Max and Jade settled in beside Savannah.

"I'm *so* glad you called," Max said, reaching for her drink. "I needed a little time away from our beautiful babies. Sometimes it's nice to be Max instead of Mom, and actually go to the bathroom alone."

They all laughed.

"I was surprised when you called," Jade said. "I didn't know there was anything going on with you and Steve."

"There isn't," Shannon corrected her. "I mean, there could be, but there isn't." She rolled her eyes and flagged down the waitress. After ordering drinks, she pointed to Jade and said, "What's the deal with your brother?"

"I've been asking myself that for years." Jade winked. "What'd he do? He seemed like he was totally into you at my wedding. In fact, Max and I were surprised you two didn't hook up when you were here before."

"Maybe that's the problem," Savannah said, waggling her brows.

"*Ugh.* No, we definitely didn't hook up." The waitress brought their drinks, and Shannon took a sip.

"Because...?" Max asked.

"How should I know? He makes it hard for me to think. I'm already having a hard time doing my research because when I'm out on that mountain alone, I get bored. And then my mind travels, and the next thing I know, I'm thinking about Steve. Then hours go by and I realize I've totally blanked on doing any research at all."

"Oh my God. You're falling for him," Max said with wide eyes.

"You won't be the first," Rachel said. "He's hot. He's smart. And he's badass."

Shannon downed her drink. "Please tell me something I don't know."

"It's just...what you see in him? So have lots of other women." Rachel paused and raised her brows, obviously waiting for something to click for Shannon.

"So...Is he a player?" Shannon guessed, but that didn't feel right unless there were forest pixies filling his bed at night.

"Hardly," Jade said. "She's trying to tell you that lots of women have tried to catch his attention, but as far as we know, he's never been the type of guy to hook up. He's not like other guys. His priority is his work. He's supremely focused. But I think it's more than that. I think he's scared to trust. I think my father's bad decisions messed him up."

"I don't think he's messed up," Savannah said. "I've known him my whole life, and I think he's just careful. It's his nature."

"I think it's both," Rachel said. "When he got back from college, he was different—more manly, of course, because he'd grown up and filled out—but he was distant. I really noticed a difference that fall when he returned home. Remember, Jade? He got that job up on the mountain, and it seemed like everything changed after that. But like I said, I think he was different from the day he got back that fall."

Jade nodded. "You might be right. I wasn't around when he came back. That was before I moved back to Weston."

Shannon closed her eyes for a second. "Oh my God. It figures that the one man I want has bigger issues than I do."

"Oh, please," Savannah said. "Those aren't big issues, if they're even true. We're all speculating. Besides, there's nothing two people can't overcome if they try. Jack and I are a prime example. He lost his wife when they were just hoping to start their family. It doesn't get much worse than that. Remember when we met? He'd been hiding out in the woods for two years. No one thought he'd come back to life, and now he's the most wonderful father and husband I could ever hope for. He's as close to his family as I am to mine. It just takes the right kind of love to get through to people. You have to take the time to figure out what's holding him back. If he even wants you to know. And then, of course, he has to want to let you in. That's the hard part. Sometimes people don't know what they want."

"You sure you're an entertainment attorney and not a therapist?" Max teased.

"I've met so many women in the birthing classes I took, and the baby classes," Savannah said. "I feel like I've heard it all. I have yet to meet a woman who either didn't have trust issues herself, or her husband didn't. I think most people are afraid of something, and I think almost everything can be overcome with patience and the desire to make it work."

"So, you think I shouldn't give up?" Shannon asked.

They all said "No" in unison.

"But it's crazy, right? We haven't even kissed. How can I fall for a guy who tells me he wants me in one breath and refuses to kiss me in the next?"

Jade and Max exchanged a smile and a knowing look that told Shannon they knew something she didn't.

"Do you even know the man I'm married to?" Jade asked. "Mr. Loyal? Mr. I Can't Touch You for *Fifteen* Years? Thankfully, my man isn't afraid of confrontation, and he forced our stubborn fathers to put an end to that ridiculous family feud. But talk about refusing to kiss someone." She shook her head and smiled. "And look at us now."

"You two can't keep your hands off each other," Savannah said. "Just as it should be. Like me and Jack and Max and Treat."

"Look, Shannon," Jade said more seriously. "Steve and I have never really talked about our personal lives, but he's always been super careful with the girls he goes out with. But you must know he's got the biggest, kindest heart. There's nothing he wouldn't do for any of us."

Shannon sighed and looked around the bar, wishing Steve would appear. Why wasn't he chasing after her? Making sure she didn't hook up with someone else? She noticed Cal sitting across the room with a group of guys. He waved, and she smiled, feeling guilty because she wished he were Steve.

Jade tapped her hand. "Rexy said Cal's got a big ol' crush on you."

"He's a nice guy," Shannon admitted. "He's just got one issue."

Rachel laughed. "You have issues with hot, wealthy guys? I've had a crush on him forever and he doesn't even know I exist."

"Trust me," Max said to Rachel. "There's no man on earth who doesn't know you exist. Bald men line up to sit in your salon chair just to be near you."

Rachel rolled her eyes. "Never the right guys."

"I have the wrong guy problem, too." Shannon didn't give a hoot about money or even looks, although in Shannon's opinion Steve was hotter than Cal. Heck, he was hotter than any man she'd ever laid eyes on.

Jade reached across the table and squeezed Shannon's hand. "Cal's problem is that he's not my brother."

"Am I a fool for being so hung up on him? We're not even very much alike." *Which is exactly why he won't take a chance on us.*

"Why do you have to be alike?" Max asked. "Treat and I were as different as the day was long. I was so broken when I met him, and he was so..." She sighed dreamily. "He *is* so distinguished, so manly, so—"

"Okay, down girl," Jade teased. "No 'O' faces at the table."

Max laughed. "I was making a point. You don't have to be alike to fall in love. Love is about discovering underlying truths. It's about caring enough about someone to put yourself last and wanting to be with them at their ugliest times as well as their most beautiful."

"That's so true," Savannah said.

"I want to find that," Rachel added.

"That sounds amazing," Shannon said. "But that would require two people wanting the same thing. Maybe I'm barking up the wrong tree and I should have gone out with his friend

Will."

"Cumberland?" Jade asked.

"Uh-huh. He asked me out and I canceled because I wanted to be with Steve, but then your do-the-right-thing brother blew me off."

"Talk about opposites," Jade said. "Will's about as brazen and risky as a guy gets, so different from Steve, but he's one of his best friends. Go figure."

Maybe there was something to be said about opposites attracting after all. Her mind circled back to last night. "I think I came on too strong to Steve."

"A Braden coming on too strong?" Max's eyes widened in feigned disbelief.

"I'm serious. He's like a calm and steady creek, and I'm a white-water rapid."

The girls laughed.

"Seriously, you guys. I talk *all* the time, and I get excited over everything. He's perfectly happy in his own world, chopping wood, climbing mountains, and probably wrestling bears, for all I know. Don't hate me, Jade, but I called him a dumbass for not kissing me."

"He *is* a dumbass for not kissing you," Jade said. "But I've honestly never seen him look at any woman the way he looks at you, so I'd be surprised if something doesn't happen between you two."

They talked for a long time and danced until they were giddy. It was wonderful to get lost in girl talk and to hear that they didn't think she was nuts for being hung up on Steve. They headed back to the table in a gaggle of whispers and giggles. A hand landed on Shannon's arm and she spun around.

Cal stood before her in a pair of low-slung jeans, a white T-shirt stretched across his broad chest. A sexy smile softened his sharp features. "Hey there, darlin'. Can I have the next dance?"

"Damn, she's lucky," Rachel said to Jade.

Maybe it was loneliness that kept Shannon from saying, *no thanks,* or maybe it was the fact that Cal wanted her when Steve didn't. She didn't know why she held her tongue, but she stood silently, debating dancing with Cal.

"Go," Jade encouraged her. "You should have fun tonight."

Savannah nudged her arm.

"Sure. Why not?" Shannon said. "I'd love to dance." As she wound her arms around Cal's neck and his arms circled her waist, she couldn't ignore the stab of guilt in her chest. Cal was the epitome of a hot cowboy, right down to his Western accent. He was a perfect gentleman, with thick blond hair and cerulean-blue eyes. And he was a sensational dancer to boot. She should be head over heels, swooning like Rachel was from their table across the room.

But he wasn't Steve.

She danced two dances with Cal, waiting for the *zing* of attraction to hit her. Her stomach didn't even flutter. Nothing. It was like dancing with her brother. She apologized for not returning his calls and spent the rest of the evening with the girls, feeling no less confused than when she'd arrived.

When she finally left the bar, she thought about Steve as she drove up the mountain. *Be careful on these roads. Turn on your headlights.* The roads were pitch-black, save for her headlights, but she wasn't scared. She felt safe knowing he was nearby. She saw a light on in Steve's cabin and debated stopping and trying to talk things out, but she was supposed to be figuring out who she was. And who she wanted to be *wasn't* the type of girl who chased down a man.

She forced herself to drive past, and as she came around the bend at the top of the hill, she was shocked to see a dozen or more glass jars with sparkling white lights illuminating the path from her driveway to the porch. Several more jars lined the steps and porch. That dangerous emotion, *hope*, came skipping in.

She stepped from the Jeep and picked up one of the glass jars, inspecting it more closely. There were no batteries, no wires, but a handful of sticks and leaves and tiny flickering lights that looked like fireflies. *How did you do this?*

She followed the lighted trail, hope soaring with every step. On the porch she found a card tucked into the doorjamb. The paper was the recycled type, off-white with dark specs like vanilla bean ice cream. On the front of the card was a sketch of wildflowers. She ran her finger over them and the pencil marks smeared.

You drew these for me?

Her heart swelled, overwhelming her.

She opened the card and saw, for the first time ever, Steve's handwriting. It was slightly slanted to the right, strong and dark. It looked confident and fluid, like him. As she read the harsh note, all those romantic feelings came to a screeching halt. Mr. Contradiction had struck again.

Predators come out at night. Keep a light on.

Chapter Six

BEFORE HEADING OUT for his morning run, Steve drew a map of the mountain, marking fox dens and landmarks, and carried it through the woods to Shannon's cabin. It had taken all of his willpower not to give in to his desires the other night. He'd slept like hell, and then she hadn't come around all day, which had been torture in and of itself. Not to mention that last night had been another sleepless night, thinking about her in that sexy little outfit dancing with Lord knew who. He'd swung by her cabin at around eleven thirty, and it was pitch-dark. He hated that she was out at a bar that late, and he worried about her coming home alone. At least he hoped she'd been alone. He'd heard her drive in about an hour later.

Didn't she know to leave her porch light on? This wasn't suburbia. Threats in the wild didn't have warning labels or flashing lights. They had sharp teeth, fierce claws, and the ability to stalk and kill in the blink of an eye. He'd wanted to wait on her porch to make sure she got inside safely, but she wasn't his to protect. And worse, what if she'd come home with Cal or some other guy? He definitely didn't need to be there for *that*.

His chest tightened at the sight of the jars he'd left for her.

The solar lights would soak up the sun today and light her way tonight—for whatever she had planned. Damn, he hated this shit. Why did the one woman he wanted have to be someone who lived halfway across the country *and* would never be content with his lifestyle? He set the map on the porch, glad there weren't *two* cars in the driveway, and went on his way.

He made the rounds while he was out for his run and found a tree had fallen across one of the trails a few miles from his cabin. There went his day. After his run he checked his email, something he hated doing for the mere fact that he abhorred doing anything online, but it was part of his job. It wasn't that he hated technology; he simply disliked the way it usurped people's lives. He read through the morning reports, noting the locations of bears and mountain lion sightings, then moved on to checking his voicemail. His mother's cheerful voice came though the line. She must have called when he was out last night. She'd found a box of his things in the cellar and thought he might want it. It was too early to call, so he made a mental note to try her later.

He hadn't heard back from the calls he'd made about the Cumberland property, but he knew he'd hear shortly. He had a good rapport with the people he'd reached out to. Of course, a good rapport didn't mean squat when it came to shelling out the kind of money needed to acquire the property.

He spent most of the afternoon taking care of the downed tree, which was a blessing in disguise. He not only needed the distraction but also the space to clear his mind. As the hours passed, his thoughts remained on Shannon. He had a feeling he could move to Kalamazoo and she'd still be right there, taking up his every thought with her vibrant smile and those gorgeous hazel eyes. Her eyes pulled him in time and time again, the way they went from excited to seductive in the space of a second.

By late afternoon, the only thing that had become clear was that being a good guy sucked.

He hiked down by the ridge where he'd seen the kids partying the other day and was pleased to see there were no signs of them. He checked on a few other trails, trying to keep his mind off of the one person he wanted to find, but it was a losing battle. Unable to resist, he finally took a detour and hiked to two of the fox dens he'd marked on the map. Disappointment welled in the pit of his stomach when she wasn't at either of them. He wondered if she was thinking about him and cursed himself for wondering. Not only had she gotten under his skin, but she'd crawled into his brain and charmed him like a snake.

On his way back to the cabin, he came across a goshawk lying among the brush. He crouched beside the seemingly dead bird and inspected it more closely. It was unconscious but still breathing. He looked up at the trees, wondering what had happened. Normally, he'd use his heavy gloves to handle a raptor, as they could tear a person up. But he had no idea how much time the bird had been out and he was still a long way from the cabin. By the time he got there and back, a predator could eat the bird. He pulled out his phone and called Jo Finney, the local raptor rehabber and a close friend.

She answered on the first ring. "How's my favorite mountain man?"

I suck. I've fallen for a woman I should stay away from but can't. "That depends. Are you tied up at the moment?"

Jo and Steve had gotten together one summer when he was home from college, but they lacked the deep emotional connection they both desired from a partner and decided they made better friends than lovers. It was the right choice, and

Steve had never regretted their very brief affair or the end of it. He'd learned a lot about himself when they were together, most importantly, that he wasn't the kind of guy who wanted casual sex without an emotional connection. That felt like a lifetime ago, and now Jo's biological clock was ticking and she was searching for Mr. Right. Steve wasn't searching at all, but he had a feeling Ms. Right was flitting around his cabin door.

"Not to a bedpost or anything," she teased.

"Sorry to hear that." *Tied to a bedpost* was their code for being in a long-term, meaningful relationship.

"Yeah, me too," she said sullenly. "What's up?"

"Found an injured goshawk. He's concussed, with a hurt wing. I'm about two miles out from the cabin, without gloves or a box to transport him."

"Got a shirt you can wrap him up in, or are you out streaking?"

He shook his head, although getting naked in the woods with Shannon had crossed his mind too many times today. Now it was all he could think about. Taking her against a tree, on the ground, in the meadow. *In my bed.* There was no room in his life for heartache and complications, but he had a feeling he was already too far gone to turn back.

SHANNON FINISHED HER research notes and looked over the map Steve had left on her porch. It was either him or forest pixies. She smiled. Steve, a player? The man wouldn't even give her a single kiss. *But he'd light up my driveway and draw me a map that looks like it took hours to make.*

She sighed. He'd detailed the locations of fox dens and

outlined routes to each one. He'd indicated landmarks along each route, including types of trees and shrubs, ridges and steep terrain, distance from her cottage, escape routes in case of fire. *Seriously? Fire?* At least she'd made progress today.

Thanks to Mr. Frustrating's map.

As kind of a gesture as it was, she'd still stewed over the darn thing all day. He'd left it on her porch without a note. Maybe after the tone of last night's note that was a blessing in disguise, although she wasn't sure what to make of anything with him anymore. The lights were sweet and romantic, as was the picture he'd drawn on the note. But that note? She couldn't get past the harshness of it. It felt cold and clipped. Like a reprimand wrapped in a pretty bow.

Was the map supposed to send the message that he would no longer go out with her when she was doing her research? Or was it meant to help her in his absence?

She slammed her notebook closed, grabbed the map, and shoved her feet into her boots. She was frustrated and she needed answers, if for no other reason than to wrap her head around the idea that he was done. *Done with what? We haven't even started. Have we?* She stood at the counter thinking about the way he'd touched her the other night, the near kiss that had sent her hopes soaring, the seductive things he'd said. It wasn't like she'd asked him to have sex with her. Okay, maybe the thought had crossed her mind a dozen or so times, but that wasn't really what she'd been after. She'd just wanted him to open up, to test the waters. They weren't kids, and there was no one standing in their way.

She looked down at the map and softened. She owed him a thank-you, and yes, maybe a little grief for not having the decency to leave a note, but definitely a thank-you for the map.

Before walking out the door, she grabbed her laptop, which was still open to the crowdfunding research she'd been doing yesterday afternoon. She could repay him for the map by explaining crowdfunding to him so at least he'd have some options to think about.

With her pulse racing, she headed down the narrow path toward Steve's cabin, wishing she'd at least thrown on jeans. She was chilly in her shorts, but she'd been hot after she'd come back from hiking all over the mountain. Even a shower hadn't cooled her off. That could have been because she'd thought about mountain-stud Steve and his *giant ax* while she showered.

A little voice in her head told her to play it cool. But she had too big of a mouth to play anything cool. She hummed to quiet the voice in her head as she navigated around tree branches. After a minute or two she realized she was humming "Legendary Lovers" by Katy Perry.

Oh boy, I've got it bad.

She forced herself to stop humming and let the warning voice in her head battle it out with her cosmic-loving heart.

When she came to the edge of the woods by Steve's cabin, she saw a green truck parked behind his, and she stopped in her tracks—but her mind kept tumbling forward. Did it belong to one of his girlfriends? Did he have girlfriends? Did he have *a* girlfriend? She had no idea, and he'd been so closemouthed about himself that it was no wonder she had no idea. Wouldn't he have told her if he had a girlfriend? Wouldn't Jade have said something? What if this was a *new* girlfriend? Maybe he didn't go into town because he was too busy making out with Green Truck Girl.

Her stomach turned over. She looked down at the map. That would explain his not wanting to be alone out on the mountain with her. *Especially after I threw myself at him.*

The cabin door opened and a pretty blonde stepped outside. She swung her hair over her shoulder, flashing a vibrant smile at Steve, who was one step behind her, carrying a big wooden box. His eyes swept over the yard and landed on Shannon. Jesus, did he have a LoJack on her? She held her breath, hoping she would evaporate into the woods.

His eyes narrowed, and a serious expression replaced his friendly smile. The blonde followed his gaze to Shannon, and she shifted curious eyes between the two of them.

"Shannon," Steve said. It wasn't a warm greeting, though it wasn't mean. He sounded sort of confused, which told Shannon exactly what the map had meant. It was his way of putting an end to the time they spent alone together.

"Hi," she managed. "I just…" *Need to turn around and go home.*

"You got the map," he said, setting the wooden box in the back of the woman's truck.

Shannon held up the map. "Yeah. I was coming by to say thank you."

He nodded.

The blonde waved and smiled. She really did have a pretty smile and eyes as green as grass. "Hi, I'm Jo Finney. You must be Shannon."

"Yes," she said, wondering how she knew her name. "It's nice to meet you."

Jo opened her truck door and said, "Steve told me you were staying up the road and doing research. I run the raptor rehab center in town. It's nice to meet you."

She kissed Steve on his cheek, and Shannon tried to turn away, but she couldn't. Watching her kiss Steve was like watching a train wreck. She was powerless to look away. She had a sick need to dissect every second of it.

"I'd better get this guy down the mountain," Jo said. "I'll let you know how he does."

"Thanks," Steve said absently, eyes locked on Shannon as he closed Jo's door. He leaned in the open window and spoke to Jo privately. Then he tapped the roof of her truck twice and Jo pulled out, waving to Shannon as she drove away.

"I didn't mean to interrupt," Shannon said quickly. "I just wanted to say thank you for the map. And the lights."

"No problem. I hope the note didn't cause you any trouble last night."

"Trouble?"

He shrugged. "If you brought someone home, I'm sure finding a note from another guy wouldn't be a good thing."

"Oh my God. You thought I would bring a guy back with me? After I practically threw myself at you? You're so thick-headed."

"Thanks. I'll take that to mean I'm thoughtful for not leaving a note that might mess things up for you." He cracked a smile as he closed the distance between them. His slate-blue eyes slid down her body, taking care of that pesky chill she'd felt earlier. "What's with the laptop?"

"Oh." *I forgot I had it.* "I, um…" Her mind was too stuck on Jo to move on to anything else. "I wanted to show you something, but was that…? Is she your…? Is Jo…?" She felt her cheeks flush, and his eyes filled with amusement.

"An alien?" he teased.

"If that's what aliens look like, we mere mortals haven't got a chance."

He took her laptop from her, then laced his fingers with

hers and led her toward the porch. His hand was big and rough, and as she had the other night, she loved the feel of it. Also like the other night, his conflicting messages confused her.

"Why are you holding my hand?"

"Because I have a feeling you're in some weird competition with an alien and I didn't want you tripping." He placed the laptop and map on the porch and stepped closer. "And maybe because I liked holding it the other night."

Her heart skipped, then skidded. She couldn't take another roller-coaster ride. "You blew me off the other night. What if I don't want to hold your hand?"

He released her hand, and she instantly regretted her comment.

"I didn't blow you off," he said gruffly.

"What would you call it?"

"Being careful." He placed his hand on her hip, drawing her closer.

He felt so good, her resolved softened.

"Look, I know I'm not like the guys you're probably used to. I'll never be a city boy, and I have no interest in living life off the mountain."

Her body ached to lean forward and press into him, but she forced herself to remain distant. "So?"

The genuine concern in his eyes caused the brakes she'd applied to slip again.

"Shannon, I can't do this anymore."

Her heart tanked. *Splat!* Right to the ground. "Can't...?"

"Can't fight it."

Her breath left her lungs in one hard exhalation.

"I'm totally into you, Shan, despite the fact that I'm not racing to the bedroom."

"I'm not trying to race to the bedroom, either." It came out too fast and defensive.

"I don't think you are," he assured her. "But I think you're used to guys who don't slow down enough to think things through, or maybe I misread that. I'm not thinking clearly lately. The other thing I know for sure is that I cannot get you out of my mind. And trust me when I say I've tried to stop thinking about you."

"And you think *I* dole out compliments?" She laughed softly, earning a sexy smile.

"I'm a dumbass, what can I say? It was unfair to say what I did the other night and not explain it. I'm sorry." His eyes went serious again. "The truth is, I'm not looking for a hookup, and I'm not looking for a wife. I'm not *looking* for anything, which is why I'm trying to be careful with what's happening between us. The sheer force of our attraction, the energy between us, has blindsided me."

His eyes grazed down her body, and he held her tighter. She felt like the trees were closing in on them, heat and torment whirring around them, binding them together in a tense, conflicted bubble.

"It's hell keeping my hands off of you in those skimpy shorts, when all I can think about is how your legs would feel wrapped around me." He drew in a long breath. "Everything about you makes me crazy, not just your looks, but...You wear hiking boots with flashy *pink* laces, which are perfectly *you* and a world away from me. And knowing you don't slow down enough to put on socks? *Christ*, Shan. I've spent a shameful amount of time wondering what else you don't slow down enough to put on."

She swallowed hard to try to stop her insides from revving

too hard.

"We're so different, but I can't stop wanting you." He stepped closer, and she stumbled back, hitting the porch railing. "I want to know so much more about you." His hands slid down her hips, pressing into the sides of her ass. "More than just how you'll feel lying naked in my arms."

"Me too." Her voice cracked. She hadn't expected to hear any of this, no matter how much she craved it, and hearing him say all these sexy things made it hard for her to think, much less speak.

"But I've seen how making hasty decisions can hurt people. I don't want that. Not for either of us. You need to understand why I'm not taking you in my arms and kissing you senseless."

Her mouth went dry.

"Christ," he muttered. "That look kills me."

"Um…" She bit her lower lip. "Can we explore the kissing senseless part a little more?"

He lifted her hand and pressed his warm, soft lips to the back of it, stepping in close again. "I hope so, but hear me out, because the last thing I want is for us to have any misunderstandings and for you to be hurt."

"Now you've baffled me." She slid her finger into the waistband of his jeans and felt his abs flex.

"Hasty decisions," he said, as if he were reminding himself what they were talking about. "Good intentions only go so far. People lie. They lose sight of priorities, or they have them all wrong from the beginning. It's a fatal flaw."

"Fatal flaw? Don't we have too many flaws to count?"

"Yes." His jaw tightened, and something dark passed over his face. "But you, my happy-go-lucky little butterfly, don't live your life avoiding relationships because of them."

Chapter Seven

STEVE KNEW WHAT he'd said was heavy, especially for a girl like Shannon, who saw the best in everyone, but he couldn't take the chance that she might hope for something that could never happen. He moved her hand from his waistband and stepped back, giving her space to process what he'd said.

"I've been the popular guy, Shannon. The kind of guy you're used to, who hangs out in crowds and at bars. Being in the middle of all that chaos, the gossip, the manipulations wasn't who I wanted to be. Once I stopped worrying about that crap, like what people might think of me, and decided to follow my passion, I found what made me truly happy. Protecting this land and the wildlife on it is more than a job to me. A forest fire that wipes out hundreds of acres, an animal that dies from a poacher, those aren't just bad days at the office. Those are tragedies to me."

"I understand that," she said empathetically. "I care about all of that, too. That's why I went into biology and natural resources in the first place."

"Then you understand why I'll probably never be a live-in-town kind of guy, why I want to fight for the Cumberland land. There's a natural order in nature. With people, any natural order is affected by things they do and sometimes by things they aren't even aware of doing. A misread look, misplaced pride, a moment of idiocy." He shot her a serious look and stepped in closer, finally giving in to the heat within him and clutching her hips. "Like when I pushed you to go out with Will."

"Aha! So you admit you sort of pushed me into that but really didn't want me to go out with him."

He shrugged. "I'm human. Flawed. What can I say?"

"Chalk one up for me not misreading you." She licked her finger and pretended to *chalk one up*.

"You're insanely cute."

She licked her finger and chalked up another point.

"It makes it really hard for me to keep from shutting up and kissing you."

She licked her finger and held it up but didn't strike a point. "I'm ready if you are."

"There's something else you need to know."

She wiggled her finger. "I get it. You're careful about trusting people. So? I'm trustworthy. I don't see the issue. Now let's get to the kissing part."

He grabbed her finger and pressed a kiss to the tip of it. "Slow down. There's the bigger reason I'm not kissing you senseless right now."

"Bigger?" She licked her lips.

He couldn't take his eyes off of her mouth. "Bigger," he stammered. "And just for the record, be careful what you wish for. Even though I've been trying not to rush to the bedroom, I have no control there either. I know once we kiss, we won't stop until we've taken *everything* from each other."

She swallowed hard. "I like the not stopping part, too. You're such a tease."

He clenched his jaw to stifle a curse. "You're killing me."

"Then spit it out, Grizz. What's a girl got to do to get a kiss from you?"

"Slow down, city girl. This is important because *you* are important." He held her tight, fighting the urge to kiss her. "My lifestyle isn't one many women want to deal with for the long haul. Especially not a woman like you."

"But I lik—"

He shook his head, silencing her. He knew better than to try to placate each other with promises they'd never keep. "I don't want to hear about how you love it up here, or how people change, or we'll figure it out. We have an expiration date, Shannon."

She scoffed. "An expiration date? That's…"

"Realistic."

"Okay. I guess you could look at it that way. But this is my body, my emotions, my choice."

"I'm not arguing that it's your decision. But a man *always* protects the people he cares about. That means I have to suck it up and slow down enough to think about how satisfying my own selfish desires might affect you in the long run."

"I'm right here, willing to do this. I want you, but you're putting on the brakes. I came here to get out from under my family's thumbs, to find myself and make my own decisions, and if I want to fall in bed with you, it's *my* decision."

"I'm trying to protect you from getting hurt. Do you think it was easy to walk away from you when the *only* thing I wanted to do was take you in my arms and show you how I feel about you? Do you think it's easy to keep my hands off of you right now and say any of this?"

He swept an arm around her waist and pulled her against

him, watching her eyes widen and then darken at the feel of his arousal.

"I don't want to be your cross-country rebellion hookup. I only sleep with people I care about, and I care about you enough to ask you to slow down and think this through with me so we don't regret it later."

"Is that what you meant when you said I was asking the wrong guy if all relationships had to lead somewhere? Because you don't do hookups?"

"I don't do casual sex."

Her brow wrinkled, and she searched his eyes. He knew she saw the sincerity in them.

"You're not my rebellion hookup. Cal could have been. Heck, Will could have been. Either of them would have probably jumped my bones if I had let them, so I'm pretty sure I could have gotten that out of my system without you if that's what I was looking for. Which I'm *not*."

"Just the thought of them touching you kills me," he ground out.

"Exactly. I *am* thinking, Steve. I want to be with you."

He held on to that with the strength of a giant but needed to know she'd thought this through and understood their limitations. Hell, *he* needed to hear it again.

"This is what it is, Shannon. Limited." His words came faster, heated. "No matter what either of us may hope for later, our lifestyles are too different. With the Cumberland deal looming, I don't even know if I have room in my life for a relationship. I don't want to hurt you. A few weeks of pleasure is not worth that. We go in with our eyes open or we don't go in at all."

She banged her forehead to his chest. "Can't you just be one of those guys who doesn't think past this second?"

"Not with you. And you don't want that. Regardless of your sexual bravado, you're a sensitive, sensual woman. You want to be loved, not used. I see it in your eyes."

She didn't say a word. She didn't have to. He saw agreement in her eyes, felt it in her fingers tightening around him.

"I won't make promises I can't keep. I know with complete certainty that being with you will be like stepping into heaven, and if you feel even half of what I do, then when you leave we'll both be falling into hell." He paused, letting the truth settle in. "I won't promise you the world, Shan. I can't. I won't promise you any more than these few weeks."

She pressed her hand to his chest, and he cupped her cheeks, tasting her desire on her breath, seeing it in the darkening of her eyes.

"Once I get my first taste of you, there's no turning back. I need to know we're both on the same page. No fantasies of my giving up the mountain to get lost in your world, or you changing or giving up what you love to get lost in mine. No dreams of a house in suburbia with a white picket fence and two point five children."

"Who are you trying to convince?" she asked breathlessly. "Me or you?"

He gazed into her eyes, and the truth came easily. "Maybe a little of both."

He brushed his lips over hers. "I have to kiss you now."

The sexiest, neediest "Yes" sailed from her lips.

"Same page?"

"Same page," she whispered.

As their mouths came together, he tried not to think about what was going to happen in a few weeks when she went back to her life and he was still on the mountain, wishing she'd never left.

THE FIRST TOUCH of Steve's lips stole Shannon's breath. He kissed her unexpectedly slowly and tenderly. With each slide of his tongue, he tightened his hold, taking the kiss deeper, claiming more of her. As the cool night air sailed over her heated flesh, his tongue searched and swept, seducing her with its perfect rhythm. He grasped the back of her head with both hands, holding her right where he wanted her, angling her head so she opened wider for him. He took the kiss deeper, probing hard and erotic, then soft and sensual, making her entire body clench, then melt, then clench again. He kissed her like he'd studied and practiced, honing the craft of kissing for this very moment. He kissed her like he never wanted to stop—and she hoped he never would. He nipped at her lips, licked them, sucked them into his mouth, until she was mewing and moaning in a deliciously delirious state.

"Love kissing you," he said in a low breath, and took her in another intoxicating kiss.

Their bodies rubbed and ground, their tongues danced, and he fisted his hands in her hair, tugging just hard enough to alight all of her senses anew. Heat invaded her core, her limbs, the very tips of her fingers and toes, stealing the strength from her legs. He held her tighter, pressing all his hard heat against her, and she went a little wild, pawing at his back and shoulders, his arms and scrumptiously tight butt. She held his hips to hers, grinding against his eager cock. He moaned into the kiss, and it vibrated through them, stirring even more scintillating desires.

Their mouths parted slowly, breathless and unwilling, stealing another kiss, then another, and—*Oh God*, she didn't want to stop. He touched his forehead to hers, and she breathed in his musky scent, salivating over the lingering taste of him. Her lips tingled and burned, and her mouth still felt possessed. She felt him *everywhere*.

"More—" Before the full demand left her lungs, he captured her mouth again, taking her hard and exquisitely passionately. She gave herself freely, kissed him hungrily, getting lost in the heady sensations rippling through her as his hot, velvety mouth claimed her neck. Every press of his lips sent her heart tumbling, her world spinning. He blazed a path around to her nape, sucking and sinking his teeth into her sensitive skin. She felt the effects pulsing between her legs.

"*Grizz*," came out like a plea.

She curled her fingers into his hair. The strength of his mouth, the sound of him devouring her, obliterated everything. When he crushed his mouth to hers again, he brought her right up to the edge. And when he softened the kiss, tantalizing shivers whispered down her limbs.

Their lips met in a series of feathery kisses. She was clutching his hair; he was holding her cheeks, and there beneath the moonlight, as their eyes fluttered open and their gazes met, a silent, powerful connection formed.

"Be mine, Butterfly," he whispered. "For a day, a week, however long you can stand it. Let's see where this goes. No other guys' hands on you. When you're with me, you're *mine*."

"I thought…" She tried to get her brain to form a rational thought, but she was still floating in the clouds. "The kisses. I thought that's what they meant."

His lips curved into a sexy smile. "I was jealous as hell the other night, thinking of you and Cal. I've never been jealous in my life."

He kissed her again, and she melted against him.

"I've wanted to kiss you since the wedding," he said, and kissed her again.

"You wasted a lot of time. We could have been kissing for all those weeks. We could have been—"

His mouth came gently down over hers in another sweet, tender kiss.

"Did you just shut me up with a kiss?"

He smiled and pressed his lips to hers again.

"I'm going to talk about nonsense now; you realize that, don't yo—"

Another luscious kiss.

"This is going to become a problem you can't keep up with, because if I have it my way, I'll—"

He scooped her into his arms and kissed her as he carried her to the porch.

"I could kiss you for days," she said. "Weeks. Months—" He captured her mouth again, laughing against her lips as he reached for her laptop.

"Your allure is dangerous," he said, somehow opening the door to his cabin while holding her and the laptop. He kicked it open wide and stood at the threshold.

"Dangerous good, or…?"

"I'll let you know when I figure it out."

He took her in another mind-blowing kiss.

"We should slow down." He moved that sensual mouth of his to her jaw. "If we do this, eventually you'll go back to your life in Maryland, and I'll still be here," he said between kisses. "Months from now, when we've both moved on, we'll see each other at extended family functions. Can we handle that? Act like nothing's changed? Move on?"

"We're adults. We'll be fine." She knew it wasn't true, but she wanted him too badly to pick it apart. She arched her neck, and his tongue glided up the center, ending in a tantalizing suck. "Oh God, Grizz."

He gazed into her eyes and said, "You should take time to think. To be sure."

"I'm done thinking."

He carried her through the living room, slowing only to set the laptop on a table. His cabin was dark, save for the moonlight sneaking in through the windows. This was the first time she'd been inside, and she inhaled deeply, wanting to take it all in at once. It smelled just as she'd imagined it would, woodsy and earthy mixed with brawn and raw desire. It smelled like *him*. Her eyes swept over the simple wooden desk and comfy-looking sofa as he carried her to the bedroom.

She breathed harder at the sight of his king-sized bed. She'd fantasized about this moment for so long, and suddenly she was very, very nervous. Her eyes skittered over the fireplace on the far wall and the picture window across from the bed. There were no curtains, which gave her pause, even though there was no one around for miles. The furniture was heavy, masculine. He sank down to the edge of the bed, cradling her on his lap, and kissed her again. His hand slid up and down her thigh in long, slow strokes, each one stealing more of her thoughts.

"I can't wait to get my mouth on these incredible thighs," he whispered against her cheek, and her breath rushed from her lungs. "Mm. My girl likes that idea as much as I do." He pulled the collar of her sweater away from her neck and sealed his mouth over her skin in a series of openmouthed kisses.

"No bra?" His hand moved beneath the back of her shorts, brushing over her bare ass, and he groaned. "No panties?"

The predatory look in his eyes nearly stole her voice, but she managed a shaky whisper. "I was in a hurry. I...I didn't plan on coming here."

"You are a sexy thing." He kissed her as he reached for the blanket and yanked it to the foot of the bed.

Oh God. Her heart was going to burst. This was really happening. In minutes all those glorious muscles, that wicked mouth, and the big, caring man were going to be all hers. He set her on the bed and knelt to take off her boots. He slipped them off and kissed the tops of each foot before removing his own boots and setting them beside hers, smiling, as if he liked seeing them side by side.

His rough hands slid up her calves, squeezing every few inches, his eyes locked on hers. Her insides didn't flutter—they raced. He trailed tender kisses from her ankle to her knee and traced the ridge of her kneecap with his tongue. She'd never felt anything so sensual, so unexpected. Her hips rocked involuntarily, heat pooling in her core. He pulled his shirt over his head, and she reached out to touch him. She'd seen him without his shirt many times, but seeing him now, in his dimly lit bedroom, looking at her like he'd waited his whole life for this moment, made everything more intense. She swallowed hard as he splayed his hands on her thighs and pushed them open, his eyes boring into her. God, he was so hot, and she was trembling like a leaf.

He dragged his tongue up her inner thigh, stopping at the edge of her shorts, and sealed his mouth over her skin. She nearly shot off the bed with the intensity of him sucking and licking so close to her sex. She fisted her hands in the sheets and slammed her eyes shut as shocks of lust burst through her.

"You are so sweet," he whispered. "So sexy. I want to love every inch of you."

He moved from one thigh to the other, and she heard herself groan. Her hips rose from the mattress as he slicked his tongue over her skin again and again, until she was a writhing, needy mess. She'd never been touched like this. Cherished, teased, *appreciated*. When he rose to his feet and took her hand, bringing her up beside him, her legs gave out.

"I've got you," he whispered, and kissed her deeply.

Holding her up with one hand, he worked the button on her shorts with the other. His palm slid down her belly, over her mound, and his thick fingers pushed between her wet lips. She moaned into their kiss, her hips bucking forward as he teased her, sliding his finger in and out of her wetness, making her sex swell and ache for more. When he found her most sensitive nerves, he played them like he'd been touching her his whole life. He sped up the kiss, taking her up, up, *up*, then slowed, kissing her softly, making her crave and plead for more. Just when she felt herself disappearing into the slower pace, he intensified the kiss, quickening his strokes between her legs at the same time, until all she could feel, all she could see, taste, or want was *him*. He kept her there, in the exquisitely painful place between release and pleasure—wanting, needing, begging for more. She was shocked and embarrassed at how quickly she neared the edge and how desperately she was clinging to him, thrusting and moaning like an addict.

He tore his mouth from hers and sucked her lower lip, groaning as he pushed his finger deep inside her. His thumb touched her swollen nerves and lights burst behind her closed lids. Her sex pulsed, her fingernails pierced his arms, and he captured her cries in another earth-shattering kiss that made her detonate all over again.

She clung limply to him, panting and shaking as she pressed her lips to his chest and said, "Sorry, it's been a long time."

He curled a finger beneath her chin and lifted her face, gazing into her eyes with so much emotion she knew she'd remember this moment forever.

"Feeling you come is magnificent. If I have it my way, you'll be so sated by morning, you won't have enough energy to be embarrassed."

He withdrew his hand from her shorts and held her gaze as he swept his glistening fingers over her lips and followed them with his tongue.

"Still on the same page?" he asked in a husky voice.

Oh, Lord, yes. It was all she could do to nod.

A devilish grin spread across his face. He hooked his fingers into the waist of her shorts and pulled them over her hips. They slid down and puddled at her feet. He loosened his belt, pinning her in place with a dark, seductive stare as he stepped from his jeans.

Her eyes fell to his eager erection, and she felt them widen at his girth and length.

"No underwear," he said softly. "Seems I was in a hurry, too. Another thing we have in common."

Underwear? That was the last thing on her mind. She'd seen enough skivvy-clad models on Pinterest to know he was *hugely* endowed. She bit her lip to keep her greedy smile from giving away her delight.

He lifted her sweater over her head and raked his eyes down her naked body.

"Lord have mercy, Butterfly, you are stunning."

He took her in another sweet, slow kiss. Her breathing quickened at the feel of his rough hands traveling up her hips, over her ribs, and brushing the sides of her breasts. She closed her eyes, surrendering to him as he explored her curves. When he kissed the corner of her mouth and trailed kisses down her neck, her head tipped back. He pressed a kiss to each of her nipples, circled them with his tongue, and as she arched forward, hoping for more, he dropped lower. He kissed her ribs, the center of her stomach, each hip. His hands slid down her torso, and he clutched her waist, kissing her above her damp curls.

When he slicked his tongue between her legs, she grabbed ahold of his hair for stability. God she loved his hair. She wanted to look, to watch him love her, but she was too lost in his breath sliding over her dampness, the burn of his hands as he splayed them across her upper thighs, drawing them farther apart. Then his mouth was on her, loving her deep and fast, teasing her with merciless mastery.

She had a two-fisted hold on him as she rocked against his mouth, shaking and gasping. "*Oh*. There. Oh *God...*"

He slid his finger inside her as he loved her with his mouth and found the spot that detonated another intense climax. She shuddered and cried out. An indiscernible stream of whimpers and moans filled the room, and he continued working his magic, making her come hard again and again. And just when she thought she'd fall limply to the ground, she was in his arms again and he was kissing her back to life. She inhaled the pungent smell of her desire. Evidence of what he'd done to her lingered on his tongue, and she didn't care. She wanted more and ate at his mouth like a ravenous nymph. He swept her beneath him on the mattress, his hard length pressing against her belly as they kissed and kissed, hard and soft, urgent and easy. She wrapped her legs around his waist. His hands slid down her thighs, making her shiver and ache.

Their kisses turned fierce and messy. Their teeth clanked, tongues tangled, and every fiber of her being burned with desire. They writhed and ground their hips together. He moved lower, sucking her nipple, caressing her breasts, and driving her out of her mind. As he shifted, the head of his cock rested against her center, and he took her in another deep, plundering kiss. The room grew hotter, their mouths pressed harder, her breathing came faster. The prolonged anticipation was unbearable.

He drew back, his eyes as erratic as a summer storm. "Please tell me you're on the pill."

"I am. But..." How could she ask what she needed to?

As if he'd read her mind, he said, "It's been a long time for me, too. I always use protection. I'm clean."

Oh, thank God.

"I want to feel all of you," he said. "Do you want to feel all of me? Feel me come when you come?"

The truth flew from her lips—"Yes"—even though the raw question had shaken her.

She grabbed his head and he took hold of her hips, guiding his thick arousal as their mouths came together. He sank into her one inch at a time, kissing her slowly and passionately. She felt the wide crown push past her entrance, felt his length claiming her, until he was buried to the hilt and they were as close as two people could be. Their mouths parted and they gazed into each other's eyes. The room pulsed around them. His steady gaze bore into her, as if he could see all the way to her thoughts. As if he knew that in that moment, all the restlessness she'd been feeling settled, and she somehow knew this was where the universe had been guiding her all along: into his arms, into his bed, into his heart. And she was there, seeding herself in his love. She could see it in the lost and somehow *found* look in his eyes.

"Kiss me," she whispered.

As their mouths came together, he rocked his hips, bringing them impossibly closer. She gasped into the kiss, and his arms slid beneath her, cradling her tight against him.

"I've wanted you for so long, Butterfly."

He kissed her deeply as they found their rhythm, stroking over all of her sensitive nerve endings. He withdrew slowly while claiming her mouth so fiercely, so completely, it stole all of her focus. And then he thrust faster, harder, and her mind reeled south again. His hips pistoned in a fast rhythm, taking her to the cusp of another orgasm, then slowed, holding her on the verge, trembling, ready to explode.

He buried his face in her neck and said, "Come with me, baby."

His kisses were hard and sweet, and when he groaned into her mouth, she lost her last shred of control. She cried out his name, clawing at his back, and her hips rose off the mattress with the strength of her orgasm. He slammed into her, growling out her name as he gave in to his own magnificent release.

He gathered her against him, and they lay on their sides, mouth-to-mouth, breathless and panting. He kissed her so hard his breath filled her lungs. When he deepened the kiss, she wanted him all over again. She'd never experienced such rampant desire. She slid her thigh over his, rocking against him as they made out like they'd just discovered sex for the first time, and he got hard again. He rolled her onto her back as their bodies came together, moving at a perfect pace.

"I was a fool," he said, kissing her softly. "Nothing will ever be the same."

He'd taken the words right out of her mouth.

Chapter Eight

STEVE AWOKE TO the sweet melody of Shannon singing in the other room. He glanced outside at the dusky morning and guessed it was somewhere around six thirty. He was surprised she was up so early after they'd made love until the wee hours. He pulled on his jeans and followed her voice, stopping in the doorway to watch her dancing as she made coffee. She wore his shirt from last night, which barely covered her ass. *Lucky me.* Her hips swung and her head bobbed from side to side as she sang a Toby Keith song about wanting to talk about what she liked. He couldn't stop smiling as she tossed her hair and poured coffee into a mug. She stepped back and played an air guitar, throwing her head forward to the beat. He bit his cheeks to keep from laughing. Adorably sexy didn't begin to describe his Butterfly.

This was a far cry from the quiet mornings he was used to. She looked like she belonged in his rustic cabin on the mountain, with the morning sun streaming in through the windows and her bare feet prancing along his worn and scratched wooden floors. He thought he knew everything about nature and the way biology worked, but their intense connection confounded him. It was bigger than sex, bigger than forbidden fruit. She was brighter than the sun and he was the shadows between the trees, and as he watched her moving like she'd lived there all her life, he began to wonder what he'd found so interesting about his solitary life that could have *possibly* been better than this.

Another sensation crept in, unexpected and mildly alarming. He'd forgotten what it was like to wake up with a sense of excitement rather than a sense of responsibility. It had been a long time since he'd felt the unique tingle in his chest, the bells of possibility ringing.

She spun on her heels and stopped cold when she saw him.

And there she was, ringing his bells without even trying.

"Hey there, gorgeous." He crossed the living room, loving the flush on her cheeks, the sexy smile curving her lips. He reached for her and she twirled into his arms as the song changed, streaming softly from her cell phone on the counter.

"Good morning, sleepyhead," she said. Parting her lips, she went up on her toes, meeting him in a kiss hot enough to melt metal.

He tugged her in closer, his hands roving over her supple body. God, what she did to him. He was already hard, eager to feel her wrapped around him again. She moaned into the kiss, and he forced himself to put a sliver of space between them before he took her right there on the kitchen floor.

"Best morning kiss *ever*." She took his hand and twirled again, dancing happily and animated. *Mesmerizing.*

His mind whirled back to the night she'd gone to Buckley's. A girl like Shannon didn't stay off the dance floor. Jealousy crushed his chest. As she danced seductively around him, he forced those ugly thoughts away. She was with him now—that's what mattered. He grabbed her hips and drew her into another kiss.

"You're up bright and early."

"Couldn't sleep." "Mr. Brightside" by Fall Out Boy began playing, and she fell into the beat, singing each word to him, stopping only to say, "Coffee? Bitter and disgusting, just the way you like it."

"Sure, in a minute." He backed her up against the counter and ran his hands up her thighs. "I guess I don't have to ask if you have any regrets about last night." He kissed her cheek.

"Not even a little."

Thank God.

"But I'm curious," she said, "because I'm a curious person and all. Have you really never had a woman in here before?"

"You mean like my sister?" he teased.

She rolled her eyes and he laughed.

"I have never had another woman in my bed. I've never had sex with another woman in my cabin. You have christened it, and I greatly appreciate that, but we still have two rooms that haven't yet been blessed."

"Wow. You have no idea how much that turns me on." She pressed her lips to his.

"Damn, I've never had sex on the porch, in the yard, or about a million other places."

"Aw, Grizz, you're such a romantic."

He nuzzled against her neck, reveling in the dreamy sigh that left her lips. "What're your plans for today?"

"Well, if you keep doing that, I think I'm going to drag you back to bed."

"Mm. We think alike." He took her in a lazy, luscious kiss, awakening all of his senses. "How about your research? Are you heading up the mountain later?"

"I'll get to it," she said absently, and turned her face away.

He moved into her line of vision and searched her eyes, sensing trouble there.

"Hey, what's going on? Want to talk about it?"

"Nope. I want to do the kissing thing again." Her eyes lit with mischief.

"After you tell me what's going on." When she didn't say anything, he kissed her softly. "Talk to me, Shan."

"*Tsk*. Party pooper." She pressed her hands to his chest and gazed up at him with a defeated look in her eyes. "It's nothing. I enjoy the research I'm doing, but I get bored and lonely out there by myself. I just don't think it's right for me, and the problem is, I don't know what *is* right for me. Doing research is what I've been working toward."

"Maybe we can figure it out together." *Together.* The unfamiliar thought prickled his skin, but as her eyes lit up again that discomfort whisked away.

"Really? I don't want to bore you with my dilemma when you have the Cumberland property on your mind."

"I think I can deal with two things at once. Besides, you're in my bailiwick when you're talking about nature."

Her face turned serious. "But the part I'm having trouble with isn't exactly high on your priority list."

"Oh, I see. The needing people part? I don't know about that." He kissed her again. "Just because I choose not to be around people as often as you do doesn't mean I don't understand. Besides, *you* are on my priority list; therefore, everything you worry about is, too."

"So you *were* listening to me the other day. And here I thought your head had been too lost in pink icing to pay attention."

Heat roared through him. He slid his hands over her silky

skin and clutched her ass. "Careful, Butterfly. Even thinking about you sucking on your finger turns me on."

Feigned surprise widened her eyes. "Really?" She bit the tip of her finger.

He pressed his hips forward. Hard as steel. They'd made love so many times last night, it should have held him over, but he hadn't even begun to feel sated.

She pushed her finger into her mouth and her eyes darkened.

"Your distraction techniques are very effective." He slid one hand to the nape of her neck. "You've done something to my brain."

"It's called lust."

No, this was far more than lust. "I want more, Butterfly." He kissed her lips. "I want to know your secrets." He kissed her jaw. "Your dreams." He nipped at her neck.

She melted against him. "You sure know how to seduce a woman."

"I want to know what makes you tick." He kissed her again. "Your favorite things." He gazed into her eyes and said, "I want to know you better than any man ever has." *Or ever will.*

She licked her lips and his cock twitched. He couldn't keep his mind on track with her soft and willing body pressed against him and her eyes pleading for what they both craved.

"After I kiss you," he whispered.

"Senseless," she said breathily. "Kiss me senseless."

Their mouths came together slowly, lovingly, in a kiss that was as sweet as it was lethal. He tried to hold back, tried to keep his hands from moving beneath her shirt, over her breasts. But kissing Shannon was like finding a hidden forest, and he wanted to discover all of her treasures. He wanted to get lost in her.

When they were together, all the tightness in his chest eased and all their differences washed away. He took the kiss deeper, filling his palms with her perfect breasts. She moaned, gyrating against him as he lifted her shirt over her head.

"Shan," he whispered in a heated breath, and brought his mouth to her breast.

She tugged at the button on his jeans. He made quick work of taking them off and lifted her into his arms. The feel of her thighs pressing on his waist, the weight of her in his arms, and the feel of her tight heat sinking down on his hard shaft had already become familiar. She'd already become *his*, and he felt like the luckiest guy on earth.

"Grizz," she panted out. "Harder."

He backed her up against the refrigerator, using it for leverage as they gave in to the heat. She clung to his shoulders, their bodies slamming together. Her head fell back, her eyes closed, and she gasped a desperate inhalation. She clawed at the back of his arms so hard he was sure she'd leave marks. But he didn't care. She felt right and true, and when she cried out his name, heat climbed his thighs, seared down his spine, and he crashed into oblivion, taking her over the edge again.

He held her through the very last quiver, buried deep inside her, his heart hammering so hard it felt like it was going to reach out and drag Shannon into his cavernous body. He took her in another breath-stealing kiss and carried her into the bedroom.

"Senseless," she panted out. "Every. Single. Time."

AFTER THEY SHOWERED together, making love again

beneath the warm spray, Shannon headed up the trail to collect data and Steve got called to rescue a stranded hiker. He spent the morning getting the injured man to safety. Immediately after handing the man off to paramedics, he got another emergency call about a lost child. He was halfway to the trail when his radio went off again, alerting him that the boy had been found. And so his morning went, handling one issue after another. When he heard back from the companies he'd hoped would take an interest in the Cumberland property and learned of their disinterest, he chalked it up to par for the day's course.

He called Mack on his way to the bank. He wasn't about to give up. "What's the status on CRH?" He ground his teeth together as Mack told him they were still sniffing around.

"Don't do anything hasty. I've still got a few ideas up my sleeve," he lied, but he had hope that he'd figure something out. He shoved his phone in the pocket of his cargoes, hoping to hell he could come up with a miracle.

An hour later his banker confirmed what Steve had already known. He earned enough to have saved a nice nest egg, but 2.4 million dollars was way out of his reach.

He walked around the brick building rubbing the crick in the back of his neck, thinking about what he could do to save the property from falling into the wrong hands. He dug his keys from his pocket just as Rex's truck pulled around the corner, coming to a stop beside him. Rex's Stetson rode low on his forehead, and one bulbous arm rested on the open window.

"How's it going?" Steve asked.

"Not bad. Hear you're talking to people about the Cumberland land."

Steve nodded. "How'd you hear that?"

Rex grinned. "Jade was at their ranch yesterday working

with a horse and Will told her." Jade was a veterinarian and equine holistic masseuse. "A conservation trust sounds like a good plan, but they're asking too much for the property."

Steve knew the property was worth only about 1.7 million, but he also knew CRH had deep pockets. "Yup."

"That why you were in the bank?"

"It was a long shot, but…" He shrugged.

"You talk to Treat?" Rex clenched his jaw.

"I was hoping I wouldn't have to go that route," Steve said, though he was rethinking that option at the moment.

Rex took off his hat and ran a hand through his thick black hair. "Shannon's only here a few weeks."

There it was, the real reason Rex Braden was parked beside him.

"Yup." Steve crossed his arms, holding Rex's stare. "She's a big girl, Rex."

"She may be, but she'll always be my younger cousin."

"Then, if anything, you should be proud that I'm the man taking her home at night." Steve opened his truck door and nodded to Rex. "See ya around, buddy."

He drove to his parents' house to pick up the box of things his mother had set aside for him, wishing he was back home with Shannon. She made everything brighter, and right now he could use a little sunshine.

He pulled up to his modest childhood home and found his parents on the front porch swing, each reading a paperback. He smiled as he ascended the porch steps. His father had worked two full-time jobs Steve's whole life. He was an agricultural engineer, and he ran their family ranch, working from sunup until well after sundown seven days a week. Sometimes he wondered if his father had worked so much to keep his mind off of the guilt he felt over breaking Hal's trust all those years ago. When his father had retired from his corporate job several years ago, he'd continued running the ranch full-time. That was around the time Jade and Rex had gotten together and the feud between the Bradens and Johnsons had come to a head. He was glad the feud was over and pleased his father had come to an agreement with Treat, who'd bought two hundred acres of his land, enabling Steve's parents to hire the help they needed so they could finally slow down and spend more time together.

"Hey, Ma." Steve leaned down and hugged his mother's slim frame. She smelled like home cooking and unconditional love.

She gazed up at him with a warm smile. His mother had the skin of a thirty-year-old, smooth and radiant. Her brown hair was now streaked with a few silver threads, the only indication of her age.

"Steven, what's that look in your eyes? You look...*something*."

Thinking about his morning, he said, "Pissed off, maybe. Mack and Will are selling their parents' property, and I was hoping to convince them to put it into conservation, but they need the money."

"It's tough, making a living these days," his father said. Earl Johnson was a serious man. Steve couldn't remember a time when his father wasn't working, organizing, or giving him or Jade a mini-lesson in something.

"Yeah, I know. I'll figure something out."

"Have you talked to Treat?" his father asked.

When Steve was younger, his father had hoped he'd take over the ranch, but Steve's dreams were too big to be contained to a few hundred acres, and his father had eventually accepted his decision. Knowing Steve wasn't interested in ranching, he'd also given Treat the first right of refusal for future sales. That had taken away worries about his parents' land eventually falling into the wrong hands.

"Not yet, Pop. I wanted to talk to you about that." They didn't often talk about the forty-year feud that had shadowed their lives.

"Son, what happened all those years ago had nothing to do with Treat." His father's face went serious. "Hell, the whole damn mess was my fault."

His father had made a hasty decision in an effort to try to save their family's ranch. He'd bought horses from a backhanded, cheating thief who had hurt Hal's wife. It didn't matter that he'd done it because he'd seen no other way out, or that he'd been too prideful to ask Hal for money. He'd wanted to make it on his own, and he'd made a bad decision. When he'd finally come clean about it, it had cost him his best friend and his reputation. *Good intentions only go so far.* One hasty decision had put a cloud over their heads for decades.

"No, it wasn't," Steve argued. "It was both you and Hal, and you know it."

He'd never blamed his father, even though he'd been the one who had made the dirty business deal. The feud had been a two-way street—a battle of pride between two men who had been best friends and had turned their backs on each other— that, along with a misguided relationship, reinforced how unpredictable humans were.

"Maybe so, son, but what I did sparked the feud in the first place." His father blew out a long breath. "That's all water under the bridge now. It's behind us, and should have no bearing on any business decisions you make. Treat's a good man, and if he is able to help preserve the history and land of Weston, you know darn well he will. It's worth a conversation."

Steve ran a hand through his hair, wishing for the first time that he had endless funds to take care of things like this on his own.

"Steven," his father said thoughtfully. "I raised you to be a prideful man, but don't let that pride stand between you and what it is you want to achieve. I know how much this town means to you. Think about it; that's all I'm suggesting."

"It's not your job to save Weston, honey," his mother said.

Sure feels like it. "I can't just sit back and watch a development come in and take over, expanding our roads, ruining the environment, and worse, demolishing the land."

"You never have been able to sit back and watch the world change." His mother's gaze softened. "I'll never forget the Save the Creek program you started in fifth grade. Remember that?"

He smiled with the memory. "Yeah, I remember. They wanted to put a bridge over Kings Creek."

"You started the effort that stopped that course of action," his mother said proudly. "I think that was when you made up your mind to make a difference. When you realized you actually *could.*" She reached up and touched the ends of his hair. "That's the year you stopped letting me trim your hair. Some things never change. Like a mother's ability to read her children. It's not anger that I see in your eyes, Steven."

"Come on, darlin'. Give the boy a break about all that." His father rose to his feet. He was a burly man, standing eye to eye with Steve. He opened his arms and embraced him.

Steve was two hundred and fifty pounds of sheer muscle. His father was down to two hundred and eighty pounds of steak, potatoes, and anything else he could get his hands on.

He'd shed a few pounds after a health scare at Rex and Jade's wedding, and Steve knew it was a daily battle for him. The man loved food like he loved the mountains.

"Your sister was here earlier," he said quietly beside Steve's ear. "Your mother thinks you and Shannon Braden are going to be an item."

Steve wondered what Shannon had told Jade the other night at Buckley's. Then again, knowing the way Shannon nearly burst with excitement over everything, she'd probably called Jade on her way out this morning. He scrubbed a hand over his widening smile.

"She'd be right," he said, and sat in a rocking chair beside them. He leaned forward, elbows on knees, and clasped his hands together.

"Oh, Steven!" His mother squeezed his hand. "I knew it. I just knew it."

"Ma, it's very new."

"Only to you, sweetheart," she said. "We have all been waiting with bated breath for you to get your head out of the trees and see that incredible woman for what she is."

Steve shook his head. "Do I want to know who the 'all' are that you're referring to?"

"This is Weston, son," his father said. "You might be better off asking who *isn't* included."

"Great, just great." His sarcasm was born of sheer habit. He sort of liked knowing whoever they *all* were already pictured them as a couple.

"Oh, honey, please." His mother shook her head. "You might live up on that mountain, but Weston roots run deep, and all the people who have loved you since the day you were born just want to see you happy."

"Thanks. I appreciate that. It's all happening pretty fast. You guys might have seen it coming, but I sure didn't. One day I was going about my life just fine, able to put her in this untouchable place in my mind. And the next? *Bam!* She occupied my every thought."

His father laughed. "Son, when you find the right woman, she doesn't saunter into your life. She invades it, silently and effortlessly, like air or steam, and before you know it, she's taken up residence in your heart," he said with a thoughtful gaze. "*That's* how you know she's your forever love, like your mother is to me." His father reached for his mother's hand and gave it a loving squeeze.

"First of all, there's no 'forever love' here, Pop. And are you really okay with this?"

He recognized the shadowy look in his father's eyes. He'd seen it his whole life. It was the stern look that made him sit up a little straighter and say things like *sir* and *ma'am*.

"Son, I've made my share of mistakes, and y'all paid the price for the biggest of them all. I'm sorry for that, but that's all in the past. I love Rex Braden as if he were my own flesh and blood, just as he loves Jade. And whomever you fall in love with will be treated the same."

"Oh, Earl," his mother said softly, and pressed a kiss to his thick shoulder.

"I didn't say anything about love," Steve said.

"You didn't have to, dear." His mother stood and smoothed her pretty fitted dress. "Come on, I'll show you where I put that box."

Steve followed her inside. "She's only here for a few weeks, Mom. You need to temper your expectations."

She led him into the kitchen, where there was a box marked

STEVE in big black letters, beside a plate of corn bread—Steve's favorite. He reached for a piece of corn bread and took a big bite.

"Mm. Delicious."

"I'll wrap some up for you." She wiped a crumb from his whiskers and searched his eyes. "Honey, I don't have any expectations. Only you and Shannon can decide what's right for the two of you."

"Thanks, I appreciate that."

"It's been a long time since I've seen you look like this." As she wrapped the corn bread, she said, "It's your expectations I worry about."

"I don't have any long-term expectations. At the end of her assignment, she'll go back to Peaceful Harbor, and I'll miss her, but I'll carry on, doing what I love. Fulfilling my life's passion."

As he lifted the box, he wondered if his mother heard the lie as blatantly as he did.

Chapter Nine

AFTER VISITING HIS parents, Steve headed up the mountain in search of Shannon. She'd told him which habitats she was visiting today, making her easy to track down. She was sitting on a rock outcropping humming as she wrote in her notebook. She had her earbuds in, and in an effort not to scare her, he went down the ridge and came up in front of her.

Her eyes nearly bugged out of her head. She squealed and jumped to her feet.

"Grizz!" She threw her arms around his neck, sending him stumbling backward. He held her tight as he found his footing and got them onto solid ground, then pressed his lips to hers.

"Miss me?"

She took out her earbuds and said, "I'm so glad you're here."

"Me too. How's your research going? I'm pretty sure you're not going to see much facing this way." He motioned toward the view of the mountains in the distance.

She sighed and handed him her notebook. He scanned what she'd written.

"Career options?" The rest of the page was blank. "Looks like you're well on your way to becoming a stargazer, Butterfly."

"Exactly." She sank down to the rock, and he sat beside her. "I have no idea what to do or even where to start."

He set the notebook beside them and held her hand. "Tell me what you enjoy doing."

"Easy. Kissing you." She smiled brightly.

He laughed and kissed her again. "Great answer. What else?"

She shrugged. "It's not that I don't love it up here. I was just thinking about how I'd love to crawl inside this mountain and experience it from its depths. See the heart of it. I know that sounds weird, but there must be energy inside it that you can feel, right? How could there not be? I mean, just look at all this *life* around us. *That* would be cool."

"Hm, that would be, but I'm pretty sure that's not a job. What else might you enjoy?"

"There's not much I *don't* enjoy. I like research, but I'm having a hard time with the solitude. And I want to do more than just research. I know it's important, but I want to make a bigger difference. I want to be *doing* more, and doing it with people. But I want to still have my hands in the rest, because I love, love, love nature."

"That's great. So you know you want to do more. Like what?"

"No clue." She opened her backpack and took out one of the cookies he'd bought the other day. She broke it in half and handed him a piece. "Right now I feel like eating this cookie. I think it'll get my brain working."

He pulled her in for another kiss. "I have a feeling your brain is always working. What about teaching?"

"I don't think I want to be confined to a classroom. Or an office, for that matter. And I think I'd go nuts staring at a computer all day."

"Have you thought about working in the forest service? Forest service techs work outside, but they work with partners. Or how about working at a nature center or a museum? There are outdoor education programs like nature and science camps for kids and teens. That could be fun. Or work as a lab manager directing and doing research in a university lab."

"I take back what I said about this not being in your bailiwick. You really know your stuff. In ten seconds you came up with more options than I have all day."

He draped an arm over her shoulder and pulled her against his side. "Please tell me you haven't been sitting here all day by yourself. I would have come home sooner."

"Okay, I won't tell you that, but you should know there are either packs of dogs or coyotes way over there on that ridge. They could have been goats. I couldn't really tell." She barely slowed for a breath before pointing across the ravine. "And there's a hawk that's been hanging out by those cliffs all day. I saw it snag something, but I couldn't tell what it was. Probably a rabbit. I felt bad for whatever he got. I hate seeing that circle of life, but at the same time, it was awesome. I've never seen a hawk capture its prey before."

She was seeing all the things city people missed, and he loved hearing the excitement in her voice.

"He's a peregrine falcon. I call him Harvey." He smiled and said, "All day, Shan?"

"Pretty much. I spent a while going over your map, which is incredibly accurate. Thank you for going to all that trouble. I have to plan time to go to the farthest dens, but it's such a long hike."

"We'll go together. We'll make an overnight trip of it and

camp."

"You would do that with me?" She didn't wait for an answer. "You may change your mind after you hear the rest of what I have to say."

"I doubt it."

"Want to know what I did yesterday?"

"Absolutely." He squeezed her hand, knowing nothing could change the way he felt about her. "I want to know everything about you."

"Grizz," she said softly. "Where's that brick wall you hide behind?"

He laughed. "A certain brunette crashed through it. Now tell me about yesterday. I want to know what you think will change my mind about going camping with you."

"Okay, but I'm telling you…there's no turning back once you know the finite details of my chattiness."

"Chat me up, baby." He leaned in for a kiss.

She smiled. "Yesterday morning I waited forever to catch a glimpse of these three kits at one of the dens, and when they finally peeked their heads out, my phone rang. I forgot to put it on silent, so I lost my chance." She shook her head. "I'm going to screw up my own data collection. And not just that, but if I had a partner, I'd talk all the time and we'd scare the foxes off anyway. I think research and I are not *one*, like you and your glorious mountain are."

"Shan, why did you accept this assignment? Why didn't you stay in Peaceful Harbor and try to figure out what else you wanted to do?"

"Because I can't figure out who I am or what I want when I'm home. There I'm *the little sister*, or *Ace's daughter*, or…I don't know. I don't want my family guiding me through life. I adore them, but I need to find out who I am without their input, and if I tell them I just spent all those years in school and possibly made the biggest mistake of my life, how will they react?"

"They're your family. They'll be supportive."

"Exactly." She huffed out a breath. "I don't want to be coddled. I want to spread my wings and figure things out for myself. I don't want anyone else fixing this for me or telling me not to worry because I can always work for my parents."

"You act like your family is oppressive." He'd never gotten that impression from them.

"They're not," she said softly. "They love me, and if they knew what I was thinking, they'd want to help. But at this point in my life, I want to help myself. I want to know that my mistakes are my own, and I know it seems weird, but I don't want that safety net beneath me right now."

"I think that's admirable. But why did you need to take the assignment to get away? You could have gone anywhere."

"That's a little harder to explain. Hold on. I need to prepare for this conversation." She took a big bite of her cookie. When she swallowed it, she took another, and another, until she'd finished it. Then she withdrew a water bottle from her pack and guzzled half of it.

"This must be big for all of that preparation."

"You have no idea." She turned toward him, pulled her knees up to her chest, and wrapped her arms around them. Her hair tumbled over her shoulders in soft waves, framing her face.

"Hey." He leaned closer and pressed his lips to hers. "After breaking down my walls, why are you erecting your own?"

"What do you mean?"

He lowered his eyes to her arms trapping her legs against her chest.

She rolled her eyes. "Because. You might think what I have to say is ridiculous."

"When has that ever bothered you?" He gently lowered her hands and moved closer, placing one leg on either side of her knees, then putting his arms around her. "You've got my full attention."

"I feel very exposed."

"Shan, you're safe with me, and you're not exposed. You were exposed this morning, lying naked in my bed." He took her hands in his and laced their fingers together. "You feel vulnerable. But there's nothing you could say that would make me think any differently about you."

She drew in a deep breath and blew it out slowly. "When they asked me to do this project, I didn't really want to take the assignment. I had spent so much time doing research alone the last time I was here, I knew I was over it. But then they offered me the cabin…"

She lowered her eyes.

"You're nervous," he said softly.

She nodded. "A little."

"Don't be."

"Okay, well, here goes. They offered me the cabin and I took it because I wanted to see what might come of us, which I know is lame. Maybe stalkerish? I can't tell."

"It's not stalkerish," he assured her, turned on, and surprised, by her confession.

"Now that I've told you, I realize it was probably a huge mistake, because now that you know, you'll feel obligated to say something comforting."

He cocked a brow. "Do I seem like the type of guy who

doesn't speak his mind?"

"No, but…"

A breeze blew a strand of hair across her cheek, and he tucked it behind her ear, then pulled her closer. "So you came out here to figure out your life *and* to see if we would amount to anything?"

She nodded with a shy look in her eyes.

"No wonder you were calling me names for putting on the brakes. You took a huge risk. Not just by coming out here, but by telling me how you felt and taking on an assignment you didn't really want."

He rose to his feet and reached for her hand.

She eyed him skeptically. "Are you going to throw me over the ridge?"

"What do you think?" He pulled her to her feet and put an arm around her. "Come on, brave girl. This is the perfect night for s'mores." He gathered her things and led her toward his cabin.

"That's it? You don't have anything else to say about me taking a job I didn't really want? Or coming out here and throwing myself at you?"

"Nope."

"Well, why the heck not?"

"Because, Butterfly." He kissed her temple as they walked. "I may not be a big talker, but I'm an excellent listener. You don't want or need anyone telling you what to do. I'm just glad you're here with me."

THE TIPS OF trees cast shadows like gnarled fingers across the grassy expanse beside Steve's cabin, where he and Shannon ate burgers he'd cooked over an open flame and shared a bottle of wine. The moon glowed orange and gray against the ribbons of rich blues and dusky clouds. The fire hissed and popped, sending curls of smoke drifting like ghosts into the night. Steve hadn't said any more about the things she'd revealed on the mountain, but she knew he was thinking about it, picking it apart, like he did with everything. She knew she was never far from his mind. He'd drawn an intricately detailed map and set up solar lights for her. He cared enough to make sure she'd thought through all the things that could hurt her down the road before they'd even shared their first kiss. And this afternoon he'd sought her out without any hidden agenda. He'd simply wanted to be with her, to see how she was doing. She may not know what she wanted to do with her life, but one thing was for sure. She'd made the right decision by taking this assignment. He obviously thought about her as much as she thought about him, and he cared for her and understood her in a way others didn't. Most importantly, he respected her need to figure this out on her own, and that meant the world to her. She didn't need to be fixed.

You want to be loved…I see it in your eyes.

She watched him now, perched on one knee at the edge of the blanket, whittling the bark from two thin branches with his pocketknife. The more time they spent together, the less guarded he became. She sensed something more going on with him tonight, and she had a feeling it wasn't just his desire to give her a wonderfully romantic evening.

She touched his forearm, bringing his eyes to hers. "We were so caught up in my nonsense earlier, I forgot to ask how your day was."

"Your stuff isn't nonsense," he said with a serious tone that surprised her, though it shouldn't. He was protective of her and of her feelings. It was a different type of protectiveness than she was used to. He wasn't overbearing, and he wouldn't let her minimize her feelings. He made her feel special, and she appreciated it.

He focused on the branch he was whittling. "And thanks for asking, but my day was hardly worth talking about."

"Did you hear back from the people you reached out to about the Cumberland property?"

He gripped the knife tighter, quiet for a minute as he shaved the ends into sharp points, his brows knitted in concentration.

"Yeah. That was a no go. I also spoke to Will. He said he knew you were going to cancel your date." His lips curved up in a softer smile and he slid two marshmallows onto each stick.

"He did?"

"Yup. Said he could tell you were into me." He handed her a stick and touched her arm, guiding her beside him, near the fire. The reflection of the flames danced in his eyes. "The man knows women."

She winced. "Was he mad?"

"Not at all. I think his exact words were 'you lucky bastard.'"

He nodded toward the fire, and they both held their marshmallows over the flames. He slid a finger beneath her stick and lifted it higher, then kissed her tenderly. She felt the tension she'd seen in him moments earlier ease.

"I still can't believe the sugar queen hasn't ever had s'mores. If you hold it just outside the flame, it'll turn golden brown."

"It takes longer that way." She pressed her shoulder against his.

"Such a city girl." He leaned in for another kiss. "I promise it'll be worth the wait."

"Well, *you* were worth the wait, so I guess I'll trust you." She realized he'd redirected the conversation from the land, and she sensed that was the source of his underlying tension. "What are you going to do about the Cumberland property?"

His jaw tightened again. "CRH isn't playing around. They're doing their due diligence, which means they'll be ready to make an offer when it hits the market. I spoke to the bank, and I called in a few favors, but 2.4 million is a huge deal." He fisted his hand and looked away. "I'm not giving up. Weston was never meant to be a town full of cookie-cutter homes."

He turned determined eyes on her. "The peacefulness you enjoy out on your uncle's ranch? The gorgeous, unencumbered views we saw from the fence that morning at Mack's? Once it's gone, there's no getting it back. Once one development is in place, more will follow. It'll be just a matter of time before Weston becomes home to Walmarts and Dollar Trees. Before schools are over capacity. I don't know how yet, but I'm going to find a way to keep it peaceful for as long as I can."

"Maybe you should reconsider talking to Treat."

He shook his head, and his gaze turned thoughtful. "It's not a good idea, Shan. Treat's a smart, well-connected man. I'm sure he made a decision about this land ages ago. If he were interested, he'd have done something. Knowing Treat, he has good reasons for letting it go. He doesn't need the added pressure of spending money because it's important to a Johnson."

Steve grabbed the plate of graham crackers and Hershey bars and set it between them. She knew he was done talking about Treat, and she respected his decision. "Are you ready for your first taste of heaven?"

"I thought kissing you was my first taste of heaven."

He shifted her stick away from the fire and pulled her into a kiss. It was rough at first, carrying the weight of the looming development invading his sleepy hometown. She pushed her fingers into his hair, earning one of his guttural moans she loved so much, and his tension fell away, replaced with the sensuality she'd come to expect.

"You have the best answers," he said with a smile.

"You give the best kisses."

He laughed and shook his head. "How did we end up together?"

"As I recall, you promised me shmores."

He kissed her again. "S'mores, no 'h.'"

"What kind of fool do you think I am? I say the 'h' and you kiss me. I'm sticking with it. Shmores. Shmores. Shmores." She laughed as he plastered sloppy kisses all over her face.

"Ready, sweet thing?" He set a piece of chocolate on a graham cracker, then held the stick, marshmallow side down, and pushed the marshmallow onto the chocolate. "Most people put the graham cracker on top of the marshmallow, but I have a feeling my sugar queen would like it better this way."

He placed another piece of chocolate on top of the marshmallow, then put the graham cracker on top.

Her eyes widened. "Ohmygod. This looks just like the pictures." She licked the melting chocolate from the edge of the cracker and closed her eyes, savoring the rich flavor melting on her tongue. "Mm."

Steve cursed under his breath.

She giggled and he kissed her again.

"You've got to taste the whole experience." He moved the

treat closer to her mouth. "Take a bite of the whole sticky thing."

"How am I supposed to fit this in my mouth? It's huge!"

"That's what you said last night, and you did just fine." He waggled his brows and she swatted him.

She took a bite and closed her eyes, moaning at the sweetness of the chocolate melting into the smoky marshmallow. She could feel the heat of Steve's gaze boring into her and opened her eyes. His eyes turned impossibly darker. He licked his lips, and a gratified smile appeared on his handsome face.

"You and that mouth of yours will be the death of me," he said in a gravelly voice.

She swallowed her bite and they both leaned in for a kiss. Just as their lips touched, she pulled back.

"Crowdfunding!"

He blinked, his brow furrowing in confusion.

"Crowdfunding! You *have* to do it now. It's the best way to get the land. Oh my gosh, Grizz!" She set the s'more on the plate and jumped to her feet. "You have to do this. You *have* to! I'll be right back!" She took off running, and he jumped to his feet and caught up to her in three long strides.

"Wait. Where are you going?"

"To get my laptop. I have to show you. This is the right thing."

He laughed, and she rolled her eyes.

"Seriously. You'll see." She tried to pull away, and he tugged her against him and kissed her—hard and deep, with a little bit of laughter.

"Shan, I have a laptop."

"Oh. Right. Let's get it!"

He looked at the fire, and she knew he was thinking about

safety first.

"I'll get it," she offered. "Where is it?"

"On my desk, but it probably won't get a connection out here."

"Hot spot," she said over her shoulder, and headed for the cabin.

"Hot what?" he called after her.

She laughed and waved him off as she climbed the porch steps, excited to be able to help him after he'd gone to so much trouble for her.

With his laptop and her cell phone in hand, she sat beside him on the blanket and connected to the hot spot on her phone.

"A little lesson in the real word, Grizz." She held up her phone and pointed to the hot spot icon. "This is called a hot spot. It uses cell service to connect to the Internet. Watch. This is how you connect it to your computer so you can work anywhere." She connected the laptop to the service and searched for crowdfunding sites.

"That's cool for a person who wants to carry around their laptop."

She rolled her eyes. "It's cool for a lot of reasons, but I'm not going to debate the value of technology with a guy who hugs trees for a living."

He leaned over and kissed her cheek. "Thank you for not making me have that painful conversation."

"Oh, you're not off the hook yet. I'm just not going to get into it *now*. We have far more important things to go over."

"Right, like begging for money."

"Ha-ha." She pulled up a list of campaigns on the FundMyProject website. "These are called campaigns, which is what you need to develop. A campaign." She clicked on one of them. "See, this singer is trying to raise twelve thousand dollars to make a music video."

"Do people really give money to someone they don't know? Twelve thousand dollars is a lot of cash. What if she's a flop?"

"What if she's a star?" She smiled and scrolled down the page. "See this list? These are things people get for donating certain amounts of money to her campaign. Five dollars gets an autographed photograph download. It costs this chick nothing to give them a downloadable image, and probably tons of her fans would pay five dollars for that. See how she offers a bigger gift for higher donations? A five-hundred-dollar donation gets a signed CD, a signed picture, a T-shirt, and a fifteen-minute group Skype. Oh, Steve! That's a great idea! You're so knowledgeable about the area and so passionate about preservation. You definitely need to do this!"

"I don't know, Shan. There's a big difference between a musician and 2.4 million dollars for conservation land."

"You should talk to Treat, even if you don't want to. He's a business genius, and he not only has the money to help, but he loves Weston."

"We already talked about that."

She crossed her arms and narrowed her eyes. "I don't understand you. You're willing to bend over backward and put yourself out there to save this land for generations to come, but you have too big of an ego, or too much pride, or *whatever*, to do the one thing that could make a huge difference."

His eyes went flat. "Not. Happening."

"Fine, but just for the record, you're being a dumbass again."

He pressed his lips to hers. "Thanks for understanding,

beautiful."

She rolled her eyes again, which she thought might become her standard answer tonight. "In that case, you'll need to reach like-minded people. You need a hook that people will care about and want to become part of." She mulled that over for a beat. "Can it be conservation land and still be used for something else?"

"Sure. It depends how you set it up with the county. Someone could use it to continue ranching, or turn it into a nature conservancy center."

"Oh, Grizz! I've got it!" She set the laptop beside her and took his hand. "Universities are always looking for money for research, right? What about making it into a research center and allowing students to use it? You could have sessions and even give tours to the local elementary and high schools. That's how I figured out what I wanted to do. It was a field trip to a research facility. I spoke to a field researcher who was so excited about what he was doing I wanted to know more, and more. This would be really helpful to students. When I was doing my master's, finding places to host me to do field research was really hard and *very* political. There's such a dire need for this sort of thing. It would take some doing to buy the property, but that would open up so many avenues."

"Shan, it sounds like a full-time job just to figure out the details for something like that, and I don't have six months. I've got sixty days to make something happen. I love your ideas, but you're talking about running a whole facility, and the word 'political' has me worried. I was really thinking more along the lines of conservation." He rubbed his chin. "This magnifies our differences, doesn't it?"

"*Please.*" She waved her hand dismissively. "This is called brainstorming, and it's what makes the world go 'round. We'll come up with something awesome like the Save the Rainforest campaigns. Oh my gosh! That's it! We can sell off the land one acre at a time, but we're not really selling. I can totally see it. Adopt an Acre. Give the Gift of Nature to Generations to Come." She blinked up toward the sky. "I see a beautiful website with pictures of the land, and wildlife, and...hikers."

"Hikers," he said with a wide smile. "Now, *that* sounds like an amazing idea. But I can't imagine it working."

"Hey, Mr. Doubtypants. Have a little faith, will you?"

"I don't know anything about setting up websites, or running programs like this."

"Well, then, I guess our magnified differences aren't such a bad thing after all. I double majored in business and biology, and I have a master's in natural resource management. I can get all of this figured out with a little input from my family. And Max handles all the online marketing for the Indie Film Festival in Allure. She can clue me in to what works, and I'll call my brother Sam about how to best capture conservation peeps online. He does tons of guerilla marketing for his river-rafting and adventure company. Ty can reach out to his tree-hugging groups. I knew one day his being a world-renowned mountain climber would come in handy. He'll love this. And you don't realize it, but you must have oodles of connections interested in conservation. Together we can totally do this. If you don't mind my helping, of course."

She was so excited she could barely sit still, and Steve was shaking his head with a wondrous look in his eyes. Before he could deny her the chance, she leaned in close and said, "Do you trust me?"

"I do," he said seriously.

"Then let me try and help you. Please?"

"What about your research? This sounds…insurmountable. I would never forgive myself if you threw yourself into this project and didn't get your research done."

She sighed but was not deterred. "I will do my research. I won't let that fall through, I promise. I'll just focus really hard. Besides, I can map this out while I'm watching the foxes. It's perfect."

"Online begging, Shan?" His brow furrowed.

Her big, badass lumberjack looked too adorable not to smooch. She pressed her hands to his cheeks and kissed him hard. "You are *not* begging. You're not trying to buy this property to live in as a vacation home. You want to conserve the beauty of Weston, Colorado, for generations to come. You're opening up a huge venture for other like-minded people to jump on board and do some good in the world. It's an admirable effort."

"You're so jazzed about this, it's hard not to get excited and believe that together there's nothing we can't accomplish." He smiled, and her heart soared. "That's an amazing feeling. But I want to be careful."

"I would expect nothing less," she said with a teasing tone, although she was serious.

"Shan, I appreciate everything you're offering and suggesting, but I don't want to stress you out over this just because I care about it. And crowdfunding sounds risky. There are so many worries. What if people pledge money and then back out?"

"I don't know how that works, but I'll research that and find out. And I *want* to do this. I didn't go into research or study biology and natural resources because it's the funnest job on the planet. I care about the environment and wildlife. And I care about you. Just because I'm not sure I want to do research for my whole life doesn't mean I'm not passionate about it."

"I didn't mean to sound ungrateful, or like I didn't believe you cared. I just don't want you to feel like you have to fight this because I am."

She laughed. "Don't you know me at all? This excitement you see." She drew circles with her finger in front of her face. "That's real, and it's for the project. It's a bonus that we can do it together, but the truth is, even if you mentioned the project and told me I'd be all on my own, I'd still want to do it. It's important. And all this talk has made me think of something else. You probably need to form a company, but I think we can get my family to show me how to do that, too. I wish you'd just talk to Treat. This is what he does for a living. He could walk you through everything."

"Jo," he said more to himself than to her.

"Jo?"

"Jo Finney. She knows the ins and outs of nonprofits and for-profit corporations. She's well connected in several conservation communities, and unlike me, she lives in the online world." He tapped the laptop. "She could help."

"Perfect! Can we call her? She seemed really nice, and it would be great to have the help."

His eyes turned serious again, and he pulled back a little. A chill ran over her skin, the kind of chill that preceded bad news.

"Shan, I need to tell you something, and you may not want to hear it, but I don't want to keep secrets from you."

"Please don't tell me she really is your girlfriend and you've been cheating on her, because that's a deal breaker for me. I'm not a relationship wrecker, and I'll end us right here and now—

"

He took her hand and gazed into her eyes with a serious—
and concerned—expression.

"I'd never hurt anyone like that. Not her, not you, not anyone, okay?"

She let out a relieved sigh and nodded.

"Jo and I have been friends since we were kids. We've both
never been into the bar scene, and we like our privacy. The
summer after my junior year of college, we were talking
about…" He ran a hand through his hair and sighed. "This isn't
easy to say, and not because I think we did anything wrong, but
because I feel like I'm breaking her trust by telling you."

With her heart aching, she said, "Then don't. I don't want
to cause a problem between you and a lifelong friend for
something that happened that long ago."

He took her hand and moved closer. "If you feel anything
close to what I feel for you, then I want you to know."

She held her breath, unsure if she wanted to hear what he
had to say, but if she didn't hear it now, it would be all she
thought about until she did.

"Okay," she managed.

"We got to talking and realized we were basically going
months without any intimacy, and we got together. We were
such good friends, we thought we could be more. But we
realized right away that we weren't meant to be together in that
way. It was like a platonic sexual affair, I guess. That's the only
way I can describe it. We never dated. No one even knew we'd
gotten together. We were kids trying to get through the
summer. We didn't call each other pet names or buy each other
gifts, or—"

Shannon had a million questions, but she tried to put them

into some semblance of order. She knew how wonderful Steve was, and clearly Jo knew, too, since she'd known him so long. How could anyone be intimate with him and *not* fall in love?

"I don't understand," she finally said. "If you two have so much in common, why was it platonic?"

"Because sex is a physical act, and being in love is an emotional connection. I love Jo the way you love Jade or Max or any of your best friends back home. And she feels the same about me."

"But..."

"Hear me out, please. Then I'll tell you whatever else you want to know." He drew in a deep breath, like she'd offered him some modicum of relief by listening.

"It was more than a decade ago, and it wasn't anything like it is between you and me. When I hear your voice, my whole world lights up. When I see you, my heart goes ballistic, Butterfly. Like I'm on speed. And when we kiss, Shan? When we make love?"

The emotions in his eyes were so genuine, so palpable, they drew her closer.

"I've never lost myself in anyone the way I do in you," he said. "I think about you endlessly. The other night, when you forgot to leave a light on, I worried about you walking from your Jeep to the house. It's ridiculous, I know."

He reached up and brushed the back of his hand down her cheek, and it was all she could do to swallow past the lump of emotions clogging her throat.

"All those things are new to me, baby. So when you ask why we were platonic, it's because none of that existed until you."

She opened her mouth to respond and closed it again to try to regain control of her emotions. Her mind was starting to process what he'd said more clearly. They were like friends with benefits, or friends who hooked up. Okay, she knew people did that sort of thing, but she'd never dated anyone who had done it before. *Or maybe they just hadn't admitted it.*

He was being honest, and that meant a great deal to her.

"It was more than a decade ago?"

He nodded. "And it'll never happen again."

"How do you know? She's beautiful, and you two were very friendly."

He smiled. "We are friendly, but not cross-the-line friendly. When I see Jo, I see a trusted friend who knows my quirks and puts up with me anyway. I see a fellow nature lover and a good, loyal person. How do I know we'd never get together again? When she and I got together and then realized it was a mistake, it was a wake-up call for me. That's when I swore off casual sex. There have been *plenty* of times when I've longed for a woman's touch, and not once did I think about filling that void with her."

She didn't want to ask who he had filled those times with, or about Rachel, the only other person she'd been curious about. Instead, she asked, "Are there other women that I've met that we should talk about?"

He laughed. "No, Shan. No skeletons in my closet. No secrets."

She felt better knowing that. "Does Jo know about us?" She didn't know why that was important, but it felt like it was.

"Yes. Before you went home for Cole's wedding, she sensed my interest in you, and we talked about it. I wasn't even admitting it to myself at that point, but girls have a sixth sense or something. And she called earlier to tell me the injured goshawk she'd picked up from me the other evening had woken up and he should be fine after his wing healed. I told her about us, and she said she'd felt our connection when she picked up the bird. She's happy for us, Shannon, but I understand if you need time and space to figure out if you still want this."

"You thought I wouldn't want to be with you because of a woman you were with more than a decade ago?"

He shrugged. "I hoped you would, but…"

"But people aren't always what they seem." *Fatally flawed.* She knew it must have been hard for him to confess what he had, and now she understood the worry she'd seen in his eyes. After what had happened with the lifelong friendship between his father and her uncle, the way it had ended over one big reveal and remained broken for more than forty years, it was no wonder he'd been worried about telling her.

But he *had* told her, and that's what mattered.

"I appreciate you telling me before I jumped on the phone with her, because finding out later would have hurt. I want to be with you, Steve. I wasn't a virgin when we got together, so who am I to judge who you slept with before me? At least you were with someone you trusted, which is better than what I can say about the few guys I was with. Two of my past boyfriends cheated. You guys had the bond of friendship. That's enviable."

She sighed and said sheepishly, "I admit, I'm a little jealous, so can we hold off on asking her for help right now?"

"Anything you want, and if you'd rather not do the crowd-funding, we can nix it altogether."

"What? No way. That's important to you, and it's important to me."

He held her closer, his blue eyes swimming with emotions. "Shan, are we okay?"

"Yes." She touched her lips to his. "Honesty trumps jealousy. I mean, it was so long ago. It's not like you were together six months ago or anything. You guys have had years to see if there was something more. And I trust you. Besides, I think I'm more envious of the long friendship you two have had than anything else."

"Because you think she knows my deep, dark secrets?"

"No," she admitted. "Because I want the strength of years behind us."

He was silent for a minute, and she worried she'd revealed too much. But she hadn't been able to hold in the truth.

"I feel like we've been together way longer than we have." He touched his forehead to hers, and she closed her eyes. "We'll have the strength of every day of the next few weeks."

What if that's not enough?

Chapter Ten

SHANNON AWOKE THE next morning in her new favorite position, wrapped up in Steve. One of his arms curled over her side, his hand resting over her breast. His hips cradled her butt, his erection nestled between her cheeks. Even in his sleep he was sexual. He was so sexually intense, she couldn't imagine him going without, but he'd said it had been a long time, and she knew Steve was an honest man. Painfully so. She ran her hand over his leg, which was bent and resting over hers, trapping her against him in the most delicious and possessive way, as if he were afraid she might disappear.

He stirred and pressed his hips forward. She smiled and tried to turn in his arms, but he tightened his grip and pressed his thigh more tightly to hers, holding her prisoner.

"I want you right where you are," he said in a sleepy, sexy voice. "You feel incredible."

He rocked his hips, his arousal moving between her cheeks, and he took her nipple between his finger and thumb, tugging it just hard enough to alight all of her senses. She felt herself go damp and closed her eyes.

"Grizz," she whispered.

"Feel good, baby?" He sucked her earlobe between his teeth.

"Oh *Lord*," she whispered.

He moved her hand to her breast, guiding her finger and thumb to replace his, and together they teased her nipple.

"So hot, Butterfly." His voice was thick with desire.

He slid his hand down her belly and between her legs, which were still trapped beneath his thigh. She tried to open them wider, but she was lying on her side and his leg was too strong. He moved his fingers in and out along her wet folds. She bit her lower lip to keep from groaning at the dark pleasures he roused. Her sex swelled and pulsed, reaching for him, but he continued his relentless teasing. His hips withdrew, and she felt him shifting angles. His thigh lifted from hers, freeing her legs. His hips thrust forward, and he guided the wide crown of his cock against her center.

She pushed down, pleading for him to fill her, but he remained perched against her sex, sliding the head along her wetness, as his fingers worked their magic. A dull ache grew low in her belly, swelling with each stroke.

"Please," she begged.

He put his mouth right against her ear and said, "Please what, baby?"

His heady voice sent shudders rolling through her. "More."

She raised her knee, opening wider for him. He pressed on her clit and pushed just the head of his cock into her, stretching her, teasing her, as he laved his tongue over her neck.

"I want to feel you come like this, with us both aching for more," he said.

His hips gyrated, his wide crown rubbing over all the right places, flooding her with need. She pushed her hips lower, but he wouldn't succumb. His tongue glided over her shoulder, up her neck, and she couldn't stop a whimper from slipping out.

"Please, Grizz. Let me feel all of you."

"Soon," he promised. "I want to feel you lose control. I want to hear my name sail from your lips as you come, before you get the rest of me."

He pushed harder with his fingers, circling her sensitive nerves, moving over them, around them, until she was panting, blinking madly, unable to focus on anything but reaching that pinnacle. He sealed his teeth over her neck and bit down hard, sending shocks of pain shooting through her core and unleashing a violent tumult of pleasure.

"Steve—"

She clutched his hip as he slammed into her, burying himself to the root. Her inner muscles pulsed. Rivers of pleasure coursed through her, consuming her as he drove into her time and time again, each thrust harder than the last. His arm circled her waist, crushing her to him, rendering her unable to do anything more than take everything he had to give—and she freaking loved it. She abandoned all attempts to gain control and succumbed to the hidden part of her he'd unearthed. The part that brought a loud, guttural moan, that drove her fingernails into his arms. The part that wanted to be rough, possessed, claimed, *owned.*

"Harder. Take everything." The words fell from her fast and unexpected, but she wasn't embarrassed. She wanted to be taken hard by him—only him—and she was getting so much more. Despite how roughly he was taking her, despite the crushing weight of his arm across her body, raw, untethered passion seeped from his every pore. Passion that was driven by more than the need for release.

He grunted with each thrust, his strong fingers pressing into her. She could tell by his fast breaths and the sheer power behind his efforts that he was as lost in them as she was. His heart thundered against her back as his hips plowed into her, sending her spiraling into another toe-curling orgasm, and when he followed her over the edge, she felt every blessed pump of his release.

He held her as she came out from under her post-orgasmic haze.

"Baby," he said breathlessly. He kissed her shoulder, her neck, her cheek. "Was I too rough?"

He shifted her onto her back and gazed into her eyes. Lust and power mixed with deep, unwavering concern stared back at her. It was overwhelming to see that much emotion in his beautiful eyes, but even more powerful was the look of pure, unadulterated affection she saw come over him. The "L" word slid to the tip of her tongue, and her throat thickened. She didn't dare believe it. Not after just two days. Not when she was leaving in a few short weeks.

"Baby, did I hurt you?" he asked again, his eyes more serious, dragging her from her thoughts.

"No. That was amazing." She reached up and touched his scruffy cheek.

"You make me feel things and want things…" His eyes were serious, his voice even more so. "Each time we're together, I lose a little more control, and I want to go further, to possess more of you. If I ever get too rough, you have to let me know, baby. Promise me."

"You would never hurt me." She knew he was just being careful with his warning.

He touched his forehead to hers and whispered, "Never, baby. Not on purpose. Just promise me, if I'm too rough, you need to tell me."

"I promise. Do you have some dark secret I should know about? A secret torture chamber? Whips or chains?"

He laughed. "No."

"Then what *are* your dark secrets?"

The spark left his eyes, and her thoughts stammered. "Grizz?"

He rolled onto his side, and she turned onto hers, facing him. His arm circled her and he tugged her closer, easing the worry that had begun to creep in.

"No dark secrets, baby. Just a life already lived. Lessons learned."

"What does that mean?"

He shrugged one shoulder.

"What does that mean—'a life already lived'? 'Lessons learned'? It sounds like you're talking about a relationship gone bad."

He shrugged again. "I don't know."

"Stop being cryptic."

His lips curved up in a troubled smile. "I'm not trying to be cryptic. I just don't know what you're asking."

"That makes two of us."

He pulled her into a loving, tender kiss. "What's troubling you, baby? Did I say something or do something that made you worry?"

"It's more what you half said."

His hand slid over her hip. "You want to know about old girlfriends?"

"I don't know. You said there was no one here. I just…"

He tucked a lock of hair behind her ear and cupped her cheek. "You want to know about old girlfriends that weren't here. I get it." He sat up against the headboard and reached for her, tucking her against him.

"Maybe a little," she admitted, and hoped she wouldn't regret it.

"There isn't much to tell. I've really only had one long-term girlfriend. Susan Nelson. We got together in our last year of college. I thought we wanted the same things out of life. I took a job in the Great Smoky Mountains and we moved in together. *Briefly.* The weekend I was going to bring her home to meet my family, she took off. End of story."

End of story? That's barely an outline. "How long were you together?"

"Couple months before living together. Two weeks of living together." His jaw tightened, and she felt his muscles tense around her.

Did you love her? was on the tip of her tongue, but she held it back. Their relationship was temporary. They had an *expiration date.* She shouldn't even want to know this much, but she couldn't help it. He looked pained, and she wanted to know how deeply he was hurt so she could soothe him.

"Why did she leave?"

"Because people suck," he said glibly.

The fatal flaw.

"She hooked up with a stockbroker, left for *the good life.* She said I'd never be able to give her what she really wanted, and she was right. I'd never have changed my lifestyle for her. The thing was, she'd led me to believe that the life I wanted was what she really wanted."

"The other night Jade made it sound like you'd never had a serious relationship." She didn't mention that Rachel had noticed a change in him when he'd returned that fall.

"Because she never knew. No one in my family did. I was

away at college, working and going to school. I was busy; our calls were brief. I didn't walk at graduation, so they didn't come out, and then I took that summer job. It never came up."

"Never came up? How can a relationship that leads to living together not come up?"

He looked right into her eyes; the honesty in his was palpable. "I have no idea, but I never told anyone about me and Jo, either. And as far as Susan goes." He shrugged. "I guess I must have known things with her weren't real, because I've already told my parents about us."

"You...You did?" Her pulse quickened.

He nodded. "I didn't even hesitate. It just came out. I was so young then. I thought I loved her. I realize now that I didn't have a clue about love, because I didn't feel for her one-tenth of what I feel for you."

"Grizz." She was overcome by his confession.

He pressed his lips to hers again and brushed his thumb over her jaw. "I was hurt when she left, but that's nothing compared to what I'll be when you leave."

Chapter Eleven

STEVE AND SHANNON immersed themselves in everything and anything having to do with crowdfunding for the next couple of days, and Steve's head was spinning. Shannon was not only determined to make this effort a success, but she'd become as entrenched in the cause as he was. Through her hard work and endless patience for Steve's distaste of social media— *Twitter? I don't want to do Twitter. Then we'll set up an account for the campaign and we'll run it together*—Steve began seeing the crowdfunding effort in a different light. It was clear that there were millions of people willing to help strangers. He was shocked at not only the number of campaigns running on multiple crowdfunding sites, but also at the wide array of campaigns—everything from college kids needing money for classes to single mothers asking for help with medical bills and kids raising funds for their school band.

Though he hoped the concept they'd come up with would pull in enough support to purchase the property, he had his doubts. Which was why he was sitting in Treat's home office trying to keep the pride he'd swallowed from coming back up.

Treat flipped through the business plan Steve and Shannon had developed, nodding every so often. He owned resorts all over the world and was a distinguished-looking man with dark hair and chiseled features. He was the eldest of Hal's six children, and he was about as even-keeled as they came. At six six, he didn't need to fly off the handle or raise his voice to demand respect. The man received it from his stature and retained it with his actions.

"I won't be offended if you'd rather not entertain the idea of going into business together. I've been wrestling with my own concerns about it," Steve said honestly. "After what went down with our parents, I wasn't thrilled about the idea of approaching you with this. Our families have come a long way, and I don't want to do anything to jeopardize the friendships we've all established."

Treat sat back in his chair and lifted his dark, serious eyes to Steve. "Neither do I. But we're not our parents, and it's clear that we both care a great deal about Weston and the community. I actually spoke to Mack and Will about the property after their father passed away, and it was clear they were going to ask too much for it. I followed up the other day when I heard about CRH, and Mack mentioned you were interested." Treat splayed his hands. "I didn't want to step on your toes, so I backed off. Needless to say, I'm glad you thought of me. A joint venture is an interesting idea. You've got the conservation know-how and I've got the business expertise. It could work out really well."

"The idea of the Cumberland land being divvied up into a cookie-cutter development turns my stomach. Obviously there's a lot on the line, and if we proceed, I want to be sure that we thoroughly outline the deal so we don't end up with any miscommunications or misunderstandings. No amount of land is worth losing good friends."

"I agree," Treat said. "I do business with close friends and family often. If we talk through the potential pitfalls up front, I'm certain we can work amicably. I like what you've outlined here for developing a land trust, and for the ranch operations to remain intact, if possible. Although I'm not sure about the crowdfunding idea. That's a tough road, Steve."

Steve drew his shoulders back and straightened his spine. "That's my only option at this point. I don't make a killing for a living, though I do all right. What I have to contribute isn't nearly enough to cover fifty percent of the purchase price, even if we talk them down to market value, which I think we both intend to. If you contribute fifty percent of market value, our campaign goal will be five hundred thousand, and I'm good for the rest."

"I respect your decision, though partners don't have to put in equal capital."

"Understood," Steve said. "I know it's a long shot, and honestly, I didn't even know what crowdfunding was until Shannon introduced me to it. And now I know only enough to be dangerous, but Shannon's taken the reins, and she's incredible. She'd like to work with Max to design an online marketing program to spread the word."

"I'm glad you two are together, Steve. I just want to throw that out there. Shannon's been hot for you for quite a while, and I know you well enough to realize you were keeping your distance out of respect not just for Shannon, but probably for all of us."

Steve scrubbed a hand down his face. "Am I that transparent?"

"Not to most people, but I've known you long enough to realize how seriously you take family loyalties."

"She's only here for a few weeks, and I didn't want to upset the apple cart, so to speak. Our families have had enough quarreling for a lifetime."

"You don't have to worry about that," Treat said with a smile. "Though I have even more respect for you for considering us. You're a stronger man than me. When I fell in love with Max, I never gave anyone besides the two of us a thought."

Steve felt a smile tugging at his lips. "Yeah, well, I obviously wasn't that strong. She's been on the mountain less than a week and we're together every night. I think that shows you where my heart lies." It sure as hell showed Steve.

They talked for a long while, hammering out details of the partnership, how it would be structured, how it would run, and they decided on the name Colorado Land Trust. Treat had been through this enough times that he knew all the ins and outs not only of trusts, but also businesses in general. He explained legal and tax guidelines, as well as general business particulars for land trusts. By the time Steve stood to leave several hours later, with his pride intact, he knew he'd made the right decision—and he owed a certain pushy brunette a hell of a lot of gratitude.

Steve saw smoke as he neared his cabin. *Shannon.* He pushed the pedal to the floor and sped up the hill. Gray plumes rose from just beyond the far side of his cabin. He threw the truck into park and flew out the door.

"Shannon!" He tore around the side of the house, praying she wasn't hurt, and found her waving a newspaper at the smoke, which was coming from a mangled attempt at a bonfire. He pulled her into his arms. "Baby. Thank God you're okay." He kissed her forehead, her cheeks, her chin, her lips, unable to slow his frantic pulse. "I thought…"

"I'm sorry. I wanted to surprise you with dinner over the fire, but I have no idea how you start the darn thing."

He drew back and searched her bloodshot eyes. "Baby, how long have you been at this?"

"I don't know." She pouted. "An hour? Maybe more. You made it look so easy."

He laughed out of sheer relief. "I'll teach you. I promise. I'm just so glad you're okay. You scared the crap out of me with that smoke."

"How can it be this hard? I've seen my father and brothers do it a zillion times. And why don't you have a grill? You need a grill. If you had a grill, all I'd have to do is push a button." She waved her hands to clear the smoke, and he dragged her away from it.

"Sorry, Butterfly. If you want a grill, I'll buy a grill. And from now on, if something like this happens, call me. Don't try to deal with it on your own."

"It's just smoke."

"And embers." He pointed to the glowing embers in the bottom of the pit. "You're in the woods, Shan. Everything here can go up in flames, most importantly, *you*."

"Fine." She put her hands on her hips and glared at him, as if he'd done something wrong. "I don't want a grill. I want to learn to do it your way. I love it out here, and I really wanted to surprise you."

"You did surprise me. You nearly gave me a heart attack."

She swatted him and he laughed.

"Seriously, it was sweet of you, and I'll teach you." He pressed his lips to hers, draped an arm over her shoulder, and headed for his truck. "I'll take care of the fire in two minutes. How about I surprise you instead?"

"I like surprises." Her eyes lit up.

"I went to see Treat."

She reached up and touched his forehead.

"What are you doing?"

"Checking to see if you're sick."

He tickled her ribs and she squealed. "Stop! Stop!"

He took her in a sloppy kiss, both of them laughing. "I'm not sick. You were right. I had my priorities all messed up. I was letting my pride guide me, and once I realized that, I went to see him." He reached into the truck and grabbed the bouquet of roses he'd bought for her on the way home.

Her eyes widened and just as quickly dampened. "Grizz. You didn't have to do that." She snagged them from his hand and breathed them in. "I love, love, love roses."

"Thank you for urging me to open my eyes and do the right thing. Treat's lawyers are going to write up the paperwork. He's agreed to put up fifty percent and to match whatever we earn through crowdfunding."

She squealed and jumped into his arms. He laughed as they kissed.

"You're changing my world, Butterfly. One pushy moment at a time."

He moved to put her down, and she wrapped her legs around his waist, clinging to him like a bear to a tree. He carried her that way back toward the fire pit.

"You can't fall for me, you know," she said more seriously. "We have an expiration date, and besides, there's no way I'm doing the whole two point five children thing. It's too mean. What would we do with the other half a child?"

God, I love you. The realization hit him like a kick in the chest, stealing the breath from his lungs.

"And we had a deal, so stop looking at me like I've hung the moon." Her eyes twinkled with delight. "All I've done is smoked up your yard and pushed you out of your comfort zone. So *no* falling for me. Got it, Grizz?"

Too late, baby.

Chapter Twelve

THREE DAYS AFTER Steve's first meeting with Treat, they met again to finalize the legal documents to establish the trust. This was really happening, and he owed it all to his beautiful girlfriend sitting on the opposite end of the couch, staring intently at her laptop. Her legs were stretched across Steve's lap as he read through their campaign plans one last time, absently massaging her feet. He and Shannon had worked late into the evenings every night since they'd made the decision to move forward with the crowdfunding effort. She and Max were almost done creating a gorgeous website focusing on Weston, the land, and the community. Shannon was going into town tomorrow to gather information about the history of the land and to talk to Will and Mack about their family's stories to include on the site, which would endear people to the property on a more personal level. She'd thought of everything. Not for the first time, and certainly not for the last, Steve was in awe of her. She'd jumped right into this project and had spent hours researching and planning while continuing to collect data for her research. Like everything she touched, the project took on a life of its own—alive, giving hope for a better future for Weston.

He wanted to give Shannon the world, and he knew his world would never offer the things that made her happiest. They had a few more weeks together, and he planned on making the best of every second.

"After we get the campaign up and running, how about we take a couple days to hike out to the two dens you wanted to see?" He didn't want to let the campaign overshadow the research she had yet to do.

"We need to make the campaign video tomorrow if you want to get the campaign started in time to get enough donations before the sixty-day window closes."

They'd talked about this a few times over the last week, and he'd even had his father weigh in on the idea. The bottom line was, he'd already learned so much from Shannon about marketing, he'd take whatever advice she gave, but he wasn't keen on the idea of being the focus of a video. "Can't we get someone else to be in the video? Or have Treat do it? He's a well-respected businessman and great with public speaking. Besides, who's going to listen to me?"

"Grizz! You *are* this campaign. All those items on the outline? Those are your words, your hopes, your dreams. No one else can do this. I've been telling you this for three days." She pointed her finger at him. "All the campaigns that do well have a video from the person asking for the donations. You're doing this—no ifs, ands, or buts."

When she put it like that, it was easy to see why she was right. Hell, she was usually right. "There you go, all bossypants on me again."

"You like my bossypants," she said playfully.

"That I do, Butterfly. Mostly when they're on the floor and the bossy woman is in my bed."

She poked his stomach with her toes, and he laughed.

"Camping, Butterfly. We need to collect the data from those other locations." He tickled the bottom of her foot, and she lifted her gorgeous eyes again. "Right after the campaign is launched. No ifs, ands, or buts. Okay?"

She smiled, and he felt it slither into his chest like a hug. "Okay."

Her eyes fell back to the laptop, and her forehead wrinkled in concentration. "I want to put together a rally."

"A rally?" Did her mind ever stop?

"Yes, to get local people involved. I was talking to Sam about it, because he hosts a huge barbecue every year to drum up sponsorships for his rafting and adventure company. He said community involvement is key with any grassroots effort, and I think he's right. He even said he'd come out for it, and that got me thinking that I could invite my whole family. I'd love for them to see this all coming together. It's exactly their type of thing. My parents started their own microbrewery business, Cole has his medical practice, Nate has his restaurant, and Tempest started her own music therapy business. And Ty loves any type of celebration."

"You should invite them out even if we don't host a rally. They'll be so proud of you for the campaign alone. It would be nice to celebrate it with them."

She sighed. "Really? You know my family. They're a lot to take in all at once."

"I love your family. Bring 'em on."

"And what about the rally? What Sam said made sense. The old-timers aren't into social media. They'll never even *see* the campaign. We can ask Mack and Will to host it on their property, and we can hold a raffle and solicit for donations, or have events, like a kissing booth or something to make money for the effort. It'll be fun."

"Kissing booth? Baby, begging our own community? It's one thing to do it online, but here?"

"Oh my gosh, Grizz. Aren't you over that yet?"

"I think you've pushed me pretty far outside my comfort zone."

She narrowed her eyes and said, "Then let me push a little farther. You're doing this *for* these people. Let them get excited to help."

He rested his head back on the cushion and sighed, staring up at the ceiling. "You know I can't say no to you."

She'd been spending the night since the first time they'd made love, and he couldn't imagine a single night without her in his arms. Everywhere he looked there were signs of her. Her favorite flavor of coffee creamers were in his fridge—several flavors, because his sugar queen liked variety. A box of Pop-Tarts sat on his counter. Her boots with the flashy pink laces sat beside his work boots by the front door, and in his bedroom, her dirty clothes were in his hamper. She'd already claimed a dresser drawer—*If I'm going to stay over, I need clean clothes*—and his shower was now home to fancy bottles with flowery-smelling shampoos and conditioners, a loofah, and a purple mesh thing called a shower puff. A bottle of organic coconut body oil sat beside the bed. She put it on each morning, making her skin, and the entire cabin, smell like paradise. He didn't even want to think about how empty his cabin—his life—would feel when she went back to Peaceful Harbor.

"This will be so fun!" she exclaimed. "You'll see. I'll call my family and invite them after we confirm the date. And I'll call my cousins in Trusty, because I know they'll want to help. You know Wes owns the dude ranch. Maybe he can hold a cattle-roping event and we can sell tickets for donations, or they can bet on it with donations. We'll figure that out. Ross and Jade could collaborate since they're both vets. Maybe pet checkups in exchange for a donation. And Ross's fiancée, Elisabeth, can sell pies. We should focus the event around agricultural things. This is going to be so great!"

He could hardly keep up with her thought process, and her excitement was contagious. "You really have a knack for this stuff, Shan. I think you've found your calling."

She trapped her lower lip between her teeth, and a worried expression settled on her face.

"What's that look, baby?"

"I want to ask Jo to help. She can bring birds of prey and give a talk about why conservation land is so important for them."

She hadn't brought up Jo since the night they'd talked about her, and even though she'd said she was okay about the whole thing, he hadn't expected her to want to bring Jo into the fold of their lives.

"Are you sure? Do you want to talk about it?"

"Not really. Unless there's more that you haven't told me?" She set the laptop on the coffee table and pulled her knees up to her chest.

Steve pulled her legs across his lap, bringing her along with them, so she was in kissing range. He didn't want her erecting any walls between them. Especially not over another woman who was truly nothing but a friend. He brushed her hair from her shoulders, and she leaned forward for a kiss. He loved how openly affectionate she was. He finally understood how a rugged man like Rex turned to mush around the woman he loved.

Shannon made him feel warm and squishy inside, even when she made him hard and horny on the outside. Their connection deepened with every minute they spent together, and he had to constantly remind himself that their being together was only temporary.

"I have no secrets," he assured her. "But you're only here for a short while, and I don't want you to be uncomfortable, so are you sure?"

"Yes, I'm sure, but will it be weird for you?"

"Not at all. She's a friend, and I hope she finds someone who makes her feel what I feel when I'm with you. Everyone deserves that." He kissed her tenderly. "No one has ever made me feel the way you do. You fulfill my every need—my brain, my body, and my heart. And I hope I do the same for you."

Her eyes went dreamy. "Grizz. That was so romantic."

"Just don't go telling everyone and ruining my tough-guy reputation." He leaned in for another kiss.

"Jade already knows just how big of a heart you have. If you're okay with it, then I'll ask Jo to help. We need knowledgeable people who care about natural resources and wildlife to really sell this to the community. Besides, what kind of person would I be if I let a little jealousy stand between you and that land?" She smiled up at him and ran her finger down the center of his chest.

That's all it took. That's all it ever took. One smile. One touch. One look. She owned him. His father's voice whispered through his mind. *When you find the right woman, she doesn't saunter into your life. She invades it, silently and effortlessly, like air or steam, and before you know it, she's taken up residence in your heart. That's how you know she's your forever love.*

He set the outline he was reading beside him and wrapped

his arms around her. "You're amazing, baby."

"Not fatally flawed?" she teased.

"Only if being lethal to my heart is a flaw." He took her in a long, deep kiss. "If you want to ask Jo for help, then I'm all for it, but if you feel at all uncomfortable at any time, nix it. Okay? Do you want me to talk to her first?"

"No. I'm a big girl. I've got this."

"I know you can handle anything." He waved at the papers he'd set down. "Look how much you've already done. You've managed to come up with an entire marketing plan. I love the idea of certificates of adoption for donators and plaques for larger contributors, naming rooms in the ranch house after them. What a timeless way to say thank you. You're brilliant, and I hope you know how much I appreciate all you're doing."

"Thank you," she said with a sexy wiggle of her shoulders. "But don't forget, you helped with these ideas. I might have come up with the concept, but you've been right here in the trenches with me. Did I tell you we already have more than seven thousand Facebook followers? Thanks to Max's advice about scheduling posts and utilizing that tweet service, we also have more than eight thousand Twitter followers."

"I still don't really get all that, but I know it's an impressive feat." He shifted her legs to the floor and stood up, reaching for her hand. "Come on. We need to get out of here."

"Why?"

"Because you've been on the mountain researching foxes all day and working on this project all night for days. You need a break." They'd been leaving the house together early each morning to take care of their *real* jobs and had sought each other out when they had breaks or as their days wound down.

She smiled. "No. I don't. I'm fine."

He lifted her to her feet. "I know my girl, and you need to get out of this cabin and off this mountain or you'll get sick of me and the mountain. Get your shoes on. We're going out."

"First, I'll never get sick of you. Second. Off the mountain? You hate going into town."

"Who said anything about going into town?" He flashed a grin and crouched to help her put on her boots. Her toenails were painted bright pink, and he wondered when she'd had time to do that. "Babe, you need socks."

"Socks, shmocks." She shoved her foot into the boot.

"Don't you get blisters?"

"No. I'm tough like that." She ran her fingers through his hair as he tied her boots. "I love your hair."

"My father thinks I should cut it for the video."

"You don't need to cut it for the video. You look earthy and artsy. People will love it."

"As long as you love it, that's what matters to me. But my father said that while it'll appeal to people like me, it's the corporate execs with strong consciences and deep pockets who we want to attract." He moved to put on his boots. "He's got a point. I mean, hair grows, right? And if we're doing this, shouldn't we do it all the way?"

She crouched beside him and pushed her hands into his hair, thrusting her lower lip out in a sexy pout. "You're my *Grizz* with this hair. And in bed I love hanging on to it when we're…" Her eyes sparked with heat.

Damn, he loved that look. "That's reason enough to leave it long. I thought you liked it when I had it cut for Rex and Jade's wedding."

Her eyes widened. "Oh my gosh, how could I forget? Cut it. You were *so* hot at the wedding. Cut it, then grow it back. Best of both worlds, because when I saw you at the wedding? Ohmygod. There are no words." She kissed him again. "But give me one more night with my Grizz."

He nuzzled her neck as they rose to their feet. "I'll always be your Grizz, no matter how long my hair is."

As their mouths came together, she tangled her hands in his hair and he lifted her into his arms. Her legs wound around his waist.

When their lips parted, she ran her hands over his biceps. "I love when you hold me. I love lying in your arms. I love watching you do anything. I just love how *big* you are."

"Damn, Butterfly. *That's* exactly what every man wants to hear."

He wondered if she realized how many times she'd said the *L* word—and was surprised that he had—*four*—and each one hit him square in the center of his chest.

STEVE PULLED SHANNON across the bench seat of the truck, tucking her against his side and buckling her in.

"You were too far away. You belong right here next to me. Always." He kissed her before buckling up and draping an arm around her shoulder.

She snuggled right in, resting her hand on his thigh. His muscles moved enticingly beneath her palm as he applied pressure to the gas pedal. How could a simple movement be such a turn-on? She inhaled the crisp air as they drove down the mountain and realized it wasn't the movement. If her hand had rested on anyone else's leg, she'd feel the simple movement, but now she felt *Steve*.

He pulled onto the highway and she asked, "Where are we going?"

"You'll see." His thumb brushed over the curve of her arm in slow, sensual circles.

She reminded herself it was just a thumb.

A digit.

Slowly stroking…

Holy cow. Shut up.

"I really appreciate everything you're doing to help me," he said. *Stroke. Stroke.* "If it's too much, or if you lose interest, just tell me. I don't want all of this to become overwhelming for you."

Did he know how that little touch made her pulse quicken? "Are you kidding? This is the first time in forever that I've been so excited about something other than *you.*"

"First time in forever, huh?"

"I forgot how much I enjoyed the business end of things and using my creative mind. The research is interesting and important, but what we're doing? Think of how many lives it could impact, not just here in Colorado, but if we get donations from around the world, then that many more people will feel good about making a difference."

He took the exit for Allure, and Shannon rested her head on his shoulder, pulling her lusty mind into a more appropriate place and enjoying the scenery as they drove into the eclectic small town. Brick-paved sidewalks, old-fashioned streetlights, and white lights strung along storefronts gave the town a romantic feel.

"I love the lights," she said. "They make the town feel like a Hallmark card."

"They leave them up year-round." He was quiet for a second, then squeezed her shoulder and said, "We could put solar lights in some of the trees by the cabin."

"I would love that. When we're together, everything feels romantic. Even when you helped me with my boots. I've never dated anyone who was so attentive or so sure of himself."

He laughed quietly. "Come on, Shan. How could any man not be attentive to you? And I'm sure the guys you dated were all confident. You're too confident to accept anything less."

"You'd be surprised. Most of the guys I know either use confidence to mask their insecurities or their egos are so overblown, it's a turnoff. But you're up front about everything. Your likes and dislikes, your strengths and weaknesses, what you want out of life." Those were just a few of the qualities she adored about him—and what had her thinking about how fast their first week together had passed. She wished she could slow down time.

"Thanks, baby. Honesty is everything in a relationship, so with me, what you see is what you get."

The sound of music floated in through his open window, and Shannon scanned the area for the source.

"It's coming from the park," he said. "Allure has outdoor concerts. They're probably having one tonight."

"Really? Can we go?" She sat up and looked for the park. "I love concerts."

"Sure, but we have to make one stop first."

"Thank you!" She pressed a kiss to his cheek.

She watched the last of the shops fade away into the distance, replaced with acres of pastures and farmland. Just as she was about to ask where they were going, he turned down a street, then another, and a few streets later golden arches appeared. She smiled, knowing exactly what her thoughtful man had in mind.

She shrieked with delight, and he laughed. She knew she talked more than he was used to and reacted to things like an uncorked bottle of champagne, while he was more like brooding wine. She worried she overwhelmed him at times, but if she did, he never let on, and he clearly listened to every word she said, making her feel special and important.

"It's Happy Pack time, Butterfly."

Fifteen minutes later they were sitting among throngs of other couples and families in the park, with two Happy Packs— one for a girl, one for a boy, spread out beside them. A band was playing country music on a bandstand that was decorated with colorful hanging lanterns, giving the event an even more festive feel. Beneath the twinkling stars, couples danced and held hands.

Shannon took it all in, swaying to the beat on the grass beside Steve. This was so different from Peaceful Harbor, with the backdrop of the mountains and the chilly night air. Sure, they had beach bonfires back home, but there was something about gathering in the center of town that made the evening feel *bigger*.

She sensed Steve watching her. He was always watching her, and she enjoyed feeling the heat of his gaze. Sometimes she caught him with a dreamy look in his eyes, but she wouldn't dare reveal that. Dreamy wasn't an adjective she thought he'd appreciate.

"Why are you always looking at me?" she asked, snuggling against him.

"Fair's fair."

She hadn't counted on him knowing she was always stealing glances at him, too.

"You're radiant, Shan. So full of positive energy and so sexy, you make me crazy." He pressed his cheek to hers and said, "Waking up with you in my arms, seeing you dance around in the mornings with a Pop-Tart in one hand and a sugar-loaded coffee in the other, your naked butt wiggling beneath one of my shirts? It's a miracle we ever get out of the cabin. I'm so into you, there's nothing I'd rather look at."

She felt a blush spread over her skin as she soaked in what he'd said. It was hard to believe he was the same guy who'd turned away from her the first night she'd tried to kiss him. He'd opened up so much to her since then, sometimes it still took her by surprise.

The band began playing another, faster song. "Dance with me later?"

"Sorry, Butterfly. I've got two left feet, and both have been banned from dancing all across the state."

Maybe she could convince him to let her teach him to dance one day.

He nodded toward the food. "Ready for your Happy Pack?"

She reached for the burger and he touched her hand, stopping her from picking it up.

"There's only one way to enjoy a Happy Pack." He picked up the toy, which was wrapped in clear plastic. "Toys must come first."

"You'll make a little boy or girl very happy one day." She snagged the plastic and tore it open, wondering if he wanted children. His words came back to her, answering that question for her and bringing an unexpected wave of disappointment. *No dreams of a house in suburbia with a white picket fence and two point five children.*

To distract herself from the thought, she focused on the tiny

Barbie doll toy. "Why do they think all girls want a doll? I like the pink streak in her hair, and her purple pants are pretty awesome, but what do you do with dolls? I never really understood them. Why would anyone want plastic friends instead of real ones?"

"I thought all little girls liked dolls."

"Not me." She set the doll down and picked up the toy from the other Happy Meal, tearing it open as she spoke. "I was into forts and swimming, riding my bike, and *anything* my brothers were doing. But Tempest loved playing with dolls." She held up the toy car she'd just opened. "At least with this you can push it around, drive it over ramps and have races."

"I assumed with your pink laces…I never figured you for a tomboy," he said with a curious look in his eyes. "But now that you say it, I can see you chasing your older brothers around, trying to keep up."

"Trying?" She waved a dismissive hand. "*Please.* I kicked ass in everything. Sammy taught me how to paddle canoes and do flips off of inner tubes. Cole and Nate taught me to throw a killer baseball and even spin a football. And Ty? When we were little he was into superheroes. He's only a year older than me, so we played together a lot. He was Wolverine, and I was Shanna. Do you know who Shanna is?"

He arched a brow. "No, and I can't wait to hear, but you should eat while you tell me, because cold McDonald's leaves a lot to be desired."

They ate as she explained. "Shanna was the only daughter of a wealthy diamond miner and grew up in the Zaire jungle. Naturally, Ty and I played this out in the woods near our house. He was the protector, and I was out to prove I didn't need protecting." She held up the burger. "This is good, but nowhere near as good as yours."

He laughed.

"Anyway, Shanna was six years old when she witnessed her father's accidental shooting of her mother, so she hated firearms, and eventually became a veterinarian. She worked at a zoo, and when her beloved leopard died, she took the cubs and raised them in an African reserve."

"Just like that?" He finished his burger.

"Superheroes can do stuff like that." She shoved a French fry in his mouth and he kissed her fingers. "Just go with it. I promise you'll love where this is headed. Her father was kidnapped and eventually killed, but while she was searching for him, she was aided by Ka-Zar. I read up on them when I got older and learned what I hadn't known as a little girl. Shanna eventually became Ka-Zar's lover, and together they fought to preserve the Savage Land from outside threats *and* pollution from technology. Can you believe it? A superhero fighting pollution and technology? I told you you'd love it!"

"I might have to start calling you Shanna." He slipped a fry into her mouth, then kissed her.

"She wore a string bikini, probably made out of animal hide."

"I think we'll skip the bikini."

As they came together in another delicious kiss, the crowd applauded and the band began playing another song.

"Well, well. Who do we have here?"

They both looked up midkiss at the sound of Rex's deep voice, and found Rex, Jade, Cal, Treat, Max, Savannah, and Jack smiling down at them with amused looks in their eyes.

Rex tilted his Stetson. "Howdy, lovebirds."

Shannon and the girls squealed as she jumped to her feet.

Steve rose and extended a hand to Rex, then Treat. "How's it going?" He shook Cal's hand. "Nice to see you, Cal."

Cal tipped his hat in the customary Weston greeting. "Steve."

"Hal's watching the kids," Treat explained. "So we came to hang out. Cal's friend's in the band."

Max's eyes darted between Cal and Steve. She pulled Treat toward the grassy lawn where couples were dancing. "Dance with me."

"Come on, angel," Jack said to Savannah. "Let's give those gorgeous legs of yours a workout."

Savannah tugged on Shannon's sleeve. "Come on! We can catch up while we dance."

"Okay!" Shannon stepped closer to Steve. "Dance with me?"

Steve's jaw clenched. "I don't dance, sweet girl."

"I do, darlin'." Cal offered an arm to Shannon. "That is, if you don't mind," he said to Steve.

Shannon looked at Steve, who shrugged and nodded. As Cal guided her into the crowd, she glanced over her shoulder, hoping to catch Steve's eye, but Cal spun her into his arms before she had a chance.

"DUDE. WHAT THE hell are you doing?" Rex asked Steve. "You just sent your woman out to dance with another man."

"Are you going to ask me how many goats she's worth, too? Shannon can dance with whoever she wants. I trust her, and I'm not going to stress over a dance when she's coming home with me." Watching Shannon dance was a whole-body experience. As she swung her hips and moved to the beat, Steve's body awakened in all the right places. He knew Cal's would be awakened, too. Steve gritted his teeth, feeling like a fast-burning wick of dynamite despite the fact that it was his own fault he'd never learned to dance. He couldn't blame Cal. Hell, a man would have to be blind, deaf, and dumb not to want Shannon, and even then he wasn't so sure they wouldn't fall for her based on her scent and electric aura alone.

Shannon moved like she was born to dance. She tossed her head back, laughing with Savannah and Max, underscoring her vivacious personality and her love of all things social. She was sexy and seductive, and he was jealous as hell that he wasn't the guy on that dance floor.

"Shouldn't you be out there dancing?" Steve asked Rex. "You two have been known to cut a rug something fierce."

"I need a few minutes for my gut to settle down. Had a big ol' steak for dinner. And you know there's no way I'd let any other man lay a hand on my wife." Rex pulled Jade into his arms.

Jade rolled her eyes. "Not all men are as possessive as you, cowboy." She turned to Steve. "Don't you wish you'd taken those dance lessons Mom tried to get you to sign up for in middle school?"

"Christ," he grumbled, watching every move Cal made.

"Treat said you asked him to go in on the Cumberland land with you," Rex said.

"Yeah. It was the right thing to do. He's a smart business-man, and I'm lucky he wanted in on the deal. I think we'll make a good team."

Steve explained how Shannon had come up with the Adopt an Acre campaign, and how she'd outlined the program to incorporate different levels of donations.

"Donations can be given to adopt anywhere from one to fifty acres, and each donator will receive a certificate of adoption. You should see the work she and Max have done on the website and the marketing plan they're working on. Shannon's as invested in this as I am. Maybe more so. I'm lucky she and Treat are involved. I don't have the money, or the expertise, to do it right," Steve admitted. "Passion only goes so far."

"Passion is the only thing that matters," Jade said.

"There was a time when I believed that." He glanced at Shannon, and he knew all the passion in the world wasn't enough to keep an effervescent woman like her on the mountain with a guy like him.

When the song ended, Shannon said something to Cal; then she hugged him, and Steve's gut churned. This was the painful price of opening himself up to such an outgoing woman. He watched them walking over. Shannon's eyes were locked on Steve's, with that coy smile he had etched in his mind. His insides heated and turned to mush, while the rest of him got hard, and he knew with complete certainty, that given the chance, he'd open up to her all over again. He could have gone his whole life and never experienced this incredible, all-consuming love, and he would have missed out on something more magnificent than all the mountain ranges in the world.

Steve reached a hand out to her. "Hey, baby." He leaned in for a kiss, settling all those jealous critters inside him.

Cal came to his side. "Thanks for not taking me down for dancing with Shannon."

"Shannon, dance with us!" Savannah said. She, Max, and Jade tugged Shannon toward the dancing crowd.

"Sorry!" Shannon yelled to Steve, but she needn't have.

Seeing her joyful smile was everything to him.

"No problem," he finally said to Cal. "She loves to dance."

"The other night, when I saw her at Buckley's, she told me she was into you. I wasn't trying to move in on your girl. But she's a hell of a dancer, and what can I say? I love to dance, too."

She told you? Before we were together? He shifted his eyes to Shannon, who spun on her heels, their eyes connecting for a split second. Enough time for his heart to take notice again.

"No worries, Cal. I know you're a good man."

Cal offered a hand, and when Steve shook it, Cal pulled him into an embrace and slapped him on the back. "You're one hell of a lucky guy, and she's a lucky woman, despite the fact that you look like Grizzly Adams."

They both laughed.

Steve spotted Rachel heading their way. The sight of her reminded him about getting his hair cut for the video. He ran his hand through his hair, thinking of Shannon's hands running through it later that night. Just like that, he went half hard. Christ, he needed to get ahold of himself.

Drawing on the techniques he'd learned in his younger years, he looked away from Shannon and thought of big hairy men. *Does the trick every time.*

"Hey, you guys," Rachel said.

"Hi, Rach. I hate to bug you with work, but is there any chance you can fit me in for a cut tomorrow morning?" he asked.

She tucked her blond hair behind her ear. "I'm booked all week, but if you can come over before the shop opens, I'll fit you in. Say, seven thirty?"

"Perfect. Thanks."

"Max asked me to meet everyone here," she said, shifting her eyes nervously away from Cal, who was looking her over appreciatively. "Where are the girls?"

"Shaking their booties." Steve pointed to the girls, who were dancing in a circle, wiggling their butts and shaking their heads like they were dancing to a rock-and-roll song instead of country.

"See ya!" Rachel jogged over to join them.

"Damn, she's fine," Cal said under his breath.

Steve's eyes were trained on Shannon. *Yes, she is, and she's all mine.*

At least for now.

Chapter Thirteen

"YOU SURE YOU want me to cut it?" Rachel stood beside Steve in her salon at seven thirty the next morning, holding a pair of shears like a weapon. "Want me to save a lock for Shannon?" She waggled her brows.

"It's hair, Rach. It'll grow. Besides, she likes it short, too."

She smiled. "Just making sure. Okay, say goodbye to these luscious locks."

Steve didn't normally think about his hair at all, much less care what length it was. When he remembered—which usually took someone pointing it out—he headed into town for a trim. But as Rachel began cutting, each crisp swish of the scissors brought flashes of Shannon to his mind. Images of her twirling her finger in the ends of his hair as they lay side by side sated from their lovemaking swam before his eyes. Last night she'd pushed her hands into his hair while she rode him, tugging to the point of sweet, titillating pain. He already longed for the feel of Shannon's hands in his hair, and Rachel had only begun to cut it.

He thought back to when he and Shannon had first reconnected at Rex and Jade's wedding. Shannon in her pretty short dress, her hair tumbling over her shoulders, begging to be touched. And those beautiful hazel eyes of hers, drawing him in like a fish to water.

He closed his eyes as Rachel chatted about the upcoming barn dance. They'd stayed out late with their friends last night, and they'd had a good time. It had been a while since he'd spent time with friends, and seeing Shannon light up at every conversation, watching her outshine every other person on the dance floor was torture and bliss. His life on the mountain was no match for her. He'd known it from day one, and still he couldn't keep it in perspective.

When he opened his eyes, he caught Rachel looking at him skeptically. Her green eyes moved from one side of his head to the other. She snipped and clipped and then stepped back so he could see the mirror. She'd slicked his hair back, like he'd worn it at the wedding, and his only thought was, *I hope Shannon likes it.*

"There you go, big guy. Clean-cut and sexily scruffy." Rachel handed him a mirror, but he waved it off. "You don't want to see the back?"

He ran his hand over the closely shorn hair on the back of his head. "Feels right to me." He rose to his feet and pulled out his wallet, following her to the front of the salon.

"You two make a cute couple," she said as he paid. "It's been a long time since I've seen you look at a woman more endearingly than you look at that mountain."

"Thanks. And thanks for coming in early to hack off my hair."

"Anytime. You look good, Steve." She smiled warmly. "You look happy."

"Yeah?" He was happier than he could ever remember being, which meant when Shannon left, he'd crash hard. He dug his keys from his pocket and reached for the door. "It's all her, Rach. My mountain's got nothing on my girl."

"Think you can convince her to stay?" she asked.

It was the one question he refused to allow himself to ponder. "She's got a whole life back in Peaceful Harbor," he said, and pushed through the door.

He couldn't ask her to give up her life, but he could sure as hell become more of the man she wanted and deserved while she was here. He pulled out his phone and called Mack. His buddy picked up on the first ring.

"Dude, I got a call from Treat's attorney. Looks like you're really trying to make a go of it after all."

Feeling the breeze against his scalp, Steve ran his hand over his head. He didn't want to talk about the property. There were major price negotiations that needed to take place in order for the deal to actually go through, and he and Treat had agreed to let their attorneys handle that end.

"Yeah, we're moving forward. A lot needs to come together for it to happen, but we appreciate the sixty-day window." He unlocked his truck door and climbed inside. "Listen, Mack, that's not why I'm calling."

"Sorry, buddy. What's up?"

"Do you...*dance?*" He winced as he said the word.

"What?" Mack laughed. "You wanna go to the prom with me?"

"Shut the hell up. Do you know how to dance? It's a simple question. Yes or no?"

"All right, geez. Settle down." Mack snickered. "No, I don't dance. Will tries, but he looks like a one-legged chicken. Why? Shannon got your balls in a knot over not dancing?"

Steve started up his truck. "No. Forget it, man. Talk later."

He fisted his hand and banged the steering wheel, pissed off that this was going to be harder than he'd thought. He clenched his jaw as he punched in Rex's number.

"Hey," he said when Rex answered. "I need a favor, but I need you to keep it to yourself. Think you can do that?"

Rex scoffed. "As long as you're not asking me to find you a herd of goats."

"Where can we meet?"

"I'm at the ranch. Come on over."

"Too visible. I'd rather do this in private."

"Do what?" Rex asked. "You make a move on me and I'll kick your ass all the way to Texas."

"I'd love to see you try. I need your help with something. It's going to take about half an hour. You got that much time?"

"Hey, Steve," Rex said more seriously. "You need my help. I'll make the time. Come to my barn. We'll have privacy there. You okay, man?"

"Hell no, I'm not okay. A certain cousin of yours has totally wrecked me."

He arrived at Rex's house twenty minutes later and was glad to see Jade's truck wasn't there. Steve felt guilty stealing Rex away from his other duties on his family's ranch, but there wasn't much he wouldn't do for Shannon.

He entered the tall wooden barn and inhaled the scents of his youth: hay, horses, and leather. He walked by the empty stalls, thinking about how much his sister had always loved horses. She preferred riding them to cars, the way Steve often preferred nature to people.

Sensing Rex's presence, he turned, catching him as he approached the barn, carrying his sleeping son in one arm. The baby had jet-black hair, like Rex and Jade, and he wore the tiniest pair of jeans and flannel shirt Steve had ever seen.

"What's going on, besides Shannon having your briefs in a bunch?" Rex's eyes ran over Steve's head. "Holy shit. She really does have your head turned around. Man, you went from Fabio to Hugh Jackman overnight."

"That wasn't because of her," Steve said gruffly, wondering how Rex could teach him to dance with a baby in his arms. "We're making a video for the crowdfunding campaign. My old man thought it would attract a wider fan base if I cut my hair."

Was he really going to do this? Ask Rex Braden to teach him to dance? Steve's gut twisted and burned. He turned his thoughts to last night.

Yeah. He was really doing this.

"He's probably right." Rex set his Stetson on a hook and shook out his collar-length hair. "Lucky for me, I don't have to worry about what anyone but my beautiful wife thinks of me. I know you didn't come here to show off your new haircut, so lay it on me. What's going on?"

"I…uh…" *I'm starting to get used to the taste of pride pie.* "I need you to teach me to dance."

Rex laughed. "You need me to *what?*"

"You heard me. Shannon loves to dance. I need to learn. But you cannot, under any circumstances, tell her I'm here. For all I know I'll suck at it."

Rex shook his head. "I am not taking you in my arms like *Brokeback Mountain.*"

"Get over yourself, Rex. I need help here."

"How do I get myself into this shit? I'm kidding about the *Brokeback* crack. I got nothing against same-love situations. But I do have something against *me* dancing with a dude." He pulled his phone from his pocket and brought it to his ear.

"Sweet darlin', I need you in our barn." His lips curved up in a sinful smile. "I wish, baby. You hold on to that sexy thought and get your sweet little body down here for me, 'kay?"

As he shoved his phone in his pocket, Steve turned his hands palm up. "What the hell? I asked you not to tell anyone."

"Jade's not going to tell anyone, and if you want to learn to dance, you need a woman."

"Don't you think if I wanted my sister to know, I would have asked her?" Steve paced, until his sister—and Max and Savannah—appeared in the doorway. "Aw, for Christ's sake."

"What's going on?" Max asked.

"Holy crap, Steve. You cut all your hair off. Look at you, all slicked back and sophisticated." Savannah stood between them, hands on hips, her auburn hair tied back in a thick plait.

She reached up to touch Steve's hair and he ducked away.

"He cleans up nice, doesn't he?" Jade hugged him. "What are you doing here?"

This was not what he'd planned.

"I...um..." No way was he doing this.

"He needs to learn to dance," Rex announced. "And you need to help him."

Steve glowered at him. "Dude, really?"

Rex shrugged, chuckling under his breath.

"Oh, this will be fun!" Max said, looking around. "Where's Shannon?"

Savannah pulled out her phone. "I've got music!"

"Shannon's doing research, and you can't breathe a word of this to anyone. Especially not Shannon," Steve insisted.

"Here we go!" Savannah set her phone on a wooden railing, and country music filled the barn.

"Why not? This is so romantic." Max's brows knitted with

confusion. "She'd love that you were making the effort. I'm going to call her."

Steve grabbed her hand. "Don't you dare." His eyes trailed over each of the girls. "I will walk out of this barn and deny I was ever here if she catches wind of this. Got it?"

"Fine," Max said. "But for the record, you have no idea how much she'd love to be the one teaching you."

"First of all, I might suck so badly that she wouldn't want to dance with me anyway. Second of all, while I appreciate y'all jumping in to help, this was supposed to be a *private* half-hour lesson," Steve said. "Just me and Rex."

Savannah laughed. "You thought Rex would teach you to dance? Do you even know my badass brother?"

"Okay, okay. Let's cut him a break. He's making a *real* effort here." Max, the ever-organized coordinator of their group took Steve and Savannah's hands. "You two are partners. He's got half an hour, and we'll need every second of it. Rex, you and baby Hal dance with Jade."

Jade smiled up at Rex, and they began to sway, melding together like candles in the sun. Steve studied them, determined to learn to dance well enough to share that type of familiarity and intimacy with Shannon.

Savannah put her hand on Steve's shoulder and guided his hand to her waist. "Don't get frisky, or Jack will kick your ass."

"Seriously?" He laughed, standing straight and still as a corn stalk. "You do realize the *only* reason I'm doing this is for Shannon, right? There's not another woman on earth I'd do this for."

"Wow." Savannah arched a brow. "You're really serious about her. Come to think of it, I've known you for more than thirty years and have never seen you dance."

"I'm not sure you will now, either." Steve had tried to dance at a fall festival when he was a kid. It was not a pleasant experience. He'd known way back then his legs were made for hiking, not dancing.

"You need to move a little," Savannah said. "You can do this, you know. The only reason you can't is because you think you can't."

"She's right, big brother," Jade said. "Close your eyes and feel the music in your soul."

Max moved behind Steve and put a hand on his hip, giving him a gentle nudge. "We're going to do the two-step. That means you have to actually move your feet."

"I knew this was a bad idea," he grumbled.

They spent the next twenty minutes passing Steve from one woman to the next, each showing him how to move his feet, where to put his hands, how to stand, where to look, and about a hundred other things they thought were helpful—and he found overwhelming. When Shannon was in his arms, everything felt natural—except dancing.

"Why weren't we invited to the hoedown?" Hal's deep voice boomed through the barn. He cradled Adam, Jack and Savannah's baby, in the crook of his arm, looking every bit the proud grandfather. Next to Hal's barrel chest and tree-trunk arms, the baby appeared minuscule. Although he was well past retirement, Hal still worked on the ranch, cared for the horses, and loved so deeply, he carried a torch for the wife he'd lost to cancer when their six children were young.

Treat stood shoulder to shoulder with his father, holding the hand of his youngest child, Dylan. Jack flanked Hal's other side, holding Treat and Max's daughter Adriana by the hand. Adriana's eyes lit up at the sight of the impromptu dance lesson.

Aw, hell. So much for privacy.

"Dad." Savannah waved Hal over. "We're teaching Steve to dance, but you can't tell Shannon."

Steve straightened his spine under the assessing gaze of the man who preached loyalty and family values and extended an olive branch to strangers more often than the sun rose. The man who had been his father's best friend and business partner until Earl made the mistake that had cost him forty years of friendship. Hal was not free from blame for that awful situation, and because of that, there had been a time when Steve couldn't look at Hal without anger rearing its ugly head. Thankfully, that anger had dissipated when the feud came to an end, and as Hal's wise eyes softened, Steve knew the feelings were mutual.

Hal placed a strong hand on Steve's shoulder, and a smile spread his sun-drenched face. "Looks like someone's heart's been snatched."

"Snatched, sir?" Steve arched a brow.

"That's right, son. Once love snatches a piece of you, you've got no choice but to surrender your heart." Hal shifted his eyes to the others. "Looks to me like my niece has got your mind good and confused. Welcome to the beginning of the best part of your life."

"She blows me away, sir," Steve said honestly. Realizing he didn't say it as eloquently as he could have, he said, "What I mean is—"

Hal looked him dead in the eye. "She blows you away. That's exactly right. The right woman blows you away, pulls you back in, and rattles you until you're too confused to know what hit you. And it's the best thing you'll ever feel. The good parts and the bad."

"Excuse me, Grandpa Hal. Are you done?" Adriana, wearing

a pretty blue dress and cowgirl boots, twirled right into the middle of the barn.

Treat reached for Max's hand with pride in his eyes, and something inside Steve shifted and settled. For the first time ever, he wanted more than his life on the mountain. He wanted this—babies, family, and a sense of belonging. He scrubbed a hand down his face with the startling revelation, but was unable to temper the smile tugging at his lips.

"Yes, darlin'. I'm done." Hal patted her on the cheek and gave Steve an approving nod.

Adriana turned adorable doe eyes up to Jack. "Uncle Jack, will you please dance with me?"

"I would be honored." He took her hand and shot a warning look at Steve. "Careful with my wife there, Johnson."

"Trust me, after she sees me dance, she'll be running for the hills."

"Don't you worry about that," Savannah said with a smile. "We'll practice until you've got it right."

"Shannon cannot know about this," he reminded her.

"I know. We'll figure it out." Savannah exchanged glances with Max and Jade.

"Oh yeah," Max said with a determined look in her eyes. "Project *Teach Steve to Dance* is on!"

Steve looked at the door, debating making a run for it.

Jack clamped a hand on his shoulder. "Don't even think about it. You've come this far."

He'd walked into the barn asking a friend for help, thinking he'd never learn to dance. Two hours later he left to meet Shannon and make the campaign video, knowing there was no way his friends would let him fail. The girls had come up with a perfectly planned scheme that made Steve wonder if they were really CIA. Their husbands were willing participants, agreeing to watch their children while their wives helped Steve turn his second left foot into a righty, no matter how long it might take. They had code words for texting to alert Steve to meet them at the barn in case Shannon saw the text, he had a mental list of dance steps he was supposed to practice, and he had new appreciation for every man on earth who knew how to dance.

When he pulled up to the cabin, Shannon was standing on her tiptoes, reaching above her head, hanging a bird feeder in a tree. Three more bird feeders hung from the low branches of other trees. *Bird feeders.* He'd lived there for more than a decade, admired the birds every single day, and never once had he thought to hang bird feeders. Maybe that was because there were bears in the area. *Only my butterfly...* He wasn't about to crush her beautiful spirit with that little fact.

He stepped from the truck and tossed his keys on the porch, noticing another new item. A welcome mat. They'd moved all of her things into his cabin the other night. He'd felt hope bloom inside him that one day he and the mountain might be enough for her. He'd known it was a dangerous thought, and seeing the mat and the bird feeders magnified that hope. He was setting himself up for a hell of a painful goodbye, but it was no use trying to change directions. His feelings for her, like the hope seeping into his very bones, was unstoppable.

He wrapped his arms around Shannon from behind and breathed her in.

Sunshine and seduction.

"A welcome mat? Are we expecting company?"

She leaned back against him, sighing happily, and she melted like he'd seen Jade melt against Rex.

"In case you ever want to be social."

"You're all the company I need, Butterfly."

SHANNON SAVORED THE feel of Steve's strong arms wrapped around her. She'd missed him more than usual today. She'd spent the day researching the Cumberland property so she could include a bit of history on the website, and every article had brought her thoughts back to Steve. When she'd read about the Cumberlands' ancestor working in the mines in the 1800s to save money to fulfill his dream of ranching, she'd wondered about Steve's family's history. When she read an article in the elementary school paper featuring a field trip to the Cumberland ranch to see the animals, she'd imagined Steve as a boy, on such a field trip, bonding with the animals and gazing out at the mountains, imagining living on them one day.

He turned her in his arms and butterflies fluttered in her belly.

"Oh, Grizz," she said breathily. He was always gorgeous, but with his hair slicked back off his face, his smoldering slate-blue eyes looked twice as seductive. Unable to form another word, she ran her hands through his short hair, over his jaw, and around to the back of his neck. Without his long hair hiding his cheeks, his dark scruff made his chiseled features appear even sharper, more defined.

"You're...*Look* at you. Will you hate me if I say you're beautiful?"

His brow wrinkled. "I could never hate you, but..."

"You're just so *hot*. Like, *forget the video and take me right here* hot."

"Now we're talking." He clutched her ass and pulled her

tight against him. He nipped at her lower lip and she felt her nipples pebble. "Glad you like it, baby. Skip the video?" He backed her up against the tree, kissing her deeply.

Her thoughts began to unravel, but they were running out of time. She forced herself to pull away. "We have to do the video."

"Later?" His talented mouth claimed her neck, wreaking havoc with her ability to think straight.

"Yes," she said breathily.

He pressed his arousal against her, and she heard herself moan, felt herself arching against him.

"Wait." She pushed back again. "No," she said with a laugh. "We *have* to do the video."

He kissed the corner of her mouth. "Fine, baby. You can video us if you're into that."

She laughed and grabbed his face—the heated look in his eyes had her biting her lower lip. How could she turn him down when she wanted him so badly? He must have seen the fissure in her resolve, because he claimed her in another mind-numbing kiss, groaning with desire and driving her right up to the breaking point.

"Grizz," she whispered against his lips. "The video."

With a loud sigh he touched his forehead to hers. "You're right. It's just... I can't get enough of you, and our time together is like a ticking time bomb."

"I know." She'd been thinking about that, too. And hating it.

"Maybe you should consider staying until winter." His hopeful smile climbed all the way to his eyes. "To figure out what you want to do with your life."

She ached at their looming reality. "I wish I could, but I

have a whole life back home. Family, friends, my apartment."

He took a step back and ran a hand over his short hair, regret swimming in his eyes as he muttered a curse. "I was only messing with you. Let's do the video. You wanted to do it at the overlook, right?"

"Wait, Grizz." She reached for him, but he kept walking. She followed him through the woods. "Shouldn't we talk about this?"

He slowed and reached for her hand. "Shannon, it slipped out. Really. We both know we have *now*, nothing more. It was a silly comment."

"Was it?" She searched his eyes, but they were shuttered. Unreadable.

"Of course. Come on. Tell me about your day on the way to the overlook."

Reluctantly trying to let his comment go, she told him how she'd spent her day, but she *couldn't* move past it. *I was messing with you.* He'd said that to her before, and he definitely hadn't been messing with her then. How could she be sure he was now?

They chose a spot on an overlook with glorious mountain views and endless blue sky. Steve read over the script she'd written one last time.

"Treat said it's perfect," she said to his back as he looked out at the mountains. His shoulders rode high and tense. His arms were crossed, his biceps straining against his cotton shirtsleeves.

"He's right. The way you've scripted it, if I weren't involved, I'd give my left arm to be part of this project. You're really talented, Shan."

She placed her hands on his shoulders, kneading the tension from them. "Nervous?"

He scoffed. "Hardly. I just hope it works. But we both know what people want one day they don't necessarily want the next."

She couldn't help but wonder if he was referring to her.

Chapter Fourteen

SHADOWS FROM TREES danced in the moonlight, cutting across the cabin floor. Country music streamed from Steve's laptop as he weeded through the campaign's Twitter feed.

"This is good, right? These tweets from other people?" Steve pointed to the Twitter stream. He and Shannon had been hunkering over their laptops ever since Treat had approved the video and they'd uploaded it and activated the crowdfunding campaign.

Shannon's side was pressed against his. Her laptop was open beside his, with windows open to the campaign, Facebook, and the website's email.

"Those are retweets and questions." She typed in a response. "Retweets are good. Every time our tweet is retweeted, we capture that person's audience. Then hopefully someone retweets and we gain the eyes of their followers."

Steve nodded, wringing his hands together, his eyes shifting to the to-do list they'd created before making the campaign live. "Now that we've sent emails to all these contacts and asked them to spread the word—"

"And my family. They're sending a link to their contacts, and Treat and his family are, too. Now we wait." She typed in another tweet, then clicked over to Facebook while Steve replied to a question about the land.

"This is so stressful," he said, moving back to Twitter. "Look at all the negative shit people say to each other. This one's ragging on some model's waist size. This one's arguing about something Kanye West said. Don't these people have lives? And how is this going to tap into the people we need to find? You worked so hard, and those tweets go so fast. How do people even focus on them?"

Shannon chuckled. "The world moves fast, Grizz."

"No, baby. People's attention spans are short, so *people* make things fast, not the world."

She sighed, pushed him back against the cushions, and straddled his lap.

"Stop worrying. We're following all the right people and the right companies and activists. We'll get there."

"I feel like I should be *doing* more. When something goes wrong on the mountain, I take care of it. An injured animal, partiers wreaking havoc, poachers, fragmenting habitats. Animals don't know about boundaries, and when they venture outside the parks to feed, mate, or migrate, I do my best to protect them, to bring them back so they're not killed. I take action; it's what I do. This feels wrong, sitting back and *tweeting*."

He gripped her hips and rocked his pelvis beneath her, but his body was too riddled with tension for him to fool her into thinking otherwise. His muscles were so tight she could bounce a quarter off of his bare chest.

"This is how the system works," she said, gently stroking his clenched jaw. "Think of it like this. Someone spots a bear ambling onto the road. News travels via cell phones and radio, and a team shows up to get him back to safety."

"Right. There's order and processes in place."

"Now, imagine that same bear ambling down the road. Someone posts a picture on Facebook, someone else posts a video on Twitter, and within fifteen minutes you have animal rights activists arguing with hunters who think they've found an easy target—and yes, you'll have idiots who think they can get there before the proper authorities to pet the bear, but you also have those activists I mentioned. And you know, now that five thousand people have seen the video, some are from around the area, because audiences usually start local, and suddenly, there's *action*. The activists stop the hunters, the police block the dummy who wants to pet the bear, and not only is the bear coerced back to safety, but now we have activists who are fighting to put up fencing so that doesn't happen again."

"Sounds chaotic, baby."

"It is, but it's also progress." She leaned down and kissed him. "And it's what's going to make this campaign succeed."

"Then I need to be distracted, because if I have to weed through the nonsense these people are tweeting about, I'll lose my mind." A devilish grin spread across his lips, and he began unbuttoning her shirt. "I know just the thing."

She felt him go hard beneath her, and when he pressed his warm lips between her breasts, she closed her eyes.

"I've been aching to be inside you all day." He finished unbuttoning her shirt and drew it off her shoulders. It drifted to the floor, and he ran his finger along the edge of her pink lace bra. "You're so beautiful, baby."

He lowered his mouth to the swell above her bra, fondling one breast while still clutching her hip. "I love kissing you."

She was breathing too hard to respond. He unhooked the

front clasp, and she arched forward, wanting his mouth on her. He slid the cups from her breasts, and she felt her nipples pebble against the cool air seconds before he took one in his mouth. Grabbing his head, she held him right where she wanted him, and he grazed his teeth over her nipple.

"Steve—" she pleaded.

He pushed her breasts together, flicking his tongue over each taut peak, and she couldn't hold back a needy moan. When he sucked one nipple into his mouth, then the other, spikes of lust darted through her. She dug her fingers into his skull. Just when she didn't think she could take another second of the exquisite pleasure, he tore her bra off and lifted her from his lap with a sinful groan. He rose to his feet, pressing their bare chests together, and took her in a punishingly passionate kiss. Thrusting his tongue to the same rhythm as he ground his hips, he made love to her mouth, hungrily and passionately, and it made her want to give him the same pleasures elsewhere. She cupped him though his jeans.

"Baby," he groaned against her mouth.

"I can't get enough of you," she confessed.

He reached down and opened his jeans, then did the same to hers. They undressed each other as they kissed. One of his hands traveled over her breasts, while the other moved to his shaft, stroking long and slow as they kissed. She pulled back with the greedy, naughty urge to watch him touching himself. His eyes went nearly black. He moved his hand from her breast to between her legs and dipped his fingers inside her. She gripped his arms, and her head tipped back with the titillating pleasures, but she wanted to watch. She forced her eyes open as he crouched by her legs.

"Open wider for me, baby."

She obeyed his sexy command, holding on to his shoulders and watching his big hand stroke his cock, one long stroke after another, as he brought his mouth to her center. His tongue dipped inside her, then slid between her wet folds, and in one long slide, he stroked over her swollen clit. He took it between his teeth, flicking it with his tongue and driving her out of her mind. Her eyes slammed shut as his tongue shot deep inside her.

"Watch, baby. Watch me love you."

She forced her eyes open again, meeting his dark stare as he opened his mouth wide and settled it over her sex, fucking her with his tongue, still stroking his cock. Her whole body was on fire. She'd never even watched porn, but she knew this was a million times hotter. Seeing her badass mountain man's enormous hand stroking himself as he took her up, up, up. He leaned back, giving her a better view of his long tongue sliding along her sex, and pushed his fingers deep inside her. She sucked in a shaky breath.

"Grizz, you're gonna make me come."

A wicked grin slid into place. "Hell, yes, I am."

He loved her with his mouth as his fingers found her pleasure spot, and her legs buckled. He released his shaft and gripped her hips, holding her steady.

"I've got you, baby. Let go. Come on my mouth. Let me taste all of you."

As if she could hold back? She was strung tighter than a violin.

He brought his mouth to her again, sucking and teasing, as his fingers invaded her, sliding over her most sensitive nerves. When he sealed his mouth over her center again, licking her around his fingers, she came hard.

"Grizz—" she cried out, and dug her fingernails into his shoulders.

He stayed with her, riding the crest with her. As the last ripple shuddered through her, he rose to his feet, his lips glistening with her desire. He wiped his palm over his lips, then lowered his damp hand to his shaft and gave it one long stroke. She. Almost. Came. Again.

His mouth swooped down and captured hers, kissing her rough and deep. Her thoughts blurred together.

"More. I want more," she heard herself beg.

"Your mouth, baby. I want it on me." He held her gaze as he guided her hand to his cock.

She loved the feel of him, long, hard, and thick. She gave him a little shove and he sank down to the couch with a seductive groan, eyes trained on hers, bordering on predatory. Her heart slammed against her ribs. She loved feeling in control, knowing the clenching of his jaw was because of the pleasure she was bringing him. She got down on her knees and swirled her tongue over the wide crown of his cock and teased over the slit. He hissed out her name, his chin falling to his chest as he watched her. She licked him low, dragging her tongue over his sac, feeling it pebble against her hand and earning another guttural groan.

"So good, baby," he said in a gravelly voice.

She licked him from base to tip, then took him in deep. He groaned louder, his hips rising as she drew him out slowly, teasing his swollen glans, before taking him in again. He tangled his hands in her hair, his hips moving with her now. She felt him swell in her hand, and she wanted to taste his essence, to feel him lose control the way he had the other morning. Raw and untethered.

He touched her cheeks and withdrew from her mouth. Without a word he reached for her and lifted her over him, guiding her down on his rigid shaft. She lost her breath as he filled her, embracing her with his strong arms, kissing her hard as he drove into her from beneath. His strength rippled through her core. She felt every inch of him, felt the power he was holding back trapped in his corded muscles. She wanted to feel all of that power. His lips moved from her mouth to her jaw and straight down to the base of her neck, sucking so hard she felt it between her legs. His hand cruised over her ass and between her cheeks, teasing her tightest hole. Between sucking on her neck, the feel of his cock pounding into her, and the titillating, dark pleasures his fingers were giving her, she lost it and tumbled over the edge. Her body quaked and shivered as a stream of desperate pleas left her lungs. Her inner muscles pulsed around him, and still he remained hard and insistent, taking her up, up, up to the peak of a second orgasm on the heels of the first.

She collapsed against him, breathing erratically, unable to think as he held her close, kissing her cheeks, her chin, her mouth. He brushed her hair from her face. She managed a small smile and rested her head on his shoulder.

He cradled her on his lap, still buried deep inside her, whispering so tenderly it brought tears to her eyes. Not for what he was saying, but because she knew the day would come when they wouldn't be together.

"I've got you, baby. You're so beautiful. I've got you." He stroked her back, holding her so close their hearts beat frantically against each other until they finally found the same rhythm.

He lifted her face from his shoulder and framed it with his hands. His eyes filled with regret at the sight of her tears. "Baby?

Did I hurt you?"

She shook her head. "Make love to me, Grizz. All of me."
Make me forget that one day we won't be together.

STEVE CARRIED SHANNON into the bedroom, worried
about the look he'd seen in her eyes. He stripped off the blanket
and laid her in the middle of the bed, following her down. He
settled his hips over hers and gazed into her eyes. Whatever
trouble he'd seen was gone, replaced with pure, unadulterated
lust.

He touched his lips to hers, cradling her head in his hands,
wanting her to feel safe and loved.

"Take me, Grizz. Don't hold back."

"Baby..."

"Don't think." She reached up and touched his cheek, a
sweet smile lifting her lips. "I can feel you holding back, and I
don't want you to."

He ground his teeth together. He was holding back, and he
was holding back a hell of a lot every time they were intimate.
She incited desires in him that made him nearly lose his mind.
"When I'm with you, I want to push us further, take more,
but—"

"Then do."

Christ, even hearing her tell him to let go, seeing the passion
in her eyes, made it hard for him to restrain himself. "I don't
know if I'll be able to pull back once we..."

"You don't have to. I want all of you," she said with so
much love in her eyes it filled the space between them. "*All* of
you, Grizz. Whatever you're holding back, I want it. I want to

feel you lose control."

She rocked her hips, nestling the head of his cock against her center. The need to drive into her was almost too strong to resist—*almost*. She'd opened a door, and he wasn't about to walk away, despite the voice in his head reminding him that the further they went, the harder it would be to say goodbye.

He pressed his lips to hers and gazed into her eyes again. "Only for you, sweet girl. You do this to me. No one else. This is only for you."

Rearing up on his knees, he drank in the sight of her lying so trustingly beneath him. Her heavy breasts rose with each breath, and her pert nipples were oh so tempting. He wanted to bring her as much pleasure as she brought him. His eyes trailed down her body to the swell of her hips. God, he loved her curves. He trailed his fingers down her ribs and over her hips, then down her thighs. Goose bumps chased after his touch. He brushed his fingers over the dips beside her hips to the gentle curve of her stomach.

"I love looking at you," he whispered, and brushed his fingers over her nipples. "Touching you." He lowered his mouth to her nipple, and as he drew it into his mouth, she inhaled sharply. He sucked in a slow, pulsing rhythm, and she arched up, urging him to take more. He drew away, and she whimpered. He wanted her to *want*, to ache and swell and go out of her mind with need.

"You're sweet, sinful perfection personified." He brushed his fingertips down her thighs, then dragged them up her inner thighs, grazing her sex.

She breathed harder, her hands moving toward her belly.

He shook his head. "No, baby." He guided her hands over her head, resting them on the pillow and pinning her in place with his gaze. He settled a second pillow under her head.

"Eyes on me." It was a low command. Her eyes widened, then darkened as he lifted her knees and spread them open.

"Look at you, baby. So wet, so beautiful."

He grabbed the base of his cock and guided the head over her wet folds in slow strokes. She rocked up, her fingers fisting in the pillows, but he didn't give in to her request. He teased her again, dragging his shaft over her wetness until it glistened with her juices. He ran his hand over the broad head, using her wetness to give it a long, slow stroke. She licked her lips and he came down over her. Perching on one hand, he crashed his mouth to hers in a rough kiss, unleashing more of his restraint.

"Touch me now, baby." He guided her hand to his hard length, stroking it with her as he straddled her waist.

"Grizz…" She met his gaze, leaning forward as she gave his shaft a gentle tug toward her mouth.

He moved up her body and lowered his shaft to her mouth. She took him in deep, loving him like she never wanted to stop, and he just about lost it. He held the headboard and she clutched his hips, urging him faster, taking him all the way to the back of her throat.

"That's it, baby. Make me yours."

She cradled his balls, teasing them and taking him right up to the verge of release. He couldn't take the one-sided pleasure. He wanted to give her just as much as he was getting. He withdrew from her mouth, gritting his teeth against her whimper. He moved the pillows from beneath her head, then turned, straddling her head as he buried his mouth between her legs.

"Oh God," she said in one long breath, and reached for his erection, guiding it into her mouth.

He nearly came undone the second he sank into her greedy little mouth. He fought against the wave of pleasure moving down his spine and pushed his fingers into her tight heat, still loving her with his mouth. She moaned, and it vibrated along his shaft. He replaced his fingers with his tongue, then moved his fingers to her most sensitive hole, teasing her there. It wasn't enough. Nothing was enough with Shannon. He needed to possess *all* of her. He eased his finger into her ass as he buried his tongue between her legs. She groaned, sending another thrum of long, low vibrations through his core. He worked her slowly, opening her, loving her with his fingers and mouth, holding back his release. He moved his mouth lower, lubricating her there, and working a second finger in. She arched off the bed.

"Too much?"

"Uh-uh," she said around his cock.

He couldn't suppress the gratified smile from spreading his lips. His dirty girl was right there with him. He sucked her clit into his mouth, moving his other hand to her center, and slid his fingers into her tight channel, loving her in every possible way. He felt her orgasm mounting, her thighs tightening, her core trembling. She cupped his sac, squeezing just hard enough to send shocks of exquisite pain radiating through him. When she cried out around his cock, he was no match for the surge of emotions swamping him as he spiraled out of control and followed her over the edge.

Their bodies bucked and shook as they rode the wave of their passion through the very last shiver. He pressed a kiss to her trembling thighs, giving himself a second to try to regain control. He moved up the bed and took her in his arms. He felt his love for her climbing up from the pit of his stomach, clawing its way through his chest, fierce, powerful, *unrelenting* in its need to be heard.

He brushed his lips over hers. "Still on the same page?"

"Yes." She held his gaze. "Every. Single. Word."

He kissed her then, long and hard. They kissed so deeply, he released all of the emotions he was holding back, pouring silent *I love yous* and *Please stays* into the kiss, burying them in her lungs.

They both pawed for purchase in an urgent fight for *more*. He stroked between her legs, eating up every sexy moan, every frantic plea. But he wanted even more, wanted to touch more of her, pleasure her in ways she'd never been pleasured.

He drew back from the kiss, eyeing the bottle of organic coconut body oil on the bedside table. A wicked little grin of approval appeared on her beautiful face. He retrieved the bottle and drizzled the oil over her belly. Her stomach flexed with the sensation.

"Smells so good," she said.

He dripped the glistening oil over her breasts, and she trapped her lower lip between her teeth. When he moved down her thighs, trailing a slick of oil from hip to knee, she closed her eyes.

He set the bottle beside the bed. "Open your eyes, beautiful girl." When she did, he stroked his hard length.

Her eyes widened, then narrowed.

"You like that," he said, gliding his hands up her thighs.

"No," she whispered huskily, and his hands stilled. "I love it."

"Then it's official," he said. "You've been put on this earth to torture me."

She laughed softly, and in that moment he fell even harder

for her. Just when he thought he loved her as much as he could, she found a way to sneak deeper into his heart.

He massaged her legs from just above her knee to the tops of her thighs, stroking, massaging, squeezing.

"Mm." Her eyes fluttered closed.

"Open, baby," he reminded her, and she looked up at him through heavy lids.

He squeezed harder as he reached the very edge of her thigh, where it met the skin beside her sex, and used his thumbs to slick oil along that sensitive skin, slow and deliberate. She made a sexy little mewing sound, rocking her hips toward his hands. He worked his way up her body, his hands gliding over the curves of her belly, along the swell of her hips, the dip of her waist. The oil warmed with his touch, and she arched toward his hands, making sweet, sexy sounds as his hands glided up her sides.

"This seems unfair," she said through heavy breaths.

He caressed her breasts, sliding over her nipples, slowing to tease and gently pinch. She bowed off the bed, and he slid slick hands up the underside of her arms and laced his fingers with hers, trapping her hands above her head. He moved his arousal over her slick belly, aching to be inside her.

"What's unfair?" He kissed her neck as she struggled for words. Her eyelids fluttered and her breathing quickened. He kissed her softly, languid and loving. Her hips rose off the mattress, rubbing eagerly against his arousal.

"This. You make me feel so good, and I'm not giving you anything back," she finally said.

"You are, baby. I take pleasure in seeing you lose yourself in me, just as I lose myself in you." He kissed her again, releasing her hands.

"Then don't stop," she urged.

He gently rolled her onto her stomach and gathered her hair over one shoulder, revealing her gorgeous, sleek back. He drizzled oil down her spine, to the crevice at the top of her ass. She ground her hips into the bed, and he dripped more oil over the curve of her cheeks to her thighs.

"Feel good, baby?"

"Yes," she whispered, fisting her hands in the sheets beside her head.

He worked his way up her spine, marveling in her beauty, her sense of adventure. He loved that she was so sexually confident, so willing to trust him. His hands glided over her shoulders, kneading her soft skin as she melted beneath him. Then he kissed her beside her ear.

"Still with me?" he whispered.

"Always," she said. As he lowered his body to hers, nestling his hard length against her ass, she said, "Yes," in one long breath.

He kissed her cheek, sliding his cock along the crease. His hands slid up her arms, and he laced his fingers with hers. Her back was slick and warm against his chest. She ground her ass into his shaft, working him in a fast, heady pace. He ground his teeth together, buried his face in the crook of her neck, trying to hold himself together. When she dug her fingernails into his hands, he nearly lost it.

With a groan, he moved down her body, massaging her sweet, perfect ass, kissing each round cheek. His hands glided fast and firm on her thighs. He spread her legs, massaging the crease beside her sex, and when she lifted her hips off the bed, he couldn't hold back from taking what he wanted. He pushed his fingers deep inside her wet center, and she cried out.

He stilled, shaking with desire. "Too hard?"

"No. Good. *More*."

She raised her ass higher, and he slid his other hand between her cheeks, testing the waters.

"Yes," she pleaded.

Holy mother of God, he was going to come unraveled. His fingers were slick with oil and slid right in. One. Two.

"More," she begged.

Three.

He was on the verge of losing it from the eroticism of what they were doing, but even with her squirming and moaning with pleasure as his fingers invaded all of her, he still needed *more*. He withdrew his fingers slowly, closing his eyes against her whimpers.

"Grizz, please," she begged.

He came down over her back, kissed her again beside her ear, telling himself to hold back, but he was no match for the mad love tearing through him.

"Shannon, I have to have all of you." *I love you too hard. It's too much.*

"Yes." She sounded relieved, as if she was fighting the same internal battle.

"Baby." He slid to the side so he could see her face, and the raw emotions he saw there slayed him. They were both shaking, and he'd never heard himself sound so dire as when he spoke. "I love you, Shannon. I love you so hard it hurts."

She swallowed hard. "Me too, you. I'm more scared *not* to do this than to do this. I can't go another day without being completely and totally yours."

Their mouths crashed together in a hard, crazy kiss that was somehow also loving and sensual.

"I love you, baby. We can stop at any time."

"No, we can't," she said. "This love is bigger than us. It's unstoppable."

Dangerous. He closed his eyes against the word and kissed his way down her spine. She lifted her hips off the bed, angling her beautiful ass before him.

"So trusting, baby," he said, tucking a pillow under her hips. He used his fingers again, kissing her back as he loved her until she was ready to receive him.

"Now, Grizz, please. I can't take another second."

He guided his slick shaft to her tightest entrance. Feeling her soft cheeks against him made him want to slam into her, but he kept control. He kissed her upper spine, and they both groaned as he breached the tight rim of muscles. Her ass squeezed around him, and it took all he had not to thrust. She gripped the sheets, her eyes closed tight.

"Okay, baby?"

"Yes. *More.*"

He took her slow and steady, until he was buried to the root, and then he came down over her back and laced his fingers with hers. She was so tight, they were both trembling, breathing hard and shallow at once.

"God," she whispered. "You're huge."

After a beat of silence, they laughed, and that humor broke the thread of fear that had held him back.

"I love you, Butterfly. So much…"

He loved her gently, and when she asked for more, he loved her harder. He slid his hand beneath her and teased her over the edge. After they'd both lost themselves to their lovemaking, he carried her to the shower and they made love beneath the warm spray.

Back in his bed, on clean sheets, with Shannon lying safely in the confines of his arms, she asked him if he'd ever done that before.

"No, baby. You make me crave all of you. I've never wanted that before."

"Oh," she said softly.

Closing his eyes and saying a silent prayer that she'd have the same response, he said, "You?"

"You know how high schools have prom queens?"

"Yeah," he said, confused.

"I was the anal queen."

He closed his eyes, biting back the anguish knotting his gut.

She lifted a finger and pretended to *chalk one up*. "Gotcha!"

He hugged her tighter, losing himself all over again in her confidence and carefree giggles. When she turned in his arms and they gazed into each other's eyes, he knew the truth before the words left her lips.

"Only you, Grizz. You own me."

Chapter Fifteen

THE NEXT WEEK passed in a blur of campaign and rally coordination, and falling head over heels in love with the area, the people, and the man whom she couldn't look at without wanting more of him. Shannon and Steve's lives had melded together seamlessly. Steve had spur-of-the moment meetings with various associations throughout the week, and she was busy every second with research and the campaign. But they'd found time to slow down for each other, making love late at night and talking into the wee hours about *everything*—with the careful exception of the future, which they tiptoed around as if it were a land mine. Lately they'd been getting up early to watch the sunrise together from their back porch. They'd even found time to go out with friends. They'd had lunch with Mack and Will to discuss their hosting the rally, and she was pleased that there had been no weird feelings between any of them about breaking her date with Will to be with Steve. They'd also met Jade and Rex for dinner, and she'd even convinced Steve to go to a barbecue at the Bradens. They'd invited his parents as well, and it was like a coming-out party.

They'd become a real couple, and it felt wonderful. Shannon's research was no longer a solo project, which made it even more enjoyable. After Steve took care of wildlife forestry concerns, he inevitably ended up where Shannon had set up for the day. He brought picnic lunches, and if they were both still on the mountain at the end of their workday, he sought her out to walk her back to the cabin. It was dating, mountain-man style, and as she was falling deeper in love, the ominous countdown to her departure loomed. They had a little more than two weeks before she had to return home, and every time she thought about it she nearly drowned in sadness.

Now she and Steve sat in a café surrounded by their friends and family to finalize the plans for the rally, Steve's hand spread possessively over her thigh. When they'd made the promise that they could handle moving on after she went back home, she hadn't fully believed it. She knew for sure there was no way she could ever look at Steve and not be madly, deeply, passionately in love with him. But she had a full life to return to in Peaceful Harbor, a family she adored, friends she'd grown up with.

Her eyes danced around the table, taking in the smiling faces of family and friends who had gathered to help them without expecting anything in return. Max, Treat, Jade, and Rex were chatting happily across from her. At the end of the table, Jo had Cutter Long's rapt attention. Cutter was Wes's barn manager, and he had volunteered to help Wes with the cattle-roping event at the rally. Jo looked quite taken with the handsome, blue-eyed cowboy. Shannon had gone to see Jo earlier in the week, and they'd had a long conversation about the rally and about Steve. Shannon had been surprised to hear that they'd been intimate only once, especially since she and Steve couldn't keep their hands off each other. And as far as she and Steve went, they hadn't revisited the sensual depths they had the night with the oil, but that night had changed everything. It had brought them to a new level, strengthening their bond and solidifying their relationship. They'd built an even stronger foundation of trust and truth that left no room for worries.

She shifted her gaze to her right, where her cousins Ross and Wes were sitting with their fiancée and wife, Elisabeth and Callie. Wes's hand rested on Callie's burgeoning baby bump. On the other end of the table, Shannon's cousin Luke and his wife, Daisy, were chatting with Cal and Rachel. Shannon had received a supportive call from her cousin Emily, who also lived in Trusty, and wished she could be there to help, but she and her fiancé, Dae, were in Italy preparing for their wedding.

Shannon wondered if it were possible for a person to have *two* full lives?

"What do you think, Butterfly?"

Steve's rough, sexy voice sent shivers down her spine. *Uh-oh.* She'd missed whatever they'd said.

"I'm happy to do it." Elisabeth's blond hair framed her pretty face, and she smiled brightly. "Rossie's assistant, Kelsey, said she'd help me with the booth. We'll make mini pies, like I made for the fair, and give them away for a small donation. Every dollar counts, and the community loved the beer cakes I made."

"That would be wonderful. Thank you." Shannon's heart swelled at the support she had here and ached at the idea of leaving it all behind. Steve was looking at her like she was the only one in the busy café. How could she leave him? How could she give him up? Could they manage a long-distance relationship? Would they want to?

She pondered that thought as Elisabeth described the pie she had in mind for the rally. "I'll call it River Pie, and use creamy white chocolate and give it a greenish hue so it looks like water, with chunks of chocolate as rocks poking out through the water and whipped marshmallow cream to add a few white-caps."

"And I'll be your taste tester," Ross said, leaning in for a kiss.

"Back off, brother-in-law," Callie said teasingly. "Pregos before significant others. I'll be the chocolate pie taste tester, thank you very much."

Ross scowled.

Wes gave him a dark look. "Don't even think it, bro. My wife wants the pie, and I'll take you down to make sure she gets it."

Everyone laughed as Wes pulled Callie into a scorching-hot kiss. Shannon's grown cousins were always wrestling like a pack of teenagers.

"Thanks for helping with this, you guys," Shannon said. "As of this morning the campaign was up to one hundred and eighty-seven thousand. Only three hundred and thirteen thousand more to go."

"I have to admit," Treat said, "I was skeptical about crowd-funding, but you two are really pulling people together. It's a different business model, but it could free up funds for renovations to the ranch and maybe even more land trust deals down the road."

Shannon's ears perked up.

"Thanks to my favorite girl," Steve said with pride. "And we have a solid plan for the event now, thanks to each of you. Mack and Will are excited to host the rally, and I spoke to the Weston Times this morning. They're going to publicize it."

"If you and Steve decide to try to buy more properties

through campaigns, or other creative means, and put them into trust, Treat," Shannon said, "I'd love to help."

"We'll plan on it." Treat slid a serious look to Steve, who gave one curt nod. "I think it's the type of work you could do remotely."

Her stomach knotted up at the reminder.

"It was a brilliant idea to hold the rally the afternoon of the barn dance," Jade added.

"Right?" Max said. "Everyone will be excited, and hopefully the dance will be a *real* celebration."

"I bet we'll see a lot of new dance moves that night," Treat added.

"Right, Steve?" Rex said with a coy look.

"Should be great." Steve turned away, but not before Shannon caught sight of the nervous look in his eyes.

She wondered if he was thinking about her leaving, as she was, or if he and Rex had an inside joke about her dancing with Cal the other night. Cal was busy chatting with Rachel. Clearly *he* wasn't worried about an inside joke.

"You guys have taken a triple two-step into this relationship," Jade said.

Steve ran a hand down his face.

"No, they didn't." Max raised her brows. "They line danced right through the barn doors."

She knew they were teasing Steve because he didn't dance, and bit her tongue because although Steve was shaking his head, he was smiling.

"You think, sweetness?" Treat said to Max. He turned a teasing grin to Steve. "I think they've been waltzing since Rex and Jade's wedding, and they've finally mastered the 'Cotton-Eyed Joe.'"

"Christ," Steve mumbled.

"Okay, that's enough, you guys." Shannon didn't mean to raise her voice, but that was *enough* teasing. "You guys are relentless. So Steve doesn't dance? Leave him alone."

Steve turned a warm smile on her. "I'm fine, baby. Are you?"

"Yes." She loved him so much she could feel the ache of it in her bones. She was glad that he wasn't crazy jealous the way Rex was. She loved Rex to pieces, but she could never stop dancing just because Steve didn't like to dance, and she didn't need everyone making such a big deal out of it.

She laced her fingers with his, feeling like the luckiest girl on earth to have found such a loving, thoughtful man who was also, undeniably, the sexiest man on the planet. If only she could take him back home to Peaceful Harbor. But she couldn't ask him to leave his life here in Colorado any more than she could step away from hers in Peaceful Harbor.

Maybe she should put her efforts into DNA cloning. Or a 3-D printer.

"Thanks to Max and Jo," Steve said, "who have offered to take over the social media *nightmare*—"

"Hey!" Shannon swatted his arm.

He laughed. "I mean, social media *mania*, Shan and I are going camping tonight," Steve said. "If you need us, wish upon a star, because we'll be sleeping beneath them."

Her throat thickened. There was no way she could stop seeing him. Could a person die from boyfriend withdrawal?

Suddenly a long-distance relationship didn't seem like such a bad idea.

AFTER LEAVING THE café, Steve and Shannon gathered their camping gear and headed into the mountains. They hiked up to the first habitat Shannon wanted to observe, and she gathered data all afternoon. While she studied the habitat, Steve made a wide sweep of the surrounding area, looking for evidence of bear activity. They'd opted to bring foods they didn't have to cook, so they wouldn't have to worry about cleanup. Subsisting on cheese and crackers, energy bars, and jerky wouldn't kill him. Steve didn't care what he ate—or if he ate, for that matter. He just wanted this time alone with Shannon and to know she was safe while out in the wilderness. Shannon, on the other hand, might die without her requisite sugar fix, which was why Steve had packed Pop-Tarts, a pink-frosted cupcake he'd picked up while they were in town, and one of those premade fancy Starbucks drinks.

She'd insisted she carry as much gear as Steve, but when she'd gone inside to use the bathroom, he'd taken half of her gear and added it to his. He admired her desire to pull her own weight, but she didn't have to prove a darn thing to him. He admired everything about her. She was sitting on a bed of rocks taking notes in one of her notebooks with a pen that wrote with pink ink. He'd noticed she had two notebooks, and in each she'd used both pink and blue ink. The fact that he'd even noticed such a thing—much less thought it was too adorable for words—told him just how far gone he was over her. As if he hadn't already known.

He moved behind her and gathered her hair over her shoulder, kissing the back of her neck.

"Mm. That's nice," she said with a dreamy sigh.

"How's the research coming?" He breathed in her unique scent he'd come to love so much.

"Good. I've got enough data for today." She looked up at the dimming sky. "We should get our tent up, shouldn't we?"

He'd brought a tent, but he had something more fun planned. "I thought we'd build a shelter."

She set her notebook down on the rock and her eyes widened. "No way. You would build a fort with me?"

"Don't you know by now I'd do anything with you?"

As he leaned in for a kiss, she sprang to her feet. He laughed and tugged her in for that kiss he wanted, and a few more to hold him over while they built their fort. "You lead, baby, and I'll follow."

She tapped her finger on her chin and scanned the woods. "We need tall branches. A bunch of them. And lots of leafy ones, too."

Steve pulled a coil of pink rope from his bag.

She shouted with glee and threw her arms around his neck, her eyes twinkling in the dimming sun. "Have I told you lately that you're the best boyfriend in the world?"

"No. In fact, I don't think I've heard the 'B' word come from your pretty mouth before." He slid his hands beneath her hoodie, beneath her shirt, and ran them up her warm back, holding her tight against him. "And I like it a whole heck of a lot."

Their mouths came together in a hot and hectic kiss. She rubbed against him like a cat, purring deep in her throat. As he roused her passion, his own grew stronger. She pushed her hands up the sides of his head, holding him possessively. Lord, did he love the feel of her claiming him—almost as much as he loved claiming her.

They came away breathless.

"Wow," she said breathily. "Kissing you is like…" She bit

her lower lip and narrowed her eyes. "It's like the difference between breathing mountain air and city air."

He kissed her again. "I want to be your *only* air." It was a risky statement, one he hadn't expected. As she melted against him, the sleek caress of her body told him how much she loved hearing it.

His hands moved down the length of her back. It was torture staving off the desire to undress her right then and watch the dusky evening roll in over her naked body. But he felt the distinct tingling beneath his skin that warned him of impending rain. They needed shelter. Once he knew she'd be warm and safe for the night, he'd make up for the time they'd lost.

And then some.

An hour later they'd gathered branches and were halfway through constructing their teepee-style fort a safe distance from the fox den, so as not to disturb them. The clearing they chose was buffered by trees, as if the space had been dropped from the sky just for them. The ground was hard and cold, still working on the springtime thaw. He couldn't wait to bring Shannon out when wildflowers were in full bloom and at the turn of fall, when autumn colors kissed every surface.

Emotions pooled inside him as they secured the tops of the branches with the pink twine. *Pipe dreams.*

Dangerous pipe dreams.

They had only two more weeks together. The end of their time lurked like a villain in the dark, threatening to tear them apart. He'd known how powerful his emotions were even before they'd kissed, but he hadn't realized she'd had the power to strip him to his very core. How would he survive her leaving?

He grimaced, pushing those feelings down as deep as he could. And then he pushed harder, forcing them further into the pit of himself as he spread their sleeping bags out inside the fort. Then he gathered their belongings and tucked them in the shelter. They'd built this fort together, and in his love-crazed mind, he saw a connection to the very heart of their relationship. They'd been laying a foundation for weeks, *building* things together. The land trust, this camping-research trip, going out with friends as a couple. They were building a *life* together. *A temporary life.* He unpacked the tent and began laying the waterproof material over the branches, wanting to stay the night in the shelter they'd built.

"I didn't think you brought a tent."

"I would never bring you out here completely unprepared," he said more sharply than he'd meant to. His emotions were eating him up, and he had to figure out how to put them in their place before he burst.

Shannon danced around in her skintight jeans and pretty yellow hoodie, alternating between humming and singing different songs, jumbling up all the lyrics as she tossed leafy branches over the material. She swung her hips and made googly eyes at him while she sang, and Steve was having a heck of a time keeping his hands to himself. He was surprised when his feet began to move to the beat of her mixed-up songs. The rally coordination was the perfect excuse for his impromptu sessions with Rex and the others, which were definitely paying off. Every one of their friends showed up for the lessons, which was embarrassing but also endearing. He couldn't believe he'd ever felt like an outsider around the people who were giving up an hour a day to help him find his right foot.

Shannon picked up a long, leafy branch and used it to fan him. "I could be your entire harem. Fanning you, feeding you grapes."

He took the branch from her hands, tossed it onto the shelter, and gathered her in his arms. As he'd counted on, as he'd sworn by, as he never wanted to forget, her soft curves accommodated him, embraced him, washing away his tension.

"We have *now*."

"What?" Shannon's brow wrinkled.

Hell. He hadn't meant to say it aloud.

He took her face in his hands and kissed her. "Now, baby. We have now, and I don't want to waste a second of it."

He lifted her knee to his hip and rocked against her. They both moaned, both grasped for more. This was how it always happened with them—a single kiss, a single spark caught fire, and they combusted. They tore at their clothes, ravenously eating at each other's mouths. Her hoodie and shirt flew from his hands, her bra shredded with a single hard yank, earning a contagious burst of giggles. Laughter was part of them— laughter, heat, *love*. There was no slowing a storm of this magnitude. He dropped to his knees and she clung to his shoulders as he wrestled with her laces.

"The one time you tie the damn things."

"Hurry," she panted out, laughing as she ran a hand through his hair. "You will always be my Grizz, right?"

He stilled for a beat. *Yes. Stay. Please stay.* "Always, Butterfly."

He tossed the boots aside, then worked his own feet free, and they both wrestled off their jeans. He hardly had time to take a breath, had to have her naked body against his. He tugged her against him and kissed her roughly, staving off the plea for her to stay. They had now. Now had to be enough.

"Long distance," she said between kisses. "We can do that, right? See each other every few weeks?"

She met his fervent efforts with hard thrusts of her tongue, moaning and pleading into their kiss.

"Yes. We'll make it work." *We have to.*

He spread her legs wide and pushed his fingers into her. She gasped, and he paused, reading her, making sure he hadn't hurt her. She bucked her hips, pushed his wrist down, forcing his fingers deeper inside her—giving him a green light. He sped right through, finding her pleasure point with lethal accuracy.

"Come for me," he commanded. "Now, baby. Come so I can take you like you want to be taken."

One perfectly placed stroke, and her eyes slammed shut as her orgasm tore through her. "Grizz!" echoed in the forest. "Oh, Grizz." She clung to his neck, her body convulsing against his hand. "I love you."

"Shannon." Her name came out so low, so heated, it sounded as if it were ripped from the depths of his soul.

Her eyes darkened, full of challenge. When she said, "*More,*" the last shred of his restraint snapped.

He spun her in his arms, and she grabbed the branches of the fort. He couldn't breathe. He needed her, needed to be inside her. She looked at him over her shoulder, and her hair tumbled over one eye. He needed to *see* her. He gathered her hair in his fist, telling himself not to tug, but how could he not when she was looking at him like she dared him to? The veins in his hands swelled like snakes slithering up his forearm from the restraint it took not to tug too hard. The burn of her stare intensified as he entered her sweet, hot center. They both groaned, loud and low. She was heaven. She was hell. She was the very air he breathed. Their eyes held as he drove into her, love and lust twining together with their frantic rhythm. She closed her eyes and he released her hair. Her head fell between her shoulders as he moved inside her, feeling her pulse throbbing around his shaft. Her fingers curled around the branches, her knuckles blanching at the force of their lovemaking. He slid one hand around her front, between her legs, and gave her the release she craved. She clung to the shelter with one hand, grabbed his forearm with the other, panting and moaning as her inner muscles clamped down around him in a sweet, erotic rhythm.

When the last of her climax pulsed through her, he wrapped both arms around her. She was trembling, her body damp with perspiration despite the chilly evening air. He turned her in his arms, stroking her back as he kissed her mouth, her jaw, her cheek.

"More," she said shakily.

"Not like this." He motioned to the fort and helped her settle on the sleeping bags, coming down over her. "I want to love you, baby, to look into your eyes and see what you're feeling."

He brushed her hair from her forehead and kissed her there. "I want to cherish you now. No more roughness, baby. Not right now."

He lowered his mouth to hers, basking in the soft press of her lips, how willingly she opened for him as he entered her. He pushed in slowly, savoring the moment and the pleasure swimming in her hazel eyes. He touched his forehead to hers, cradling her body against him, and breathed her in.

"I love you, Butterfly," he whispered. "I will always love you."

She sucked in a breath, and her eyes dampened.

"I *love* you with every ounce of my soul. I'm so full of you I'm not sure where I end and you begin."

She smiled, and tears escaped down her cheeks. "We'll be okay, right?"

She was so strong and so vulnerable. He wanted to protect her from the world, but he knew he had to protect her from his begging her to stay, too, because beyond the love, beyond this unstoppable connection, was a woman who needed more than the mountain.

He kissed her salty tears and then he kissed her beautiful mouth.

"We will." He kissed her again. He knew what the future held, knew it would drag him under when she left and leave him wrecked, but he didn't care, couldn't care. They had *now*— and she *loved* him. God, she *loved* him. He could barely wrap his mind around this beautiful, vivacious, smart woman *loving* him. A man who didn't dance, a man who was as gray and brown as she was pink and yellow.

As cool air whispered over his skin and he gazed into her gorgeous, trusting eyes, things in his head shifted. He didn't know how, didn't know if it was possible, but he'd damn well try to find a way for her to have it all—the world she loved and him.

He swallowed past his thickening throat as the first raindrops fell, and whispered, "I want to kiss you like the sun rises: slow and soft, then wild and tantalizing. And just when you think you've experienced all there is, I'll take it deeper, until you feel it in your bones. Until our love is inescapable." He kissed her softly and said, "And then I'm going to start all over again."

He sealed his promise with a kiss as thunder rolled in, and loved her through the storm.

Chapter Sixteen

THE TWO WEEKS leading up to the rally passed too quickly as schedules were rearranged and last-minute preparations were put into place. Steve got called into town for so many spur-of-the-moment meetings with business owners to pitch the project, she thought he might get sick of it before the rally even took place. But not only had he come back rejuvenated after each meeting, but on several occasions she caught him humming. *That* was a side of Steve she'd never expected.

Shannon's family was arriving later tonight and staying at Hal, Rex, and Treat's houses. She was excited to share this time with them and for them to finally see her and Steve as a couple. She wondered if they'd see how happy she was, and she was nervous about how her brothers would act. But Cole assured her they weren't going to embarrass her, which was good, because she'd hate to have to embarrass them right back by putting them in their places. They were as excited about attending the rally and the barn dance tomorrow night as she was. She tried to focus on that instead of the fact that the following afternoon she would join her family on a flight back to Maryland.

How could the time have passed so quickly?

She'd managed to complete her data collection and bring

the campaign and rally to fruition, all while falling desperately in love. She still needed to decipher the data and write the paper on her findings, which she'd take care of back in Peaceful Harbor, but the finalization of the project signified the beginning of the end of her time with Steve.

She sat on the edge of Steve's bed remembering the first time he'd carried her into his cabin and how nervous she'd been. The way he'd fought his feelings for her so vehemently those first couple of days, how he'd tried to convince her to fight hers, too. They were no match for their connection, and now she almost wished they had been stronger. How could she leave a man she loved with her whole being? How would she sleep in a bed that didn't smell like Steve? How could she sleep without his strong arms wrapped around her? Without his sweet murmurs whispering into her ears?

As if he could feel her thinking about him, Steve sauntered into the bedroom with an easy smile. "Hey, Butterfly."

How could she face a single morning without seeing his handsome face? Without hearing his sexy, love-filled voice?

He eyed her open suitcase lying empty on the floor by the dresser. She thought she'd start packing, but she hadn't been able to muster the courage to begin deconstructing their lives in a way that felt so final.

"Maybe you should leave a few things here for when you visit," he suggested.

They'd decided to try a long-distance relationship, but hearing him refer to her *visiting* brought tears to her eyes.

He crouched before her and brushed away her tears. "Hey, baby. We'll get through this. We'll Skype, and—"

"You hate the Internet," she said with a pout.

"But I *love* you."

He sat beside her and draped his arm around her, pulling her in close. His scent invaded her senses, drawing a stream of fresh tears. He kissed them away, but more came. Is this how she'd be for the next million days? Crying a river of tears? That wasn't fair to him. She sniffled, drawing her shoulders back a little. It didn't help. Like a needy girlfriend, she curled against him.

"I'm going to miss you so much. Who will buy me cupcakes?" It was a stupid, selfish question, but she was too brokenhearted to think straight.

"I'll have them delivered fresh to your apartment door," he promised. "Jazzy Joe's delivers."

She wiped her tears. "How do you know about Jazzy Joe's?"

"My girlfriend forced me to become Google friendly."

She smiled at that. He put up with the Internet; he did not embrace it. "But why were you looking up Jazzy Joe's?"

"I wasn't. I was looking at the Peaceful Harbor Pinterest board, another thing my wonderful girlfriend introduced me to. I wanted to see the place I was losing you to." He pressed his lips to hers, and his sweet words brought even more tears.

"You're not losing me."

He framed her face with his rough hands. She loved his rough hands. She was going to miss them. God, was there anything about him she wouldn't miss?

"I know, baby. I didn't mean it. The truth is, I only started on the Pinterest board to see the area and what it had to offer. Then I moved on to the local help wanted ads. I contacted the park service, and I even called your brother Sam and asked him about finding jobs outside of the park service. I figured if anyone knew about jobs in my field, it would be him."

"You called Sam? You looked for a job there?" Tears burned

in her eyes.

"I tried. But it's a small beach town. A really cute town, too. A town where I can see you frolicking in the sand and swimming in a sexy little bikini that makes guys go wild."

She laughed, and a tear slid down her cheek. "Grizz..."

He brushed her tear away. "I'm sorry, baby, but unless I grow fins, I have no chance of finding a job in my field there."

"I can't believe you did that for me."

"I did it for us, baby. And I'll be counting down the days for the next three weeks until you come back." He kissed her again. "Come on, I want to take you someplace special."

She swallowed past the lump in her throat and looked at her evil suitcase. The darn thing was just waiting to be filled up like a ravenous stomach. "But I have to pack."

"I'll help you later. You've done enough already." A playful grin spread across his face. "Besides, I'm still hoping you'll leave a few things for the next time you come."

"Well, I don't wear underwear very often, so I know you're not referring to that." She swiped at her tears with the back of her hand.

"Your pink shoelaces. Your yellow hoodie. That light pink shirt you wear to bed sometimes. You know, the one that I take off the minute you hit the mattress."

She felt her cheeks flush. "You want my shoelaces?"

"No." Rising to his feet, he took her hand and brought her up, hugging her to him. "I want you, but since you have responsibilities elsewhere, I'll make do. I'll tie one of them here." He touched the wooden spoke on the headboard. "And I'll put one in my wallet. That way you're always with me."

A sob escaped her lungs, and she covered her mouth. "And my hoodie?" she asked through her tears.

"It's what you wore the first night we stayed in the wilderness together." He shrugged. "I know I can't have you here all the time, but I need pieces of you."

She touched her hands and her forehead to his chest. "How can I leave you?"

"I wonder that myself." He lifted her chin and gazed into her eyes.

She had to go home. That's where her family was, her life. Well, her *other* life. She couldn't just pick up and move. What would happen after the research assignment and the campaign ended? When she didn't have projects to keep her busy?

"We can do this, Shan. We'll Skype. We'll talk on the phone. And we'll make the best out of the time we have together." He kissed her again. "Now come on. No more tears. Let's get out of here. No more packing, no more talk about donations or campaigns or rallies—not for the next few hours, at least."

"But we should check the campaign page before we go."

The crowdfunding campaign gained donations by the thousands every day, evidence of social media and a giving society in action. Every so often Steve still lost it over a nasty post, but Shannon waylaid his anger with patience and love. She didn't expect him to ever fully embrace social media, or the idea of completely trusting people he'd never met, even after he was beginning to realize how much good it did in the world.

He led her out of the bedroom. "I already did."

"You checked the campaign?" She couldn't hide her surprise.

"Yes. We're at four *hundred* and thirty-five *thousand*. Now it's time to let your boyfriend take you someplace you can't go through an Internet connection."

"Holy crap! Four hundred and thirty-five thousand dollars? Grizz!" She leapt into his arms, and they laughed and kissed.

As her feet touched the ground, he said, "Now can I kidnap my girlfriend for something not-campaign, not-Internet, and not-dollar-sign-related?"

"Absolutely." She went up on her toes and kissed him again, loving the value he placed on enjoying their natural surroundings. More often than not, they cooked dinners over the open fire. They'd begun setting aside *couple time*, taking nightly walks, stargazing, and making private wishes. Steve's love of the outdoors made her realize how much of it she took for granted. Shannon didn't miss her overly plugged in lifestyle. She'd been so busy with the rally preparations and the campaign that by the time she'd settle in for the evening, all she wanted was Steve.

They drove a long way out of town. Steve followed a web of narrow, winding roads. The truck rocked and rumbled over the change from pavement to dirt. Unlike the woodsy, mountainous area where Steve lived, this area was low-lying and arid-looking, with few trees and an abundance of verdant, prickly looking bushes.

"This looks spooky," Shannon said as the truck ascended a steep hill, then careened around a sharp turn and followed a grassy path down another hill. "Where are we going?"

"You'll see." He continued driving, slowing as a ravine and large jagged rock faces appeared in the distance.

Layers of coarse-grained rock spanned as far as she could see. The setting sun cast an orange glow over the rock face, giving it an otherworldly appearance. Tufts of sparse trees and bushes capped the rock formation like a toupee, and two dark enclaves appeared like villainous eyes not far from the ground.

"Fifers Canyon," Steve said. "Isn't she beautiful?"

"Incredibly. It's so different from where you live. It's a little mind-boggling."

He squeezed her thigh. "That's nature, baby. Let's go inside."

Her pulse quickened. "Inside? We're going *in* there?"

"Sure." He pushed open the door and reached for her hand.

"Um…" She gulped down her fear. "I don't know."

He unhooked her seat belt and shifted her legs so she was sitting on the edge of the driver's seat, then cupped her cheek. "Trust me?"

"Always," she said honestly.

"This will be one of the most spectacular things you've ever seen." He lifted her under her arms and set her on the ground. Then he dug around behind his seat and came out with a lantern.

"What if the cave collapses?"

He draped an arm over her shoulder and began walking. "Then we'll die together."

She gasped.

"What happened to my fearless girl?"

"She's back in the truck, where we should be." She slowed her pace, hoping to dissuade him, but he was having no part of it. He laughed, kissed her again, and continued walking, tugging her along with him.

She slid her hand into his back pocket. "How about we make out for a while?"

"Nice try." He stopped walking and kissed her. When she moaned, he took the kiss deeper. She felt the tension leaving her limbs; her breathing shallowed, and she dissolved against him.

"Feel better, baby?" he asked with a satisfied look in his gorgeous eyes. "Just like Valium."

Holy smokes. "Yeah, if Valium made girls wet."

He stilled. His jaw clenched repeatedly, and his fingers tightened around her shoulder. He adjusted his very eager erection and shook his head before continuing toward the cave. She couldn't help but giggle.

"Think that's funny?"

"Hilarious," she admitted.

He turned, his eyes glistening like liquid heat. "A billion years ago this gigantic rock formed below the earth's surface and was forced upward," he said in a voice thick with lust. "That's nothing compared to what you do to me with a single kiss."

And just like that, all thoughts whooshed away—except the dirty ones.

THE PAST WEEK had been one distraction after another, the biggest of them being Steve and Shannon's decision to have a long-distance relationship. Steve hoped this mini excursion would take their minds off of their impending separation. He'd considered proposing to her in this cave, trying to convince her to stay with him in Colorado, but she was so vehement about going back to Peaceful Harbor—to the life that had confounded her so badly she'd come across the country to try to figure it out—he'd buried that hope.

He lifted Shannon over the rock ledge at the entrance of the cave. Cool air seeped out of the darkness. Shannon peered inside with a fearful look.

He lit the lantern and took her hand, pressing a kiss to the back of it. He wanted to take her in his arms and hold her until the fear left her eyes—hell, until she agreed to stay in Colorado with him. But any more discussion about her staying would only bring more tears.

"Ready for your next adventure, Butterfly?"

She gazed up at him with trusting eyes. He didn't think anything could make him contemplate leaving the mountain, but the idea of Shannon being on the other side of the country had done just that. Even though the small beach town didn't hold *any* possibilities of a future in his field, he was nowhere near ready to give up on the chance of winning her over to the idea of one day living in Colorado permanently. But she had to want his lifestyle—and therein lay the problem. How could he compete with her family? With beaches and the ocean? With lifelong friendships?

Long distance it was.

For now.

"I've got you, baby. I promise this will be something you'll never forget."

He led her into the cave, feeling her hesitation in her tentative gait. He tucked her beneath his arm and kissed her temple. He smiled down at the woman he'd once thought was too damn cute, too damn social, and too damn temporary for the likes of him. He was wrong on at least two of those counts. She was supremely cute and perfectly social. It was the third one that twisted him into knots, but he'd take two out of three and make do with seeing her once a month until they could figure out the rest.

"It starts out narrow, but it'll open up quickly," he said as they walked deeper into the cave. He understood the claustrophobic feeling that came with entering a cave for the first time. He still got a tingle in his chest from it.

"It's cooler than I imagined," she said, sounding a little less nervous. "I know caves aren't like mines, with poor air circulation and lack of oxygen, but I didn't expect it to feel so…easy to breathe."

"Most caves have more than one entrance, so there are lots of fractures and conduits to circulate the air." They followed the uneven rock as it dipped and wound around protruding walls. The lantern illuminated only a small area.

"Look!" Shannon pointed up to the ceiling as they entered the area he wanted to show her. "Stalactites." Her eyes widened, and she pointed to a flowing formation cascading along an overhung surface of the sloping ceiling. "What is *that*? It's gorgeous!"

"They're called draperies. They're formed from calcite-rich solutions. The surface tension allows them to cling to walls or sloping ceilings and stream downward. Loss of carbon dioxide in the atmosphere causes them to become supersaturated and deposit in these thin trails. The different colors are caused by the changing supply of organic acids."

"This is beyond gorgeous," she said.

"Like you, baby. You said you wanted to see the heart of the mountains or the cliffs. This is about as close as I could come."

She slid an arm around his waist and rested her head against him. "I'm glad I took Tempest's advice and came out here."

He thought about his next question for a beat before asking it. Not only was it a loaded question, but her answer could shatter him, no matter how much she loved him. Despite her tears and her confession that she'd miss him after she left, she was still leaving. "Did you find what you were searching for? Figure out what you want in life?"

She tilted her beautiful face up, silently looking him over. Did she feel their pulses pounding in the air around them? His heart lying in wait?

He reached over and stroked her cheek, no longer needing her answer. "Don't say it, baby. Just let me know you're happy."

"Grizz," she said softly. "I found what I was searching for, but I've only made my life, and yours, more complicated."

"Then stay." He couldn't help it—he had to ask. He had to *try*.

Her lips curved down at the edges. Her expression turned doleful, almost pleading. "Grizz…"

He heard her unspoken words—*We talked about this. I can't leave my family, my life.* He touched his forehead to hers and closed his eyes.

"I'm sorry. I just can't fathom a day without you." He opened his eyes and saw hers were damp, hating himself for being too weak to hold back his feelings. "When you went home for the wedding, the mountain was *too* quiet, the air was *too* still, and we hadn't even been together yet. I can't imagine what it will be like when you leave for good."

"Not for good," she said forlornly. "For three weeks, and then I'll be back. And after I go back home, you'll come to see me three weeks later."

The back-and-forth travel—missing her effervescence, missing her loving, missing the sweet melodies she hummed and her excited squeal at every little thing—wasn't the life he'd envisioned for them.

Because I envisioned something I couldn't have, and I knew it from the start.

"Besides, Grizz, what happens in the winter when the mountain becomes too treacherous to navigate and you're stuck with me *all* the time? I don't even know what this mountain looks like in the snow. Will I go stir crazy being that far away from people, when the Internet goes down and cell coverage is spotty? Will I resent you for asking me to stay? Or hate myself for wanting to?"

"What if you love it here in the winter?" he asked, knowing full well she needed more than the mountain. More than him. He told himself to man up and stop acting like a lovesick kid.

He could face wild animals, hike for days, and work in iceberg temperatures, but when he tried to imagine three weeks without Shannon, he felt like he couldn't breathe.

Chapter Seventeen

THIS WAS IT, Shannon thought as she gazed out at the mountains while waiting for Steve to return from the emergency call he'd received at five thirty that morning. She hadn't even heard the phone. She must have been fast asleep when he'd received the alert that a hiker had reported an injured mountain lion on one of the overlooks. How Steve always knew exactly where to go on this enormous mountain range still amazed her. But this mountain was his life, and he knew every trail, every tree, where water gathered when it rained in the same way she knew the back roads of Peaceful Harbor. She closed her eyes and tilted her chin up toward the morning sun, pulling her sweater tight across her chest. It was chilly now, but the sky was clear and it promised to be a perfect day for the rally and hopefully for the dance later that evening.

She should be packing for her flight tomorrow, but she still hadn't been able to muster the gumption to do it. She'd tried to pack last night after they'd gone to her uncle's house to have dinner with her family, but every time she approached the dresser with the intent to fill her suitcase, she shook and her throat thickened. She drew in a deep breath, trying to gather the courage to go inside and face what she had to do.

She pushed from her perch on the back steps of the cabin and scanned Steve's yard. *Our yard. It feels like our yard.* The stump where he chopped wood still had a log lying on top of it. His ax, however, was neatly stored in his shed. Everything had a place in Steve's life. There was order and process, things she'd never been very good at establishing for herself, and she found comfort in being with someone who knew exactly what he wanted.

Including me.

Her chest constricted. She wanted him, too. She wanted him so badly she'd almost agreed to stay when he'd asked her to last night. But that wouldn't be fair to either of them. The truth was, she hadn't figured out her life beyond falling in love and finding out that she was really good at, and thrilled with, the work she was doing for their trust. But this exciting project would end soon. Steve and Treat would make the final purchase of the property, and that door would close. They'd have saved two hundred acres from development, given back to the community where Steve had grown up, and forged another bond between the Bradens and the Johnsons.

She wanted a bond between one Braden and one Johnson.

So does he.

She closed her eyes and breathed deeply. She'd accomplished a lot, and she'd fallen in love with an incredible man. Three weeks apart wasn't the end of the world—even if it felt like it right now.

As she walked toward the front of the house, she hummed Taylor Swift's "Last Kiss." She paused by the fire pit, remembering the night they'd shared s'mores and the day she'd created a smoke bath when she'd wanted to surprise him. True to his promise, he'd taught her how to start a fire on their camping trip. He was patient and loving and…

She covered her face with her hands as tears began to fall, giving in to the clutch of her heart.

Stop it. Just stop it. She couldn't do this. She didn't want him to come back and find her bawling her eyes out, especially when he wanted her to stay and she knew she just couldn't. She'd never lived this far away from her family. She'd never been away from home this long, other than when she went to college, and that was less than an hour from Peaceful Harbor *and* a handful of her closest friends she'd grown up with had gone away to school with her. She couldn't risk not having a job and becoming a burden, or being stuck up there on the mountain and finding she couldn't handle the solitary lifestyle for the long run. It would be ten times as hard to leave then. Love was supposed to conquer all, to fulfill every part of a person's soul. So what was wrong with her? Why did she worry about those things? She loved him wholly and completely, but was that really enough?

She wiped her tears and fisted her hands, holding them up toward the sky.

"What kind of stupid test is this?" she said through gritted teeth. "Why wasn't I born *here*? Or he born *there*?" She groaned as her last words tore violently from her lungs. "Where the hell is the answer in all of this? Where's that cosmic shit Tempest believes in?"

She hammered her fists against her thighs and closed her eyes. Suddenly there were arms embracing her, bodies pressing in on her. Shannon's eyes flew open and she burst into tears.

"We're right here," Tempest said reassuringly. "We brought a box of pastries. All your favorites. And don't say 'cosmic shit.' It's not shit."

Shannon laughed through her tears. "I can't believe you're here, witnessing my meltdown." Her family was supposed to meet them at the rally, and here they were, exactly where she needed them.

"Of course we are, sweetheart," her mother said, brushing Shannon's hair from her tear-damp skin. "Last night at dinner we saw how broken up you were about leaving. You can't fool your mother."

She took in her mother's wild blond mane, her bohemian top and skirt, and she sank into her open arms.

"I think the fact that your eyes filled with tears every time she asked about it tipped her off," Leesa said, pulling a much-needed smile from Shannon as she stepped out of her mother's arms.

"We're here to help you pack," Tempest said. "After seeing you and Steve together, I know you won't be able to do it. I guess you don't hate me for encouraging you to leave Maryland."

"No. I love you even more for it, but I hate myself. I came back to Colorado wanting to see what might come of us, and what came of us is so perfect, it's..." Tears slipped down her cheeks again and she swiped angrily at them. "God! I need to stop this! Tempe, what if I'm making a mistake by going home? Or if we take forever to figure out where to go from here?"

"You'll know if you've made a mistake and you'll come back," Tempe assured her.

"Baby girl," her mother said with the tone she'd used when Shannon was little and worried about all the fish in the sea being killed by fishermen. "You and Steve are beautiful together, and it's clear how much he loves you. He told you last night there was no rush to figuring out your plans. Take some time to breathe and trust things will turn out how they should."

"And those answers you're looking for, Shan?" Faith touched her hand and smiled. "They'll come to you when you're ready to hear them. Mine did."

Tempe gave Shannon a nudge toward the front door. "Come on. Let's get you packed up so you can come back in three weeks."

Ugh. "Fine, but I'm leaving my pink shoelaces, my yellow hoodie, my pink cami…" *And my heart.*

THE CUMBERLAND RANCH had been transformed into a rally to end all rallies. Balloons and streamers decorated the tall fencing around the grounds. A gigantic banner, donated by a local graphics company, hung over the entrance and read, BE A PART OF HISTORY—ADOPT AN ACRE, and below it were the words COLORADO LAND TRUST. Pride swelled in Shannon's chest. She and Steve had done this. They'd taken their ideas, melded them together, and created all of this. They were good together. Really, really good.

The rally had opened at eleven o'clock, and five hours later they were still packed. The event was scheduled to run until six, with the barn dance starting at eight at the festival ground. Shannon stood at the top of the hill taking it all in. Crowds gathered around the riding ring where Luke and his wife, Daisy, were giving rides on their *girls*, their gypsy horses. The overly affectionate horses were gorgeous, with feathering completely covering their hooves, their abundant silky manes and tails flowing in the breeze as they circled the ring. Ross and Jade were giving veterinary exams to pets in exchange for donations while baby Hal slept in a playpen beside Jade. A line of people with leashed pets waited their turn. The line stretched up the hill, almost reaching Elisabeth's booth, where she and Kelsey were selling cakes and pies—including the new River Pie, which was sinfully delicious. Beneath an awning beside Elisabeth's booth, Shannon's and Steve's mothers were running the refreshment stand, while Rex and Treat grilled up burgers and hot dogs. Callie sat on a blanket reading to a swarm of excited children while they ate. Shannon watched her mother chat with Steve's as they doled out drinks and paper plates piled high with chips and burgers. She wondered how much of their conversation was about her and Steve. *Probably most of it.* She smiled at the thought, because her mind was one hundred and ten percent on her hunky man.

Down by the corral, Jo was holding a red-tailed hawk, giving a lecture on birds of prey to a crowd, while Cutter leaned his tall frame against the corral, his legs crossed at the ankle, as he watched her. In a few minutes, the cattle-roping event would begin. Shannon could hardly believe how well the events had come together and how many people had turned out to support their effort.

Her eyes slid to Cutter's right, catching on the tall, muscular man whose eyes were locked on her, and her heart skipped a beat. How long had Steve been watching her? And what was he saying to her uncle Hal, who was also watching her? She started down the hill as her father and brothers came out of the barn.

"There's my girl," her father said, stopping her from descending the hill. Thomas "Ace" Braden, with his closely cropped dark hair, button-down shirt, and slacks, was as conservative as her mother was bohemian. He pulled her into his strong, familiar embrace. "You and Steve have done an incredible job, sweetheart. Mom and I are very proud of you."

"Thanks, Dad." She looked at her four handsome brothers and felt her two worlds colliding. Cole was as conservative as his father, in dress and in nature, while Sam and Ty were like bees trapped in a glass, always ready to fly off and do something exciting. Nate tugged her into a hug, and she reveled in his embrace. Even though he'd been back from overseas for almost two years, she still felt the need to cling to him a little longer than the others.

"Everyone here is talking about you and Steve and how great a team you make," Nate said. "I guess you'll have a date for my wedding."

"Damn right she will. Steve hasn't taken his eyes off of her all day." Ty lifted his camera and snapped a picture of her and Nate. "Beauty and the beast."

Nate coiled back to punch him, and Cole grabbed his arm.

"Let him go," Sam said with a laugh. "Ty's been a big pain in the butt today."

"What?" Ty smacked Sam on the back of his head. "I wasn't the one Hal caught making out with Faith in the barn."

"Jealous?" Sam teased.

Ty scoffed. "Hardly. You see all the hot women here?" His eyes shot to Jo.

"Don't even think about it, Ty," Shannon warned. "Cutter's been eyeing her for two weeks."

"When's that ever stopped me?" He headed down the hill.

Shannon shook her head. "He's going to get himself in trouble."

"Damn it," Sam muttered. "I've got him." He hustled after Ty.

"Aw, hell. That's like sending Dumb after Dumber." Nate

jogged down the hill after Sam.

"Cole," their father said, and lifted his chin in the direction of their brothers.

Cole sighed. "Really, Pop? All because Ty might hit on some girl?"

"And then he gets into it with Cutter, someone says something that pisses Nate off, and Sam jumps in just for fun," their father said. "Go on, son. Be the voice of reason."

Cole rolled his eyes and dutifully followed in their wake, grumbling about how he was *too old for this crap*.

Their father laughed and draped an arm around Shannon. "Think he bought it?"

"Probably." *But I didn't.* "Why didn't you just tell him you wanted to talk to me in private?"

He shrugged. "Maybe I like knowing they've got each other's backs."

"You taught us well, Dad. Family comes first, no matter what." She watched her brothers slapping each other on the back and laughing. Ty shook Cutter's hand, and they fell into line along the fence beside Steve.

"How are you really doing?" her father asked. "Are you ready to come home, or do you need more time?"

"What I need and what I want have nothing to do with reality." Shannon drew in a deep breath, preparing for the onslaught of emotions that had been wreaking havoc with her all day.

"They're your reality, Shannon. That's all that matters."

"Not really. I have a whole life back home, Dad."

He gazed down the hill at the people making their way across the field toward the corral. Rachel and Cal were talking with Max and her children, following the crowd. Max and

Rachel looked up at them and waved. Shannon waved back. Tempe came out of the barn carrying a cat and joined them.

"I didn't know you were in there," Shannon said.

"I was checking out the horses, but then I found this lovable little guy." She scratched the back of the cat's neck. "What are you guys looking at?"

"Shannon's other life," their father said.

He'd always had the ability to know what each of his children were thinking. It was spooky when they were younger. He and her brothers would eye each other a certain way, and the next thing she knew, her brothers were confessing something or apologizing for something she had no idea they'd done.

"Looks like a good one," Tempe said. "And here comes the best part of it." She nudged Shannon with her elbow and nodded at Steve, who was heading their way.

"He sure is taken with you," her father said, hugging her against his side. "Sam told me he tried to find work in Peaceful Harbor. I'm sorry, honey. I know how hard it's going to be to leave him. But he's doing the right thing. He's worked hard to achieve what he has in his field, and back home he would have to start a whole new career." He kissed the top of her head.

"I know, Dad." She took in Steve's purposeful stride, his broad shoulders, the square set of his jaw, which was clean shaven today, giving him a different type of allure. His short hair was brushed back from his face, and his eyes—those gorgeous slate-blue eyes that spoke louder than words ever could—were making her insides quiver.

Everything Steve did was with her best interests in mind. *You tried to move with me.* She swallowed past the love swelling inside her, the torment of the weeks ahead, and focused on making it through this moment without falling apart.

Steve was ten paces away. *Breathe.*

Eight. *Inhale. Exhale.*

Treat came out from the other side of the barn, joining Steve. The two fell into a conversation, but Steve's eyes remained trained on her.

She could barely hear past the blood rushing through her ears as he approached. She could practically taste his lips as they curved into a loving smile. He took up the space beside her, and her rocking world began to right itself. Her body instinctively keeled toward him.

Her father bent, speaking quietly in her ear. "Roots run deep, darlin', and they don't come unearthed because of a little distance." His words caused the first tears to spring free.

"Baby? Are you okay?" Steve took her hand, searching her eyes.

She blinked away her tears, wondering if a person's love could consume them to the point of rendering them mute. He was really ready to give up the mountain for her. Seeing him now, among the rally whose sole purpose was to save the land he loved, realization hit her harder than before. She didn't know how she was still standing. How she was managing to blink her eyes dry or how her voice still worked when she said, "Yes, just happy it's all coming together so well."

"Look at what you've done, baby. You made this all happen." Steve waved his hand toward the crowd below, then pulled her in tight.

She melted against him. This was how she made it through. One breath at a time. One hug at a time. One second at a time.

"You made your dream come true, baby."

And you were willing to let yours go to give me mine. "We made *our* dream come true," she managed.

"We've already hit our goal," Treat said. "Congratulations, Shannon. You and Steve made this possible. You've given Weston their happily ever after."

She nodded and smiled, trying not to fall apart as the news of their success sealed the end of another thing she loved.

Where's our happily ever after?

Chapter Eighteen

THE BARN WAS lit up like a Christmas tree on the sprawling fairgrounds, with colorful lights strung from exposed beams along the ceiling and around the windows and doors, bringing a whimsical, romantic feel to the special night. Country music filled the air from the band playing on a stage in the back of the barn. Women wore their prettiest dresses and men donned their best jeans and boots, dancing and mingling, but no one was as captivating as Shannon, twirling in her short pink halter dress. Silver embellishments formed delicate designs along the hem, glistening under the lights as she stomped out a country dance in her pink and white cowgirl boots. Her hair lifted from her shoulders as she, Jewel, Faith, and Leesa moved in time to the beat.

She was beautiful. She was his. And she was leaving.

Sam sidled up to Steve. "My sister can dance, can't she?"

"I have yet to come across a thing she can't do." He crossed his arms, more nervous than he could ever remember being. He'd been learning to dance for weeks now, and from what Rex and the others told him, he was pretty good. He just hoped *pretty good* was good enough for Shannon. He wanted tonight to be unforgettable.

"Except make a life decision," Sam said with a serious look in his eyes. "She came out here because she was into you. She fell for you, and now she's afraid she's going to screw it up."

"She can't screw this up. There's nothing she could do that would change my feelings for her."

"It's not what she might or might not do. It's what she thinks she can handle." Sam motioned across the room to Tempest.

Tempest waved, smiling as she crossed the room toward them. Her blond hair was pinned up in a ponytail, revealing her long, graceful neck. She carried herself more primly than Shannon, appearing acutely aware of her surroundings at all times, where Shannon flitted from one happy moment to the next. Except recently she'd been on the verge of tears every time they talked about her leaving.

"Why aren't you dancing, Sam?" Tempest asked.

"Faith's having too much fun with the girls. Besides, you know Steve doesn't dance, so I thought I'd hang out with him."

"Who told you I don't dance?" he asked.

"Shannon, who else?" Sam answered. "She told us not to give you a hard time about it."

Steve got a funny feeling in his stomach knowing she was watching out for him. He couldn't take his eyes off of her as she swayed to the music. She caught him staring and lifted a hand in a half wave, looking sweet and sexy and moderately shy. In her eyes, sadness rode just below the surface, but love led the way, reaching out to him across the room. She was worried about leaving, and probably about dancing without him. *Don't worry, baby. Soon enough you'll be in my arms.*

"Tempe, tell Steve about Shannon and life decisions," Sam said.

Tempe's lips pressed into a firm line. She narrowed her eyes and said, "Sam, that's not my story to tell. Or *yours*."

Sam chuckled and turned to Steve. "Trust me on this—she's scared to leave her safe little hometown for good."

"Sam," Tempest chided. She turned a softer gaze to Steve. "It's a big move for her. She just needs time."

"Don't worry, Tempe. I'll give Shannon whatever she needs. Including time, even if it kills me." He had a few surprises in store for her before she got on that plane tomorrow, and when Mack waved him over he knew at least one of them was ready.

The song ended while Steve was talking with Mack. He watched Shannon come off the dance floor. Her family gathered around her. Her eyes skittered nervously around the barn, and he knew she was looking for him. He raised a hand over the crowd, and when she saw it, her eyes lit up. *Soon, baby.*

"Thanks for the key, Mack," Steve said. "And for helping with the other stuff."

"No worries, buddy," Mack assured him. "It's amazing what can happen over the course of several weeks."

Thinking of Shannon, he said, "It is, Mack. It truly is."

Rex stepped up to the stage with his baby in his arms and took possession of the microphone. Baby Hal gurgled, and it amplified over the mic, drawing the crowd's attention. A low laugh rumbled through the barn as Steve weaved his way toward Shannon.

Rex kissed his baby's head. "My boy's got a lot to say on this special night," Rex said, earning another group chuckle. "I think I speak for everyone here when I say thank you to Steve, Shannon, and Treat for putting the rally together and for allowing all of us to become a part of their monumental effort toward preserving Weston's heritage. How about a big round of applause to bring the three founders of the Colorado Land Trust up for a dance?"

Applause and cheers sounded around the barn.

Shannon shook her head, confusion riddling her brow as Treat and Max walked onto the dance floor and Steve took Shannon's hand in his.

"Steve, you have to correct him," Shannon said urgently.

"You were more a part of this than either Treat or I were. Congratulations, Butterfly. The three of us are partners now, if you want that."

"But..." She shook her head, her eyes filling with tears again. He'd seen enough tears from her for a lifetime, but at least these were tears of joy.

"I love you, baby."

She covered her mouth with her hand, blinking away tears.

He gently lowered her hand and cupped her face. "Do you want this? To be part of what we've created?"

She nodded emphatically, her eyes full of love. "But how...?"

"Remotely. Treat and I agreed that the Colorado Land Trust wouldn't have come to fruition without you. You're the heart and soul of it, and we'll make it work any way you need us to."

More tears fell, and he pressed his lips to hers. Everyone was watching them now, and he proudly offered her his arm. "I believe this is our dance."

"You don't dance," she whispered. "You don't have to..."

"For you I'd walk through fire, baby." He walked her to the middle of the dance floor, his nerves buzzing like live wires as dance steps played out in his head.

"Grizz?" Her eyes moved nervously over the crowd. Everyone seemed to be waiting for his next move as much as he and Shannon were.

Steve slid an arm around her and began dancing. "Triple-step, Butterfly. Try to keep up."

"Ohmygod," she said as they glided across the floor. More happy tears fell from her eyes. "You can dance? How...?"

He twirled her around and she laughed—music to his ears.

"You can dance!" She looked out at the crowd and said proudly, "He can dance!"

Everyone cheered and clapped, and as couples joined them on the dance floor, making supportive comments—*I knew you could do it! Hear you're good at swing dancing. Save me a dance. We're so glad we can talk about it now!*—it became clear to Steve that the Weston grapevine had been buzzing all this time. And they'd protected his secret—and by doing so, they, too, were giving Shannon an unforgettable night.

"How?" she asked again, and he told her the whole embarrassing story.

"I'm sorry I had to lie about attending all those fake meetings, but I had to go when everyone was free."

"Oh, Grizz! I love you so much. All those stolen hours were worth it." She threw her arms around his neck and kissed him.

Rex danced over with Jade and baby Hal and cleared his throat, interrupting their kiss.

"The story of Steve's dance lessons will be told over holiday meals for generations to come," Rex teased.

If Steve had his way, he and Shannon would be telling the story together over holiday meals for years to come.

Now that the cat was out of the bag, every woman in Steve's life wanted to dance with him. "Go, go!" Shannon urged him as he was passed from Jade to Savannah, then Rachel and Jo.

"Isn't it strange?" Jo said as they danced. "I'm looking for Mr. Right and your soul mate saunters into your life?" Shannon didn't *saunter* anywhere. She was the very essence of life itself. She flitted, burst, or charged, but saunter? Not a chance. Remembering his father's words, he smiled. Shannon had indeed invaded every aspect of his life and his being.

He danced with Tempest and Shannon's mother, and after dancing with almost every female in the darn town, he sought out the only woman besides Shannon who had been on *his* dance card.

"Mom?"

His mother's expression warmed. "Steven," she said softly. "I never thought I'd see the day my handsome son was gliding across a dance floor. I'm so proud of you, honey."

"Will you dance with me?" He reached for her, and she placed her delicate hand in his. As they walked onto the dance floor, he caught sight of his father watching them and felt a strange sense of pride. *Every man should dance with his mother.* It was a strange and out-of-place thought, and he realized he'd had several of them lately—thoughts of the future, of a family of his own. And now, of something he'd want to pass along to a son of his own one day.

"You're a lovely dancer, Steven," his mother said. "When I heard you were learning to dance for Shannon, I knew this was the real thing. I'm so happy for you, honey. I know how hard it must have been for you to turn to Rex for help."

"Nothing is too difficult where Shannon is concerned. And, Mom? I was wrong the other day."

"About?" Her thin brows furrowed.

"I thought when Shannon went back to Peaceful Harbor I'd be able to carry on doing what I love most. But *she's* become what I love most. *She's* my life's passion."

"I know, honey." She gazed up at him with a smile that told of wisdom Steve had yet to learn. "You'll figure it out. The two of you will. When it's time, when it's right, you'll both know."

His eyes drifted to Shannon, talking with her father, Ty, and Tempest. She was so close to her family, he wondered if she'd ever be ready to move away from them. He promised himself he wouldn't pressure her, but as her time to leave neared, it was proving to be harder than he thought.

"What if our *right times* never fall into sync?" he asked through a thick throat.

"Then you'll change your life to accommodate hers."

As the song ended, he touched the key in his pocket. *I already have.*

MOONLIGHT SPRINKLED THROUGH the treetops, dotting the road as they drove up the mountain. It had been a perfect night, one Shannon would never forget.

"You learned to dance for me," she said as Steve reached for her hand. "From my family." She still couldn't believe he'd gone to Rex. What she wouldn't have done to have been a fly on the wall in that barn.

"I did." He gave her hand a little squeeze.

"You and Treat want to make me a partner." She still couldn't believe that either. Treat and Steve told her that they were toying with the idea of expanding the Colorado Land Trust to all of Colorado and making more deals under the business model the three of them had put together. There was a lot to do legally, but the idea of being involved and doing what she'd loved doing for the past few weeks thrilled her.

"We do, baby."

She gazed up at the man who never stopped thinking about her. Not for a minute. "It's a big commitment."

"Yes, and you have plenty of time to think about it on your long flight home tomorrow, but tonight," he said as he parked the truck, "I want to show you something."

He leaned in and kissed her. Then he opened his door, and a roaring, thunderous sound boomed around them. Before she could ask him what it was, he closed his door and walked around the truck. She saw it now, the way he moved more fluidly than he had before he'd learned to dance. The pieces of his secret dance lessons were all falling into place. His sporadic humming, the way he seemed to fight to keep his feet still when she'd danced around him the past week. How had she missed all of that?

He opened the passenger door, and she put her hands up to her ears to block the noise. Steve flashed a Cheshire-cat-like grin and helped her put on the sweater she'd brought with her.

"What is that?" she hollered over the roaring noise.

He helped her from the truck and said, "Close your eyes, baby."

She did as he asked. "Usually you tell me to *open* my eyes. What do you have up your sleeve, mountain man?"

With an arm securely around her, he guided her toward the backyard.

"Just a little something for my favorite person."

The noise grew louder. Then Steve's cheek touched hers and his deep voice penetrated through it. "Open your eyes, Butterfly."

She opened her eyes and inhaled a mouthful of snow. *Snow!*

She held her palms up toward the sky, in complete and utter awe of the winter wonderland before her. She blinked against the cold snowflakes shooting out of the snow machine. The backyard was covered with fluffy white snow. It glistened off the back porch and the steps where she watched the sunrise. Snow covered the tips of the tree branches, and when she turned her face up toward the sky, snowflakes rained down on her cheeks. And there, basking in the moonlight, his short hair covered in white, was her knight in snowy armor.

"Grizz!" she yelled over the noise, and launched herself into his arms.

He caught her and stumbled back, both of them laughing. "Now you've seen what the cabin will look like in the winter."

She squealed and pushed from his arms. Then she packed snow into the worst snowball ever and threw it at him, starting a battle of awful snowballs that fell apart like fairy dust. They laughed and ran around beneath the falling snow until they were out of breath, their skin pink from cold. He tackled her in the snow and spread her arms out wide. She was shaking, but not from the cold.

He pressed his lips to hers. "My very own snow angel."

"You love me," she said with a smile so big her cheeks hurt.

"More than you know," he said, and then he kissed her, melting the snow from her limbs. Just like that, the spark between them caught fire, and he picked her up and threw her over his shoulder like a sack of potatoes.

"Grizz!" She laughed as he turned off the snow machine and then slid her down his body and cradled her, kissing her as he carried her inside.

He set her feet on the floor, and they stumbled into the living room in a tangle of limbs and crashing of teeth and tongues. Their clothes were drenched. Steve peeled her sweater off and tossed it aside, then fumbled with the tie on the back of her dress. Finally he gave up on the stubborn knot and tore the dress over her head. She'd purposely forgone underwear to remind him of their first night together. She was still wearing her boots, which made her feel naughty. He stepped back with a predatory gaze, drinking in her nakedness. His eyes moved slowly down her body, lingering on her breasts, and she felt her nipples rise in anticipation of his touch.

"Grizz," she said breathily.

"Shh. I'm not rushing our last night together."

His words made her wanton and sad at once. *Our last night together.* His gaze slid lower, then lower still. She trembled with need and he hadn't even touched her yet. He grabbed his collar with two hands and tore it open, sending the buttons *ping*ing across the room, and dropped the black button-down to the floor.

His abs flexed as she reached a shaky hand toward him. He caught her wrist and lowered it down to her side. Oh, how she loved when he took control.

"I've been waiting to touch you all night." He kissed her deeply, sensually.

She watched as he unbuttoned and then excruciatingly slowly unzipped his jeans, exposing a hint of dark hair, his thick arousal outlined by the denim. She was so eager for him, her body felt electric. She'd watched him dancing with all those women, and all she could think about was getting back to the cabin and making love with him. Her insides quivered as he pushed his jeans over his hips, off his powerful thighs. He was a thing of beauty, a masterpiece.

He pulled off his boots, stepped from his jeans, and slid a

finger beneath her chin. One finger. A single touch—she felt a *zing* all the way down between her legs. He lifted her chin, bringing her eyes to his, and a sexy grin curved his perfect lips as he stepped closer. He gathered her against him with a heady grunt, one hand splayed across her back, the other sliding deliciously up and down her torso. His arousal grazed her belly, the hair on his legs tickled her thighs, and his hand slid over her hip and clutched her ass—*hard.*

"I love you, Butterfly," he said so softly she had to strain to hear it. His eyes were drenched in love, reflecting all of the emotions backing up inside her.

She sucked in a breath when his fingers slid between her legs, teasing over her wet flesh.

"I loved dancing with you," he said, pushing his fingers inside her.

She trapped her lower lip between her teeth as he moved in and out of her, treacherously slow.

"I loved watching you dance in those sexy boots." He pressed a kiss to the edge of her mouth. "Wanting you from afar." He kissed the other side of her mouth, his fingers stroking over the magical spot inside her that made all her nerve endings flare to life. Her lip sprang free from her teeth, and a satisfied smile rose on his face.

"The way you move your hips is like sex personified." The hand on her ass moved between her cheeks, bringing her thigh tight against his, teasing her from behind.

Her eyes fluttered closed, and he claimed her in a slow—oh, Lord, so slow—kiss. He moved his tongue at the same pace as his fingers thrusting inside her. Her thighs flexed; her hips bucked. She was almost there.

"Open your eyes, baby," he said gently. "Look at me."

Her eyes fluttered open, and his face was right there, his seductive eyes boring through her as he masterfully brought her to the edge of ecstasy. Her eyes closed again.

"Open," he said sharply, pressing his arousal firmly into her upper thigh.

She fought to keep her eyes open, to hold his hungry gaze, as his finger pushed past the tight rim of muscles from behind, and the world careened away.

"Open, baby," he said gently but firmly. She opened her eyes, struggling to see through the lusty fog consuming her.

"Come," he said roughly, and pushed his finger deeper into her ass as his thumb pressed on her clit. A wave of heat and cold crashed over her, dragging her under. She was spinning into oblivion, clinging, panting, and pleading incoherently. He captured her cries in a loving kiss, invading her body *everywhere*. He slowed the kiss, making love to her mouth—and then she was in his arms and her boots fell to the floor with a *clunk*.

He laid her on the bed and came down over her. "I need more of you."

"You're a greedy boy. What if I need more of *you*?" She playfully pushed at his chest and he willingly flopped onto his back.

"Take it, baby," he said in a gravelly, lustful voice. "I'm all yours."

"I've wanted to taste you all night." She kissed him, then turned, facing the foot of the bed, and licked the crown of his hard length, earning a guttural moan.

He reached between her legs and she stilled, enjoying the slow sweep of his fingers. *Our last night together.* She forced her mind into submission.

"I want to please you," she said brazenly. "Then I want you

to make love to me roughly, so I feel you long after I leave."

His hips pistoned up with her dirty talk, and he pushed his fingers inside her again. "Love me, baby, and I promise I will love you until you feel me in your sleep."

She lowered her mouth, taking all of him in, and he shifted them both onto their sides, driving deeper, hitting the back of her throat.

"That's it, baby. Love me like you never want to stop." He gripped her hips, and then his mouth was on her, his tongue thrusting into her sex.

"Ohgod." Her eyes closed. "Grizz."

He rocked his hips, and she loved him with her hand and mouth as he ate at her throbbing sex. He shifted and rolled onto his back, bringing her up onto all fours over him. She took him in deep, sucking and stroking as he made sweet love between her legs with his glorious mouth. Then his mouth moved back to her other hole, and she groaned. He licked her there, then pushed his finger in deep, bringing his mouth back to her sex. Within seconds she was coming on his mouth as his finger invaded her. She felt him swell in her hands, stroked him faster. His thighs and abs flexed, and his hands stilled as the first salty jet shot down her throat. He groaned, bringing his mouth to her sex again, as she loved him through the last pulse of his release.

He gathered her against him and wiped her lower lip with his thumb, then dragged his forearm over his mouth before taking her in a mind-numbing kiss. They kissed for what seemed like hours, though she had no grasp on reality. Her thoughts were frayed, her body was exhausted, and still, deep inside her core, she craved more of him. He pressed her into the mattress with his body, kissing her fast and hard, then feathery light and sweet.

"I love you so damn much," he whispered into her ear.

She wrapped her legs around his hips as he entered her, and he kissed her again. His mouth was hard, but his lips were soft and warm. It was a kiss of possession, their emotions driving them up to a frantic pace. Each taking and giving in equal measure, staking claim. He loved her into the wee hours of the morning, and then they made love again until they were both sated and too tired to move.

And as she drifted off to sleep, she prayed a miracle would happen and tomorrow she'd wake up and find they'd gone back in time and had another few weeks together...

Chapter Nineteen

THE NEXT MORNING Steve awoke alone and bolted upright. *It's too soon.* He shook his head to wake himself up and jumped from the bed.

"Shan," he called out as he threw on a pair of jeans and a shirt.

The cabin was too quiet. This was what it would be like after she left. An icy shiver slithered down his spine. He gritted his teeth against it and opened the back door.

Shannon was sitting on the steps wrapped in a blanket. An empty Pop-Tart package was on the porch to her right. She looked adorable wearing one of his sweatshirts. It was so big it hung over her hands, between which she clutched a steaming mug of coffee. He smiled as he sat beside her and drew the blanket around both of them to ward off the chilly morning air.

She rested her head on his shoulder and sighed.

"You okay, baby?"

She had on the pair of flannel pajama pants she planned on leaving at the cabin and her hiking boots, with no laces, since she'd left them for him. He caught a glimpse of bare skin and remembered the first morning after she'd come back to Colorado and how he'd known even then he wouldn't be able to resist her.

"Mm-hm. I just wanted to watch the sunrise."

"You should have woken me." He kissed her temple.

"We were up so late. I was just thinking about how different it's going to be at home. Waking up to the smell of the ocean instead of the crisp mountain air. Everything at home is a two-minute drive or walk from my apartment. It's going to be weird to go back to it."

"It's home. It'll feel good." The statement sounded supportive despite the fact that he felt like her home was here now, with him. But he was determined not to say or do anything that would put pressure on her.

"I guess, but I'm not so sure anymore." She sipped her coffee. "I love the way the mountains come slowly to life in the morning. At home everything comes alive at once. Cars, people, noise. I knew I was going to miss you, but this morning, as I was lying in bed, I realized I'm going to miss all of this, too."

She'd fallen in love with the area, just as he had. He held her close, trying to stave off the ever-present plea for her to stay, which had been on the tip of his tongue for days. "I know, baby."

"I feel like I've finally figured out who I am and what I like." She turned and faced him with warm, loving eyes. "Who I love," she said. "Part of the reason I came outside was that I knew if we made love again this morning, I wouldn't want to leave your bed."

His chest constricted. He wished she'd stayed in bed. "Our bed, baby."

"Our bed," she whispered.

"I'm going to miss watching the foxes. I want to see them grow up."

"I'll text you pictures while you're gone," he said, feeling the ache of the three lonely weeks ahead of him.

She lifted her head from his shoulder. "Thank you. Can you keep me up to date on Jo and Cutter, too? They danced a *lot* last night. I wonder if that will go anywhere. And why isn't Cal with Rachel? What's going on there?"

He smiled. That was his girl, thinking about so many different things at once.

"I don't know, but I'm sure you'll keep in touch with them and figure it out."

She fell quiet for a long while, and as the sun began to rise, she said, "You know I love you, right?"

"Absolutely."

"And you know I'm only going back because I have to? I can't just give up everything, and…"

Her words faded, reality hanging in the silence between them. She was leaving in a few hours, and in the end, it was her decision.

LATER THAT AFTERNOON they met Shannon's family at the Weston airport to wait for their flight. Thank God they didn't have to go to the Denver airport. The Weston airport had only one gate, and Steve was able to wait with Shannon until her flight was boarded. Everyone was clearly trying to appear as if they were in good spirits, but sadness hung like a cloud over the entire group. Steve and Shannon had spent the last few hours vacillating between promising to be there for each other regardless of the miles between them and staring silently into space, each lost in their own thoughts. Now, as their time together ticked down to minutes rather than hours, each passing second felt like a noose tightening around Shannon's neck. She looked at Steve, talking with her parents, Cole, and Leesa. Steve was wringing his hands, his eyes hooded. He met her gaze, and the love in his eyes, the distance between them, it was all too much. She needed to be in his arms.

"Shannon said you're coming out to visit in seven or eight weeks," her father said to him.

"Yes, sir. That's our plan."

Our plan sucks. "Excuse us, Dad, but they're going to call our flight soon. Do you mind if I steal Steve for a few minutes?"

"No, sweetheart, not at all." Ace pulled Steve into an embrace. "We look forward to seeing you soon."

"Thank you. I do as well."

"Okay, now he's mine." Shannon dragged him over by a bank of windows, and the minute his arms circled her, she finally felt like the vise in her chest eased.

"I've been dying to hold you," he confessed. "But I didn't want to take you away from your family."

"The only one I want to be near is you." She pressed her hands to his chest, reveling in his strong, steady heartbeat.

He gazed into her eyes, and sadness overcame her. She touched her forehead to his chest as tears slid down her cheeks. "I would move to Peaceful Harbor if I could find work."

"I know you would."

He slid a hand to the nape of her neck and whispered, "Don't go."

She held her breath. He'd asked her to stay so many times, but he'd stopped asking recently. She lifted her eyes, feeling her heart shred anew. "We have now. We agreed to that. I have my—"

"Your apartment, your job, your friends. I know." He ground his teeth together. "Goddamn it, Shan. I would go if I could. Please stay. You can get a job here doing any number of things. Stay with me. We'll go back and get your stuff."

"We..." *We what? Agreed? Agreed not to fall in love?*

He drew in a deep breath and pressed his hands to her cheeks. She loved that. That possessive, look-at-me-I-love-you hold.

"What if now's not enough?" he asked. "What if I want tomorrow, next week, *forever?*"

She was shaking all over. Tears flooded her eyes. "Steve, we agreed..."

Shannon's flight number rang out over the loudspeaker. They were boarding the plane.

"Shan, we promised these weeks together would be enough. We agreed. I know. I get it. I'm sorry. But we're humans. Fatally flawed. Remember? We made an error, but it's fixable. We need more. I need more."

"Shan, honey." Her mother waved her over to the line, which was moving way too fast. What ever happened to airports dragging ass? Everyone was there, watching them. Waiting for her. Sam tapped his watch and mimed a kiss. Faith grabbed his face and kissed him. For three weeks, Shannon wouldn't be able to kiss Steve like that.

"Damn it. I'm sorry, baby. I promised I wouldn't pressure you."

She couldn't process her thoughts. They were clouded, and her family was waving her over, shouting her name, getting in line to board the plane.

He pulled her against him, holding her so tight she could barely breathe again. Maybe that was because of how conflicted she was; she couldn't be sure.

The announcement rang out again, and she clung to Steve, afraid to let go and equally afraid not to.

"I'm sorry, baby. I just can't imagine a day without you." He took her by the shoulders and put a few inches between them. She wanted to climb beneath his skin and stay there.

"I shouldn't have pressured you. You're right. We'll be fine. Three weeks isn't the end of the world."

Now she wasn't so sure.

"Shannon!" Sam hollered, waving her over. The rest of her family had already disappeared down the Jetway.

This was it. This was really it.

How can this be it?

"Kiss me goodbye, baby."

Grizz. She couldn't speak. Her voice was lodged beneath her heart, which had clogged her throat. Gripping his chest, she went up on her toes, and he met her halfway in a toe-curling kiss that tasted salty from her tears.

"I love you, baby." He guided her toward the Jetway. "Call me when you get in so I know you've arrived safely." He hugged her again, speaking into her ear. "You've changed my world, Butterfly. I don't know how I existed without you for so long, and I'll count down the minutes until you're in my arms again."

And then she was in the line, following strangers through the narrow Jetway.

"There you are." Tempest was pressed up against the side of the Jetway, waiting for her. "Are you okay?"

No. Did she say it? She looked over her shoulder, staring into a sea of people. "I can't," she said. Her feet stopped moving. People bumped into her, pushing her farther away from Steve.

"What?" Tempest asked. "Did you forget something?"

She spun around and pushed through the crowd. "Grizz!" she yelled. "Grizz!"

"Shannon!" Tempest called after her.

She kept going, bumping into shoulders, saying *sorry* as she pushed between families and couples. She saw the entrance to the Jetway. "Sorry. Sorry. Sorry," she said, pushing through. Her heart thundered against her ribs as she ran out of the narrow tunnel.

"Grizz!" she hollered, scanning the waiting area. Her stomach plummeted.

And then she saw him standing by a bank of windows outside the gate, looking at something in his hand. Tears sprang from her eyes, and she grabbed her chest, sure it was going to explode.

"Grizz!"

He turned, his eyes full of sorrow. She ran toward him and he came for her. And then she was in his arms, and he was kissing her, holding her, asking her what was wrong and kissing her again.

"Did you forget something?"

"Yes," she said through her tears. "I forgot that this was *my* life. *My* choice. And my life is here, with you. I choose you, Grizz. I choose you."

He spun her around as he kissed her, both of them laughing.

"You're sure, baby?"

"Yes! I want today and tomorrow. I want *forever* with *you*, Steven Johnson. You may have to buy me a snowmobile so I don't go stir crazy in the winter, but yes, I'm sure."

"We won't be needing that snowmobile, Butterfly." He

opened his fisted hand.

She stared at the silver key in his hand, unsure of its meaning. "What's that?"

"A key to Mack's house. Walking distance to town. I rented it for us. I can commute, and we can stay in the cabin when you feel like it."

Sobs bubbled up from her lungs. "You rented a house? Near town? You love living on the mountain."

He shrugged like it was no big deal, but she knew exactly how much living on the mountain meant to him and she wasn't about to let him give up all that he loved for her. She knew he, like everyone else, probably thought she was giving up everything for him, but the truth was, *he* was her everything. A life without Steve, even for just three weeks at a time, would be a miserable life. She loved him, and she loved the man he was, which included his love of all things natural. No, she couldn't let him walk away from that.

"You need people, baby. And I need you."

"And I love you too much to let you give up living on the mountain. We'll compromise, maybe stay on the mountain during the week and in town on the weekends. Or on the mountain in the summer and in town in the winter. Or—"

His mouth came lovingly down over hers. Standing within his strong embrace, feeling his heart beating steadily against hers—knowing her family was on the plane toward her *other* home, probably toasting her last-minute decision—Shannon finally understood the meaning of what her father had said at the rally.

Roots run deep, darlin', and they don't come unearthed because of a little distance.

At the time she'd thought he meant her relationship with

Steve could survive a little distance. But she'd been wrong. He meant that everything she knew and loved wouldn't disappear just because she moved away.

Steve gazed into her eyes and said, "It doesn't matter where I lay my head at night as long as it's next to yours. Let's go home, baby."

Home. She took his hand and said, "Grizz, can we make one stop on the way?"

He flashed a sexy smile, and she could tell he knew exactly what she needed. Didn't he always?

"Pop-Tarts or bakery items?"

"Bakery, of course. I have an urge for pink frosting."

Epilogue

THERE WAS A time when Steve couldn't imagine swaying to the beat of any music, much less a Jimmy Buffet melody like Sam and Ty were playing on their guitars. Then again, he never imagined himself sitting on a beach in Peaceful Harbor, Maryland, hundreds of miles from his beloved mountains. Shannon had not only changed his life, but she'd become his world. Spending this cool September evening with the woman he loved, after watching her brother Nate and his new wife, Jewel, standing barefoot on a bed of rose petals, exchange vows on the beach at sunset, Steve wanted that, too. He wanted Shannon to become his wife, and he to become her husband, in front of all the people they loved most.

The bonfire crackled and sparked, lighting up the faces of Shannon's family. Her mother, Maisy, rested her head on Ace's shoulder, smiling as she looked at each of her children. The pride and love in her eyes was palpable. On a blanket across from them, Cole and Leesa held hands beside Anita, Jewel's mother. Tempest and Faith shared a blanket with Sam and Ty, while Jewel's younger siblings, Patrick, Krissy, and Taylor, played with a lighted ball near the water's edge a few feet away. A cool breeze rolled off the ocean, bringing the salty scents of the sea and sweeping red rose petals over the beach. They fluttered to the sand beside Steve and Shannon's bare feet like gifts from the wind.

"Kiss! Kiss! Kiss!" everyone cheered.

After the sun had gone down and the breeze picked up, the rose petals began to take flight—and the wine Steve and the others were drinking began to take effect—inciting the *kiss* chant, along with sharing tales of embarrassing family stories.

Steve wanted more of *this*, too. Shannon had opened his eyes to how much he'd been missing out on while living his peaceful solitary life on the mountain.

He set his wineglass down beside him and took Shannon's beautiful face between his hands. Gazing into her hazel eyes, which were alit with amusement, he said, "I love you, Butterfly," before planting a sloppy, loud kiss on her warm mouth.

Everyone cheered. Shannon giggled.

"Remind me to invest in rose petals," Steve said, causing another uproar of laughter and cheers.

A single rose petal flitted over Steve's foot. He placed it on Shannon's toes and kissed her softly before the cheering began again. Everyone was barefoot tonight, as they had been at the wedding. The men wore gray slacks rolled up at the cuffs and white button-down shirts. The girls wore pretty fall dresses. Shannon's was pink, of course, and she sported a sassy silver toe ring with an *S* inside a heart in the center.

He touched his toes to Shannon's, looking around at everyone's bare feet. "Now I know where Shannon gets the barefoot thing from."

"It's a Peaceful Harbor thing," Ty said. "When I'm climbing, I miss being barefoot, and when I'm barefoot, I miss my climbing shoes."

"Speaking of climbing," Nate said. "Do you remember that time Ty and I made homemade parachutes and climbed up to the roof?"

"You mean the trash bags?" Cole asked. "The ones I got in trouble for?" He glared at his father.

"Hey, don't get on me, son," Ace said. "As I recall, you *said* it was your fault."

"You *knew* it wasn't my fault," Cole insisted.

"Yes, but you came to me with that cockamamie story about how Ty heard you talking about doing it yourself and he and Nate just beat you to it." Ace laughed and shook his head. "You *told* me to punish you, remember? You were being honorable. Why would I steal that proud moment from you?"

Leesa hugged Cole. "Forever the hero."

Cole scrubbed a hand down his face and shot an amused look at Ty, who continued playing his guitar with a smart-ass grin on his face.

"They landed in rosebushes and couldn't walk for days," Tempest reminded them. "The universe always steps in."

Steve squeezed Shannon's hand and leaned in close. "Yes, it does."

"Universe my butt," Shannon said with a playful smile. "I set my sights on you and wrangled you into submission."

"And how's that working out for you?" Sam asked.

"Couldn't be happier," Shannon said.

"And what does your man have to say about that? How's life with our sister going for you?" Ty asked.

"Oh, please." Shannon waved her hand dismissively. "You *know* I'm awesome."

Steve and her brothers laughed. He'd been around enough to know they weren't looking for real answers. This was all part of the big-family dynamics that Shannon had tried to escape. In the end, there was no escaping the very people who loved her most. She'd confided in Steve that she'd never wanted to *escape* them. She'd just needed to find her own wings before she could feel comfortable under theirs.

"There's never a dull moment in either of our houses," Steve said. He and Shannon had been staying at the house in town about every third night. Steve had acclimated to living in town surprisingly well—much easier than Shannon had. She'd missed living on the mountain too much to commit to more than three nights away.

"So, she's a pain," Ty teased, winking at Shannon.

"Hardly," Steve said. "Living with Shannon is nothing short of amazing. I'm truly the luckiest guy on earth. She decides she's going to do something, and she doesn't allow any negative thoughts to slow her down." They'd finalized the purchase of the Cumberland property *and* Shannon's partnership in the Colorado Land Trust, which they'd expanded to handle deals throughout Colorado. Shannon was now working part-time for the trust, learning falconry from Jo, *and* doing research for a local company. Steve had never seen her so happy.

"She created her own career, and thanks to your gorgeous, brilliant, and yes, a little lovingly pushy sister, we've created an incredible life together." Steve pulled Shannon against him, breathing in her floral shampoo and the scent of *home*. "I love you, baby, and I wouldn't change a thing about you."

"Thanks, Grizz." She pushed her hands into his hair, which had grown out and was sufficiently scruffy again. "I wouldn't change you, either."

Sam laughed. "You already have."

"Only in the very best of ways," Steve said with a warm

smile. "And she didn't change me. She reminded me of who I used to be—and who I want to be for her."

Tempest sighed dreamily. "I hope I find that sort of happiness one day. Watching Cole, Nate, Sam, and now Shannon fall in love makes me long for a soul mate."

"If you hung out with me more often," Ty suggested, "I'd break that train of thought for you. We could go hit a few bars, party it up. You'll never want to settle down."

"That makes me want to fall in love even *faster*." Tempest smiled at Steve and Shannon. "I'm happy for you guys. I guess now's as good a time as any to let you all know that I've expanded my music therapy practice, and starting next month I'm going to be working in Pleasant Hill, too."

"Oh, Tempe," their mother said. "That's wonderful, honey."

"Thanks, Mom. Cole referred me to a few physicians there, and I figured it couldn't hurt to expand my network, meet new people." Tempest nodded, like she was trying to convince herself that this was a good idea. "I've called our cousin Jillian, and she's offered to let me stay with her if I don't want to commute. It's only an hour away without traffic, but with traffic it could take much longer."

"That's great," Shannon said. "I don't regret moving away at all, although I do miss everyone, as you know by my Skype and FaceTime calls."

"We love those calls, honey," her father said. "I have to admit, it's strange having my little girl so far away, but I know Steve is watching out for you."

"He is," Shannon admitted. "But I *can* keep myself out of trouble, you know."

"Like the time you snuck out to meet Tommy, or Timmy,

or whatever that kid's name was?" Ty said.

Shannon rolled her eyes. "It was Frankie, and you guys were jerks."

"Your brothers were just looking out for you," her mother said.

Shannon rolled her eyes again. They'd been sharing *Shannon stories* all weekend, and Steve would never tire of hearing them. He could imagine the spitfire she must have been as a teenager.

"What happened?" Steve asked.

"I snuck out my window." Shannon pointed to the second-story window of her parents' house behind them. "It was a pain, too. I tied sheets together, secured them to the foot of my bed, then climbed down them and had to jump the last ten feet. Then I ran all the way down the beach to his father's boathouse. I was so nervous and out of breath by the time I got there, I thought I was going to throw up. I was only thirteen, and I knew I was going to get my first real kiss."

Sam cleared his throat, and she shot him a death stare.

"*Kiss*, Sam. Nothing more." She turned her attention back to Steve and said, "Anyway, I pushed the boathouse door open and it was pitch-black. So I stepped inside, shaking like a fricking leaf, and I whispered something. I don't remember what—"

"You said"—Sam spoke in a higher pitch—"'Frankie spanky, I'm here.'"

He burst out laughing.

Shannon covered her face. "Ohmygod."

"Frankie spanky?" Steve cocked a brow.

"Ugh! It was a joke!" She scowled at Sam. "I walked in, and these numskulls were standing there. Nate had Frankie in a headlock, and Frankie looked like he was going to pass out or throw up. I was mortified."

"You were also dead meat," Ty said. "She got grounded for a month."

Shannon sighed loudly.

"I think it's time for a change of subject." Tempest picked up Ty's guitar and began playing.

Steve rose to his feet and reached a hand out to Shannon.

"May I have this dance, beautiful?"

She bounced to her feet. "You can have every dance."

"I want to dance with my *husband*," Jewel said. Still wearing her knee-length white lace wedding dress, she tugged Nate up to his feet. Nate went gladly, with a look of love in his eyes.

Cole and Leesa followed, as did Shannon's parents. Ty offered a hand to Anita, who graciously took it. Steve held Shannon in his arms, dancing beneath the moonlight, thinking about how lucky he was. Not only for falling in love with such an incredible woman, but for having friends who'd taught him to dance, so he could feel her melting against him like a candle in the sun. *Pure bliss.*

"I CAN'T BELIEVE they told the *Frankie* story." Shannon gazed into Steve's eyes, recognizing the flicker of nervousness that usually sent his hand cruising through his hair. "Are you okay?"

"I wish I'd known you then," he said thoughtfully.

"Why? Because you think I would have made out with you in a boathouse? By the way, we *all* called him Frankie spanky because his little brother called him that."

He kissed her softly. "Making out in a boathouse does sound pretty hot, but that's not why. You once said you wanted the strength of years behind us. I want that, Shan. I would have loved to be your first kiss, your first date…"

The sincerity in his voice made her insides go soft. "You were the first person to have shmores with me, and a Happy Pack, and some sexy things we won't talk about here." Her cheeks flushed. "You were also not just the first but the only person I've ever fallen in love with. That's a lot more important."

"You're right, baby. And I want you to know that I understand how important your family is to you. If you ever want to move back here, I'll make it work. I'll figure out a way. I want you to be happy, and I'll do whatever it takes to give you the best life you could possibly want."

"I know you would do anything for me, but I love our life in Colorado. This is all I need, a few days here and there to touch base. You saw how much I missed the mountain when we tried to move into town. I can't imagine moving this far away from the place we fell in love. My heart is on that mountain now."

"I want this with you forever, baby. Everything. Family get-togethers, our own family." He reached into his slacks pocket and pulled out a red velvet bag.

"Grizz?" she said with a shaky voice.

He withdrew a gorgeous rose-gold ring with tiny white and yellow gold butterflies along the band and a teardrop-shaped diamond in the center.

Her hand flew to her chest, and she choked out, "I can't breathe."

He dropped down on one knee and held her left hand. She

was trembling all over, vaguely aware of her family gathering around as he said, "Marry me, Butterfly. Be mine and let me be yours forever. I want to see you in a wedding dress and round with our babies. I want to grow old and gray together listening to your endless sentences and waking up with you in my wrinkled, arthritic arms."

"Grizz," she whispered. Tears slid down her cheeks. She'd dreamed of this moment, but nothing could come close to the love filling her veins as she gazed into Steve's loving eyes. His hands were shaking, as were hers. "Kids," she said softly. "You want kids?"

"As many as you want, sweet girl."

She choked past her thickening throat. "As many as I want? Sugared-up baby Grizzes? Can we give them Happy Packs and teach them to make shmores and to dance?"

"Baby," he said, rising to his feet. "If you marry me, there's nothing we can't do."

"We'll need more space. Not now, but when we have kids. Maybe we can add on to the cabin. Married! Grizz, we're getting married!"

He held the sparkling ring in front of her finger. "Is that a yes?"

She pushed her finger into the ring and squealed, leaping into his arms as she said, "Yes. Double yes. Triple yes. Quadruple y—"

Her final words were smothered in the most delicious kiss of them all. The kiss of promises to come, hopes, and dreams from the only man who could ever make them come true.

Ready for more Bradens?
Tempest Braden is waiting for you!
WHISPER OF LOVE

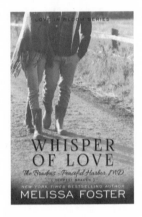

From New York Times bestselling author Melissa Foster comes a new sweet and sexy romance, WHISPER OF LOVE, in which Tempest Braden, a music therapist, sets her sights on a reclusive artist with a secret past.

Have you heard about Braden Flirts?

What is a Flirt?

The Love in Bloom big-family romance world has become so widely enjoyed, I have been asked by thousands of readers to write the stories of our beloved side characters. While I couldn't possibly fit in writing full-length novels for each of them while maintaining my normal publication schedule, I've created *flirts*. Flirts vary in length and cover twenty-four to forty-eight hours of two side characters' lives on their path to their happily ever after, while also updating readers about their favorite main characters. Flirts vary in length and heat levels. I hope you love these quick, fun, sexy stories as much as I enjoy writing them.

Love at Last follows Cal Hayden and Rachel Gray, friends of the Bradens, and also features several of the Colorado Bradens. *Love at Last* is a great way to get to know the Braden family, and then you can go back and read each of their love stories. Like all Love in Bloom books, flirts are written to stand alone, so jump right in and enjoy the fun, sexy, and emotional ride.

Cowboy Cal Hayden has loved Rachel Gray practically since the first time he set eyes on her. But Cal's a careful, responsible man who knows better than to start a relationship before he can give it his all. He bided his time while caring for his family through his father's terminal illness. Now his father is gone and his mother is settled, but has Cal waited too long to make his move? Find out in *Love at Last*, and catch up with many of your favorite Colorado Bradens, including much-anticipated news about babies for the Bradens in Trusty, Colorado!

Fall in love with Seaside Summers
SEASIDE WHISPERS (Seaside Summers)

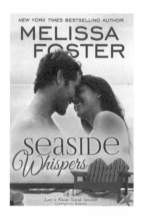

Having a mad crush on her boss's son, Matt Lacroux—an intriguing mix of proper gentleman and flirtatious bad boy—is probably not the smartest idea for single mother Mira Savage. Especially when the company, and her job, is already on shaky ground. But as a Princeton professor, Matt's life is hours away from Mira's home on Cape Cod, keeping him safely in the fantasy-only zone. And as a single mother to six-year-old Hagen, with a floundering company to save, fantasies are all she has time for.

With hopes of becoming dean off the table, and too many months of longing for a woman who lived too far away to pursue, Matt's publishing contract couldn't have come at a better time. He heads home to Cape Cod on a brief sabbatical, intent on starting his book, and finally getting his arms around sweet, seductive Mira.

A surprise encounter leads to white-hot passions and midnight confessions. The more time Matt and Mira spend together, the deeper their relationship grows, and the love and attention Matt showers on Hagen is more than she has ever dreamed of. But Matt's sabbatical is only temporary, and Mira's not saving his father's company so she can leave it behind. Will their whispers of love be enough for one of them to change their life forever?

Don't miss Melissa's sexy new stand-alone romance
Tru Blue

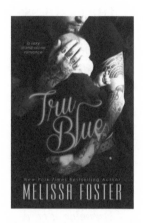

He wore the skin of a killer, and bore the heart of a lover...

There's nothing Truman Gritt won't do to protect his family–
Including spending years in jail for a crime he didn't commit. When
he's finally released, the life he knew is turned upside down by his
mother's overdose, and Truman steps in to raise the children she's left
behind. Truman's hard, he's secretive, and he's trying to save a
brother who's even more broken than he is. He's never needed help in
his life, and when beautiful Gemma Wright tries to step in, he's less
than accepting. But Gemma has a way of slithering into people's lives
and eventually she pierces through his ironclad heart. When
Truman's dark past collides with his future, his loyalties will be tested,
and he'll be faced with his toughest decision yet.

For more on Tru Blue and Melissa's other releases, visit: www.
MelissaFoster.com

LOVE IN BLOOM SERIES

SNOW SISTERS
Sisters in Love
Sisters in Bloom
Sisters in White

THE BRADENS
Lovers at Heart
Destined for Love
Friendship on Fire
Sea of Love
Bursting with Love
Hearts at Play
Taken by Love
Fated for Love
Romancing My Love
Flirting with Love
Dreaming of Love
Crashing into Love
Healed by Love
Surrender My Love
River of Love
Crushing on Love
Whisper of Love
Thrill of Love
Promise My Love (novella)
Daring Her Love (novella)
Our New Love (short story)

THE REMINGTONS

Game of Love
Stroke of Love
Flames of Love
Slope of Love
Read, Write, Love
Touched by Love

SEASIDE SUMMERS

Seaside Dreams
Seaside Hearts
Seaside Sunsets
Seaside Secrets
Seaside Nights
Seaside Embrace
Seaside Lovers
Seaside Whispers

THE RYDERS

Seized by Love
Claimed by Love
Chased by Love
Rescued by Love
Swept into Love

SEXY STAND-ALONE ROMANCE NOVELS

Tru Blue (Set in Peaceful Harbor)

<u>BILLIONAIRES AFTER DARK SERIES</u>

WILD BOYS

Logan
Heath
Jackson
Cooper

BAD BOYS
Mick
Dylan
Carson
Brett

NICE GIRLS
Phoebe
Francine
Nicole
Genevieve

<u>HARBORSIDE NIGHTS SERIES</u>
Includes characters from the Love in Bloom series
Catching Cassidy
Discovering Delilah
Tempting Tristan
Chasing Charley
Breaking Brandon
Embracing Evan
Reaching Rusty
Loving Livi

More Books by Melissa
Chasing Amanda (mystery/suspense)
Come Back to Me (mystery/suspense)
Have No Shame (historical fiction/romance)
Love, Lies & Mystery (3-book bundle)
Megan's Way (literary fiction)
Traces of Kara (psychological thriller)
Where Petals Fall (suspense)

Acknowledgments

Writing a book is not a solo endeavor, and I am indebted to my fans, friends, and family, who inspire and support me on a daily basis. Many thanks to Fan Club member Alexis Bruce for our incredibly fun brainstorming sessions, Molly Izod Finney and Jo Venison for allowing me to borrow their names for character Jo Finney, and to Ana Paula Medeiros for giving me Shanna, our superhero. Please continue to keep in touch. You never know when you'll end up in one of my books, as several members of my Fan Club have already discovered. www.Facebook.com/groups/MelissaFosterFans

A heap of gratitude goes to Shannon Pascone for "shmores" and "Happy Packs" and Aurelia Kucera for your in-depth knowledge about all things biology, fox, and research related.

If you don't yet follow me on Facebook, please do! We have such fun chatting about our lovable heroes and sassy heroines, and I always try to keep fans abreast of what's going on in our fictional boyfriends' worlds. www.Facebook.com/MelissaFosterAuthor

Remember to sign up for my newsletter to keep up to date with new releases and special promotions and events and to receive an exclusive short story featuring Jack Remington and Savannah Braden. www.MelissaFoster.com/Newsletter

For a family tree, publication schedules, series checklists, and more, please visit the special Reader Goodies page that I've set up for you! www.MelissaFoster.com/Reader-Goodies

As always, heaps of gratitude to my amazing team of editors and proofreaders: Kristen Weber, Penina Lopez, Jenna Bagnini, Juliette Hill, Marlene Engel, Lynn Mullan, and Justinn Harrison. And, of course, to my main heartthrob, Les.

~Meet Melissa~

www.MelissaFoster.com

Melissa Foster is a *New York Times* and *USA Today* bestselling and award-winning author. Her books have been recommended by *USA Today's* book blog, *Hagerstown* magazine, *The Patriot*, and several other print venues. She is the founder of the World Literary Café and Fostering Success. Melissa has painted and donated several murals to the Hospital for Sick Children in Washington, DC.

Visit Melissa on her website or chat with her on social media. Melissa enjoys discussing her books with book clubs and reader groups and welcomes an invitation to your event. Melissa's books are available through most online retailers in paperback and digital formats.

Made in United States
Troutdale, OR
06/09/2023

10511423R10174